Mountains
Between Us

OTHER BOOKS
BY JENNY PROCTOR
The House at Rose Creek

Mountains Between Us

a novel

Jenny Proctor

Covenant Communications, Inc.

Published by Covenant Communications, Inc.
American Fork, Utah

Printed in the United States of America
First Printing: September 2014

20 19 18 17 16 15 14   10 9 8 7 6 5 4 3 2 1

ISBN: 978-1-62108-660-4

This one is for my kids
because they are awesome
and totally deserve it.

Acknowledgments

It was a surreal experience sitting down to write the acknowledgments for my first book. But now a second book? I wasn't sure I would ever get here. There are so many people who deserve mentioning.

I work with an incredible team at Covenant. My editor, Samantha Millburn, is brilliant *and* tactful, a rare combination. I have beta readers who are beyond valuable. Sure, I'll take credit for writing this book. But it's good because Kimberly Vanderhorst was willing to comb through every single word—more than once. There aren't many in this world like you, Kim. Not many at all.

Kiesha Corn, thank you so much for answering all of my questions and for giving me insight into what life at a rehabilitative boarding school is like. DeNae Handy, Valerie Walz, Lindsay Anderson, I'm forever grateful for your willingness to read and share your opinions. Emily, I know you were swamped with other important life events while I was editing this time around, but the story was born from your willingness to endlessly hash out plotlines, and I never stopped feeling your encouragement and love. As far as sisters go, I'm pretty sure I've got the very best one.

All of these people are incredible, and I'm pretty sure I couldn't write like I do without them. But closer to home, it's my family who allows me to pursue this dream. They are the ones who listen to my story ideas and pretend like all of my imaginary friends matter to them as much as they do to me. They encourage and uplift. They pick up the slack when I spend a particularly long night (or day) catching up on revisions or finishing a chapter I just can't leave alone. They help me keep all the plates spinning. And that's huge. Josh, I love you. And, kids, I think you're all rock stars.

Chapter 1

HENRY JACOBSON WATCHED HIS SEVEN-year-old son throw rocks into the still water of the Little Tennessee River. AJ was only a few yards away, close enough for Henry to reach him in a mere moment should he step any closer to the water—still, Henry couldn't shake the feeling his son was somehow too far away. Close to the water or not, it felt as if AJ were slowly, quietly slipping beyond his reach.

Henry turned and looked down the asphalt path that wound through the dense green foliage next to the river. It was a beautiful summer day, warm but with enough of a breeze to keep the heat from feeling stifling. For a Sunday afternoon, Rose Creek's Greenway Park was relatively quiet. Henry saw an older couple walking a small dog that hopped energetically between them and a family riding their bikes farther down the path. Otherwise, he and his son were alone.

"AJ," Henry called. "Do you want to go back over to the playground? I could push you on the swing?"

AJ scrunched up his face in consideration. "Naw, I don't really feel like swinging."

"What about your bike? I could walk beside you while you ride, catch you if you come close to falling."

AJ turned and looked at him, disbelief on his face. "Dad, it's been forever since I fell off my bike. I can go really fast by myself."

"Ah, that's great, AJ." Henry was ashamed to have missed such a milestone in his son's life. "Can I see you ride, since you've gotten so good?"

"I don't really feel like it," AJ said. "Can we just go home now? I'm starting to get hungry, and Grandma has apple pie."

Henry glanced at his watch. It was just after four, a full two hours earlier than AJ's mom expected him home. He sighed.

"All right, if that's what you want to do." Henry watched as AJ tossed one final rock into the river. Close to the size of AJ's fist, the rock made a noisy splash when it hit the water.

"I'll go get my soccer ball," AJ said.

Henry drove through town with his heart heavy in his chest. He had hoped the park would provide enough of a distraction that he and AJ could enjoy the entire afternoon together. Week after week, it was growing more and more difficult to fill the time, to find things AJ wanted to do.

His son was only seven. Henry knew it was his fault. *He* was the dad. He was the only one who could make things better. But what could he do if his own son didn't enjoy spending time with him? He couldn't force him to have a good time. When he gave in to the impulse to try, it only pushed AJ further away. Henry stopped the car at an intersection beside the construction site for the new elementary school.

"Are you excited about the new school?"

AJ shrugged his shoulders. "I guess so. They're supposed to have a field for nothing but soccer. That'll be cool."

Henry had never been a soccer player, but in moments like these, when relating to his son felt like grasping at straws, he wished that he had. "When's your next soccer game? Maybe I'll be able to come."

Henry watched AJ in the rearview mirror, hoping the idea would elicit even a hint of excitement. But AJ appeared indifferent.

"I don't know. You could ask Mom or Grandma. I think it's on Wednesday, so you'll probably be working."

"I'm done by four thirty on Wednesdays. If your game is after that, I'll be there."

"Cool."

AJ had mood-ring eyes, just like his father. That's what Henry's sister had called them when they were kids because their color seemed to fluctuate so frequently from gray to blue, then back again. Henry wished he could get a glimpse of how AJ was feeling by observing his eye color.

If only it were so easy.

Aside from the eyes, AJ looked very much like his mother. He had her sandy blonde hair and the same dusting of freckles across his cheeks and the bridge of his nose. Henry couldn't help but notice the similarities, and it made him grip the steering wheel just a little tighter. He wondered how much time would have to pass for the sting of rejection to fade every time he saw the woman he'd loved—even still loved—in his son's face.

* * *

"Is Allison not here?"

"She's out with Robert." AJ's grandmother Lila shook her head. "I expect she'll be back by six. I daresay she didn't think you'd bring AJ home before then."

Henry wearily rubbed his fingers through his hair. He looked through the living room into the kitchen, where AJ and his grandfather were already eating a piece of Lila's homemade apple pie.

"He said he wanted pie." Henry watched the expression on Lila's face soften.

"You look like you could use a piece yourself." She pulled Henry out of the entryway. "Come on in and sit down. I'll fix you up a slice, and you and I can talk a bit."

Henry sank into the couch in Lila's small, familiar living room. He'd spent hours of his adolescence sitting in this room. It was where he'd kissed Allison for the first time, where they'd fallen in love over old movies and bowls of popcorn. To his left, in front of the old fireplace, the two of them had stood in cheesy prom attire for both junior and senior prom pictures. One of those pictures still hung to the left of the big bay window behind the couch in an outdated gold frame, the paint chipping around the corners.

Lila returned to the room, a big piece of pie in hand. She gave it to Henry, then placed a glass of milk, a napkin, and a fork on the coffee table. She moved around the table and sat down next to him on the couch.

"Henry, how are you?" Her words were warm and sincere, rolling out with the typical softness of her Southern cadence. "You seem a little discouraged today."

Lila had always been good at reading his emotions. For fifteen years, she'd been asking the same question: "How are you, Henry?" She had a way of making him feel like she really wanted to know.

"I'm good," Henry lied. "Work is good, church is good. Things with AJ . . ." He hesitated. "I guess they're good too."

"That's not what I asked," Lila said. "I didn't ask about work or church or even AJ. I asked about you."

Henry gave her a small smile. He always appreciated Lila's concern. It was a welcome reminder that even though his marriage with her daughter had ended, Lila, and even Jim, still considered him family.

"You always ask the hard questions, don't you, Lila?"

"I just want you to be happy, dear. You know if you're happy, it will be easier for you to have a good relationship with AJ."

"I do have a relationship with AJ." Henry knew he sounded defensive and tried to dull the edges of his words. "I see him twice a week, every week. I like spending time with him."

"Does he know that?"

"Of course he does. Why wouldn't he?"

"Henry Jacobson, if there is one mistake you should never make, it's assuming a seven-year-old knows how you feel." Lila gave him a pointed look, her hands folded primly in her lap. "Just make sure you're talking to him. Don't ever hesitate to tell him how much he means to you."

Henry didn't say anything. He kept his eyes on his plate, pushing the crumbs of his pie from one side to the other.

"Are you seeing anyone?"

Henry looked up, surprise in his eyes. "You mean dating?"

"Of course I mean dating. It's been two years. You're thirty years old, Henry. You're in the prime of life, and you shouldn't waste these years. Surely there's a nice girl at your church, someone you could spend some time with. Allison is moving on. So should you."

Your church. The words still stung. Allison's parents didn't share Henry's faith, but for a while, Allison had. When she'd walked out on Henry, she'd walked out on her faith too. Now it was *his* church. At least she still let AJ attend.

Henry knew perfectly well that Allison was moving on. She'd been dating Robert Franklin, a local attorney and old high school friend of Henry's, for nearly six months. Henry had run into them once in town, shopping at the grocery store, with AJ chatting animatedly between them. To any stranger, they would have seemed a normal, happy family.

Just thinking of Allison dating someone made Henry flush with anger. She'd claimed she needed to live life for *her.* They'd fallen in love so young; she didn't even know who she *was* anymore. Funny, she'd seemed fully aware of who she was when she'd jumped into a serious relationship not six months after their divorce had been finalized.

Henry shook his head. "I don't think I'm ready for that yet." He stood. "I should go. Do you know what time AJ's soccer game is on Wednesday?"

"I think it's at six, but let me check the schedule to be sure. Come on into the kitchen and say hello to Jim before you leave. You can say good-bye to AJ too, and I'll box up a few more pieces of pie for you to take with you."

Jim looked up when Henry entered the kitchen. "I finished the book." He leaned back in his chair, resting his hands on his substantial midsection and furrowed his brow. "Didn't like it."

Henry laughed. "It was a history book. What was there not to like about it?"

"History according to who? I was over there in Vietnam, and I remember what it was like. You can write a book about politics and maneuvering and who said what and when, but that's not the real story. Only those of us on the ground can tell the real story."

Henry shook his head. There wasn't anything wrong with the book he'd given Jim. But no book was going to be good enough until Jim sat down and wrote one himself. No other version of history was ever going to measure up. "Why don't you tell the story, then? I'll even help you write it. It'll be good for you."

"Beh," Jim said gruffly. "I'm not a writer."

"But I am. I mean, at least I teach about writing. I know enough that I think I could help."

"You're a very good writer, Henry," Lila said gently. "You should let him help you, Jim. He knows what he's talking about."

Henry laughed to himself. Lila meant well, but the only writing of his she'd ever read was an essay he'd written in the eleventh grade. It had been an adequate essay, Henry remembered, but an old high school paper hardly justified her labeling him a "good writer."

Jim pushed his chair back from the table. "I gotta mow the lawn." Jim ended the conversation in typical Jim fashion—just as abruptly as he'd started it. "You want to help me, AJ?"

"Sure, Grandpa; I'll go get my old shoes." AJ dropped his plate into the sink with a clatter. "Bye, Dad!" His hurried farewell tossed over his shoulder as he raced down the hallway toward his room felt like little more than an afterthought.

Lila walked Henry to his car.

"Can you tell Allison I'll be at AJ's soccer game on Wednesday night? Maybe I can take him for a cheeseburger or something afterward."

Lila nodded. "I'll let her know. And, Henry, don't forget what I said. Don't forget to take care of *yourself*."

He gave Lila a hug before climbing into his car. "I'll try."

Henry knew Rose Creek was where he needed to be. Having a closer relationship with his son eclipsed any doubts he'd ever harbored on the matter. As long as it was AJ's home, it would be his home too. And yet, as he pulled out of Lila's driveway and drove the winding streets he knew and loved from his childhood, he wondered how a place he'd called home for so many years could feel so desperately lonely.

Chapter 2

"So how did Beverly take it?"

Eliza turned away from Lexie and tried to appear nonchalant. "Fine, I guess."

"You guess? We're talking about your mother. You're not allowed to give me a three-word answer and leave it at that."

Eliza picked up a sweater—a spring-green cropped cardigan—and held it against her, turning toward the mirror. "What else do you want to know? She's happy for me. She knows it's a good job. What about this one?" She motioned to the sweater. "Should I take it?"

"I haven't seen you wear it in months," Lexie said. "The color brings out your eyes though. And it's cold in the mountains. You'll need it." She pulled the sweater out of Eliza's hands and folded it, adding it to the growing pile of clothes inside Eliza's suitcase. "So that's it, then? She's happy for you, and now you're on your merry way?"

Eliza sighed and sank onto the bed next to her friend and longtime roommate. "Not really. She was sad and a little discouraged, I think. I could tell she doesn't want me to be so far away. The thing is, even though I'm happy about where our relationship is now and I wish it didn't have to change, this job . . . even Mom agrees it's too good for me to pass up."

"You know, just because there'll be more physical distance between you doesn't mean your relationship has to change." Lexie gave Eliza's shoulder a gentle nudge.

Of course, Lexie was right.

But things with Eliza's mother still felt fragile. It was only recently they had been able to repair the splintery remains of a relationship that for years had been fractured beyond recognition. They'd made so much progress Eliza might even say they were close. It wasn't a typical mother-daughter relationship. They were more like good friends. But after all they had been through, Eliza would take good friends. It could be so much worse.

"I hope you're right," Eliza said. "We're going to have lunch together today, and I don't want things to be awkward when we say good-bye. I just want everything to be okay, you know?"

"It's going to be fine. It *has* to be. Besides, there's no turning back now. Your suitcase is already packed." Lexie glanced at her watch. "Shoot, I gotta go. I'm meeting Jason in twenty minutes." She paused in the doorway and looked back. "Speaking of Jason, you're coming back for the wedding, right?"

Eliza cocked an eyebrow. "Wedding? When did the engagement happen?"

Lexie grinned. "It hasn't yet, but it will soon. And when it does, I'll say yes, and then there'll be a wedding, and you'll come back for that wedding. Right?"

Eliza laughed. "Of course I'll come back. I wouldn't miss it for the world."

"Will you call me after lunch with your mom? Tell me how it goes?" Eliza nodded.

She watched Lexie walk down the long hallway of the two-bedroom condo they had shared for the past three years. Lexie disappeared into her own bedroom at the opposite end of the hall, then reemerged only moments later, her purse and keys in hand.

"I'll be home later tonight if you want to go through the stuff in the kitchen."

Eliza waved from the doorway of her bedroom. "Sounds good."

Leaving the condo—leaving Lexie—was going to be hard. Eliza had moved in just weeks after finishing her master's degree in social work, wrapping a new job, a new condo, and a new roommate all into one action-packed week. Working for Davidson County Child and Family Services right in the heart of Nashville, she'd been lucky to find a place so perfectly situated. But the apartment's close proximity to her office had seemed like bonus points when Eliza realized how much she enjoyed having Lexie as a roommate. They had been instant friends.

Sorting through the last of her closet, Eliza boxed up the clothes she no longer wanted and carried them out to her car. If she hurried, she'd be able to drop them off at Goodwill before making the forty-five-minute drive to Ashland City for lunch with her mom.

* * *

Once they were settled over caesar salads and minestrone, Beverly voiced the same concerns she'd been clinging to since Eliza had told her mother about the new job.

"And you're sure this is the right place for you? It just seems rather . . . remote."

Eliza took a deep breath and tried to keep her tone light. "It *is* remote. But I'm kind of excited about that part. It feels a little like an adventure. Besides, there's a town thirty minutes away."

"With three whole stoplights, I'm sure." At least her mother smiled then. "What's it called again? Rose Hill? Rose . . ."

"Rose Creek."

"That's right—Rose Creek. You won't live in town though, will you? You'll live at the school?"

Eliza nodded. "There has to be a counselor on site at all times, so yes. But I'll have time off when I need it. There will be four of us who live there full-time." She paused and looked at her mom, willing her to recognize the sincerity in her voice, the hope she had for the work she would be doing. "Mom, this is the kind of job I've been waiting for. It's why I got my degree—so I could do *this* kind of work, with *these* kinds of kids."

"And there isn't anything you could do here in the city that would provide the same opportunity? Something not quite so rustic?"

Eliza shook her head. "This is it, Mom. I'm sure of it. It's the opportunity I want."

Eliza knew the remote location wasn't what was bothering her mother. She suspected she simply felt the same desperation Eliza did. They both understood the possibility of distance damaging the relationship they'd been working so hard to build.

Still, Eliza knew she had to go.

Five hours east of her home in Nashville, Rockbridge Academy was a therapeutic boarding school for troubled teenagers. The school was an island of civilization in a sea of wilderness, buffered by National Forest land on three sides, making the remoteness of its eighteen-acre campus feel magnified.

But everything about the school—from the administrative staff to the counselors Eliza would be working with, even the atmosphere and energy of the place—led her to conclude the job was just the opportunity she was looking for. It *was* remote but not so remote that her mother couldn't visit. That was her hope, anyway.

Eliza pulled a package out from under the table, where she'd stowed it before her mother arrived, and handed it across the table. "Here—this is for you."

"What on earth is this for?"

"Just open it."

She watched as her mother untied the string and carefully removed the brown wrapping to reveal a framed photo. "It's the mountains in North Carolina," Eliza said. "Not far from Rockbridge."

"It's lovely." Her mother paused, her eyes focused on the picture in her hands. "You know, I think I might have you worried that I don't want this for you. That's not really it. I want you to be happy, and if this job makes you happy, then it's what I want too." She looked up. "But I can't pretend I don't hate this. You've been my anchor, Eliza. Even when you were a little girl, you were the one solid thing . . ."

Eliza reached across the table for her mother's hand.

"Logically, I know I'll be fine. The distance doesn't have to change anything." Beverly took a cleansing breath and pulled the napkin from her lap to wipe the tears from under her eyes. "But I will miss seeing you."

"I'll miss you too, Mom."

"I've just been thinking how ironic it is that after all you went through, now you're on the other side of things—you're the one *helping* instead of being helped." Her mother shook her head. "I'll never stop wishing things had been different."

"Mom, stop. I don't have any regrets, all right? We had it rough for a while, but I'm okay. *We* are okay."

Her mother's smile was bittersweet. "You've told me that a thousand times. I wonder if I'll ever start believing it."

"It's always hardest to forgive ourselves." Eliza leaned her elbows on the table, and her mother gave her a funny look. "What? What is it?"

"Nothing. That was just the kind of thing your father would have said. And then the way you leaned on your elbows—for a moment, you looked just like him."

Eliza brightened. Her mother could pay her no higher compliment.

The tragedy of her father's cancer had been an agonizing blow for Eliza's entire family. Eliza was young and confused in the wake of his death, but her mother's grief had been insurmountable. In her silent, suffering world, alcohol had become the only drug that could dull the pain, leaving no room for her two daughters—daughters who were adrift, looking for a lifeline to help them through their own mourning. But they'd found no lifeline in their mother. As a result, Eliza had turned to her father's memory for comfort, idolizing him, imagining the parent he would have been if he'd never been ill.

As a grown woman, she was wise enough to know that had he lived, he would have been just as flawed as her mother—as anyone. But the sheen of Eliza's youthful adoration still clung to her memories. In her heart, her father would always feel just a little bit better than perfect.

Eliza watched the frown lines on either side of her mother's face deepen. Beverly cleared her throat and shifted in her seat. "So, Gina came home last night."

"What? Why didn't you tell me? Is she all right?"

"I still haven't seen her. I only know she's home because her things were all over the kitchen when I got up this morning. I knocked on her bedroom door, but it was locked, and she didn't answer."

"You really should change your locks. She can't keep doing this to you."

"Change the locks? Why? So she can sleep in the street? She only comes here when she has to. If I turn my back on her, where will she go?"

"Maybe she'll finally get the help she needs." As she always did whenever they discussed her sister, Eliza quickly grew frustrated. "Mom, this has to stop. She's wasting her life away, and you're letting her."

Her mother's face turned stony. "She'll figure things out. I got better. So will she."

"You got help," Eliza said sternly. "You went to rehab. You stopped drinking. You got better because you tried. Gina isn't trying. She's hiding, and she's drowning herself in alcohol. Before long, it's going to be too late. Not to mention how brutally unfair it is for her to show up at your house every day reeking of alcohol. Do you let her drink in the house? How is that good for you?"

"Now you stop that." Beverly's voice was sharp. "You stop turning therapist on your family. Your sister's doing the best she can. She didn't handle things like you did, but she's going to be all right. She'll come out of it soon enough." She crossed her arms tightly across her chest, an indication to Eliza that as far as she was concerned, any conversation on this particular subject was over.

Eliza wondered why her mother even bothered to tell her about Gina. Their conversations always ended the same way. Her mother had been sober eleven years. Eliza wished her mother's experiences made her more aware of the seriousness of Gina's condition, but it was far more complicated than that. Her mother felt *responsible* for Gina's struggles. She hadn't been there when Gina had needed a mother most, and Eliza knew her mom felt guilty for it every single day.

The guilt made her soft, even indulgent to Gina's whims. She was too gentle, too tolerant. But Gina needed something more than just a shoulder to cry on or a bed to sleep in. She needed help.

Eliza offered. Over and over she offered to help. But Gina just pushed her away. She pushed everyone away.

"Just be careful, all right? Don't let her take advantage of you. And don't let her—" Eliza looked up, waiting for her mother's gaze to meet hers. "Mom, I just don't want her to pressure you or make you feel uncomfortable."

"Oh, Eliza, I've been sober long enough to know that I have no desire to go back to where Gina is now. I appreciate your concern, but I can't abandon her. I'll be fine. I promise."

Eliza only nodded.

"When do you leave?" They both seemed happy to change the subject.

"Early Saturday morning. I've got the rest of this week to pack my room at the condo, and then I'm off. Are you coming to the going-away party on Friday night? Lexie said she invited you."

Beverly smiled. "Of course I'll be there. I wouldn't miss it for anything."

* * *

Eliza climbed out of her SUV and stretched her arms over her head. She'd made the trip in just under four hours and was stiff from being in the car for so long. It was a beautiful day. The sky was a brilliant blue overhead, the trees a vibrant summer green. Eliza couldn't help but feel invigorated as she took in her surroundings. She was parked in the lot behind Rockbridge's main administration building, just in front of a row of small apartments, where the on-site staff resided. Her apartment was on the very end of the north building, number five.

Her heart rate quickened with anxiety as she thought about how alone she was in this new chapter of her life. Sheer momentum had pushed her through the past few days, but now, with no one but the birds for company, she found her solitude a little overwhelming. She took a deep breath and closed her eyes. *This is right*, she reminded herself.

Knowing she couldn't stand in the parking lot forever, Eliza reached in through the open driver's side window of her car and pulled out her purse. The keys to her new apartment were inside, and she was anxious to get settled in. She pulled out her cell phone to check the time. Six thirty-four—still plenty of time to unload before dark.

"I hope you're not trying to find a signal." Eliza looked up. An attractive, sandy-haired man stood in front of her, hands on his hips, broad smile stretched across his face. "When I first started working here, I searched the campus high and low for even one bar of service and never came close."

Eliza smiled. The man spoke with a subtle accent that she couldn't immediately identify. It was charming though, as was his warm and welcoming smile. "I was just checking the time." She extended her hand. "I'm Eliza."

"The new therapist," the man said. "I recognize your name. Glad to have you here. I'm Flip Marshall."

"It's nice to meet you. Do you live on site?"

"Down there in number two. Can I help you carry anything in?"

Eliza moved to the tailgate of her SUV and opened it, handing the largest suitcase to Flip. They walked to her apartment together, and Eliza held the screen door open with her hip while she unlocked the main door to her new home.

The apartment had a large front room and an efficiency kitchen in the back corner, as well as a small table with two chairs and a sitting area with a matching couch and chair. The floors were polished oak, and a soft blue area rug filled the space directly in front of the couch. Eliza was surprised to see a small television on the back wall.

Flip must have been watching her gaze. "Satellite television, high speed Internet, and don't forget your trusty landline telephone," he said. "It's the same number for everyone—the school's main number—but you'll have two different extensions, one for your office and one for personal use." Flip placed the suitcase he was carrying by the door to the bedroom just off the sitting area.

"So your bathroom is through the bedroom, and everything else you can see from here. Not too bad, is it?"

"It's perfect."

Flip moved back to the door. "What else can I carry?"

Eliza willingly accepted his help, and the two made fast work of moving her boxes and various belongings into the small apartment. When they finished, Flip ran down to his own apartment and grabbed a couple of cold water bottles, bringing one back for Eliza. The weather was much cooler in the mountains than it had been in Nashville when Eliza had left that morning, but it was still warm enough to work up a good thirst.

"So what do you do here at Rockbridge?" Eliza asked Flip. They sat companionably on the steps in front of her apartment.

"I'm a wilderness team leader." Flip's cargo shorts and hiking boots matched well with his responsibilities.

"So you're the one who takes them off into the woods. Do you bring them all back?"

Flip smiled a little half smile. "So far, so good. Though I won't say I haven't been tempted a time or two to leave someone behind—at least long enough to give 'em a good scare." He put his empty water bottle on the stairs between his feet. "In all seriousness, I'm always amazed at how much the kids change when they're out in the woods. When they're free from distractions and all the regular pressures they're used to—I don't know. They all seem like good kids. It's a good program."

When Flip strung several sentences together, it was easier to hear the slight lilt to his voice and pick up on the roll of his *r*'s and the way he clipped the end off many of his words. "So, obviously you're not from around here," Eliza said. "What brought you to Rockbridge?"

"What? My Southern accent not convincing enough, is it?"

"Not hardly. I'm guessing Irish?"

"Look at you," Flip said. "I'm impressed. Not everyone guesses right the first time."

"I watch a lot of British television. I'm pretty much an expert."

Flip laughed. "Is that so? I didn't realize they let the Irish onto British television, though I guess *someone* has to drive the cars and run the pubs."

It was Eliza's turn to laugh. "You said it, not me."

"And you better not either. I'd be insulted if you did. But since I've the blood of an Irishman, I can say what I want about my fair homeland." He nudged Eliza and gave her a good-natured grin. "I moved to the States with my parents when I was thirteen. I've been here long enough that if I try really hard, I can almost sound American. But where's the fun in that? Besides, girls like the accent."

Eliza shook her head. She wouldn't deny the certain charm Flip's accent gave him, but she wasn't about to let him know she felt that way. "Where did you move to? To North Carolina?"

"No, we moved to Richmond, up in Virginia, not too far from here. Virginia was home until I came to Rockbridge. What about you? Where's home for you?"

"I grew up in Ashland City, Tennessee. It's just west of Nashville, but I've been working for Davidson County in downtown Nashville for the past few years."

"A big-city girl, are you? I hope the quiet mountains don't put you to sleep."

"No, I'm looking forward to a quieter life." Eliza looked around the near-empty parking lot. "Not everyone lives on site, do they? Are you required to live here?"

"I don't have to, no. It's just you, Natalie, Jeff, and James who are required to live on site. And, of course, the dorm managers too. I guess Frank and Dr. Adler won't ever move away either—they live in the cottage over by the entrance."

Frank and Elena Adler were Rockbridge's owners and directors.

Flip continued. "We're not kept on quite so short a leash, but there are a few more of us who live here by choice. It's almost too convenient not to if you're on your own and don't have a family to go home to."

"What's Jeff like?" Eliza asked. "I met James and Natalie when I interviewed for the job, and they seem really great, but Jeff was away when I was here, so I didn't get to meet him."

"You'll like Jeff too. He's a little rough around the edges, but once you get to know him, you can't help but like him."

"Who else lives on campus?"

"Jeff lives down in one. I'm in two. Henry Jacobson, he's the English teacher, lives in three, Natalie in four, then you, here in five." Flip paused and ran his fingers through his hair. "Let's see. One of the teachers—history, I think—she just moved into number six of the south building across the parking lot, and then James is in seven. I think the last three on the end are empty. No, that's not true. The maintenance man—Gerald, a prickly old man, that one—he lives at the very end, in ten."

"You know I'm not going to remember all of that, right?"

"Sure you will." Flip cracked his knuckles with a flourish. "Here's your first quiz. Pulling up right now is the resident who lives in apartment number three."

Eliza rolled her eyes and looked up to see a dark sedan pull into the parking lot. It came to a stop just a few spaces down from where she and

Flip sat. A man in khaki dress pants and a light-blue button-down shirt climbed out of the car, keys bouncing in his hand. He moved to the trunk of his car and lifted the hatch, momentarily obscuring Eliza's view.

"Well, I haven't met him before, so it could be Jeff, but he looks a little too polished for anyone to call him 'rough around the edges.' So that would make him the English teacher, yes? I can't remember his name."

"Very good; that's Henry Jacobson. And no, he's not rough around anything. He might actually be the most cautious man I've ever met." Flip raised his arm over his head to wave. "Ho, Henry! How are ya?"

Henry closed his trunk and looked up, lifting his hand in brief acknowledgment. Without another glance in their direction, he moved to his apartment, unlocked the door, and swiftly pulled it shut behind him.

Eliza raised her eyebrows and looked at Flip. "Nice guy?"

"When he's anything at all, he's very nice. But most of the time, he just keeps to himself. He's into books and things. You know the type."

"I like books." Eliza's tone was light. "What does that say about me?"

"It's not just the books. He's just so reserved and quiet. And he never wants to hang out with any of us. I don't know. I just imagine him sitting in his apartment with his nose in a book. A bit presumptuous of me, huh? Don't get me wrong—I like the guy, but I guess he just seems . . . sort of boring."

"I don't know. I think he sounds kind of mysterious. Who knows what he's really up to?"

"Well, if you want to know about mystery, there's one other thing I should probably tell you about Henry." Flip had an air of mischief about him, a playfulness that led Eliza to believe he wasn't being completely serious. "Though don't tell him you heard it from me."

Eliza matched his conspiratorial tone. "What's that?"

"Henry . . . is a *Mormon*."

"Really?" Eliza filled her voice with feigned disbelief. "Well, in that case, you'll have to introduce me."

"Why is that? You got a thing for Mormons?"

Eliza smiled. "I do—especially ones that will give me a ride to church."

Chapter 3

Late the following Friday afternoon, Dr. Elena Adler sat across her desk from Henry, her expression full of concern.

"Mr. Jacobson, I want this job to work for you. I know it's been a little difficult for you to find your footing here at Rockbridge. I share the staff's concerns with you because I want you to stay. I want you to work through these challenges, not be beaten by them."

Henry finally released his breath and relaxed. When he'd responded to Dr. Adler's request for a meeting, he'd been certain he was losing his job. She was right. He *was* having a hard time finding his footing. In truth, Henry wondered if he wasn't in over his head. And yet, he wasn't ready to give up. He liked living at Rockbridge. He loved the area and atmosphere of the school, and most importantly, he needed to stay in Rose Creek to be close to AJ. He was grateful Dr. Adler wanted to keep him on board, though what he could do to improve, he didn't yet know.

Dr. Adler was often admired for her unassuming gentleness—her ability to breathe peace into those around her. Sitting across from her, seeing the compassion in her kind, gray eyes and experiencing the grace of a second chance, gave Henry a perfect understanding as to why.

Elena and her husband, Frank, had opened Rockbridge twenty years ago on a piece of inherited family land. They'd built the retreat from the ground up, turning it into a reputable institution, respected for both its rehabilitative programs and its quality of education. But at the root of it all, Rockbridge succeeded not because of prestigious recognition but because of the Adlers' kindness and sincerity—because they believed, just as Henry did, that people *deserved* a second chance.

"I appreciate your faith in my ability to improve," Henry finally said. He leaned back in his chair, his shoulders slack with defeat. "This is just so different from any teaching I've ever done before. Some of these kids—they just don't respond. I don't know how to get through to them."

"These kids are here because they *don't know how* to respond. When you teach at Rockbridge, you are more than a teacher. You are part of a team that is dedicated to healing and rehabilitating. We don't give up on kids here." Dr. Adler leaned forward, fixing Henry with her gaze. "We dig, and we push, and we find ways to reach every single student. You have to think outside the box—tear down every expectation of what you think a regular classroom in a regular high school should feel like."

Henry shook his head. "I don't know how." He hesitated. "I've just never been very good with people—I don't know that I *can* relate."

Dr. Adler folded her arms. "Mr. Jacobson, I mean this as gently as possible. If you want to keep working at Rockbridge, you'd best *find* a way to relate."

When she stood, Henry followed her example.

"Thank you, Dr. Adler," he said. "I'll try not to let you down again." He shook her hand, then turned to leave but looked back when Dr. Adler spoke again.

"Henry? Can I call you Henry?" Her tone was different, gentler, as if she regretted the sternness of her last comment.

Henry nodded. "Of course."

"What made you apply for this position?"

Henry looked down and pushed his hands into his pockets. After a moment, he decided the situation warranted a truthful answer. "My wife and I divorced two years ago. She moved back to Rose Creek—we grew up here—and I followed to be close to our son, AJ. He's only seven."

"I see." She paused as if to consider her words. "Henry, I wouldn't have hired you if I didn't think you were capable of handling the job. The kids here are too important for me to jeopardize their learning by hiring the first teacher who walked through the door. I know it can be difficult, but trust me—teaching here can be more rewarding and more fulfilling than anything you've ever imagined. I promise as long as you don't give up on these kids, I won't give up on you. Do we have a deal?"

Henry forced a smile. He knew Dr. Adler was trying to be kind, but she'd wounded his pride. He'd much prefer retreating in silence, perhaps giving himself a few minutes to sulk before putting on his game face and jumping into a deal. But she was right. If he wanted to stick around, something was going to have to change.

"Deal."

"Good." She returned his smile. "Then I'll see you back at five for staff meeting. Have you had the chance to meet our new counselor, Ms. Redding?"

Henry shook his head. He'd seen her around campus, but their schedules hadn't provided an opportunity for them to meet directly. "No, not yet."

"She'd be a valuable friend for you to make. She's a remarkable counselor and recognizes things in these kids that, even with all my experience, I don't often see. She might be able to help if you have specific students you're struggling with."

"I'll keep that in mind."

Henry glanced at his watch as he left Dr. Adler's office. It was four thirty. Rather than leave the administration building, he decided to wait on the front porch until the staff meeting started. The wide porch wrapped around the front of the building and continued around the western side to the back, where it joined a large sun deck. The deck was full of picnic tables and was a frequent gathering place for students and staff alike. But Henry preferred the split-log benches that sat just east of the main entrance. The porch didn't wrap around on this side, eliminating any through traffic and creating a quiet corner, where Henry was often alone.

Henry stretched, enjoying the growing coolness that accompanied the approaching evening, and set his black leather bag on the bench beside him. He would never grow tired of North Carolina mountain summers. He'd missed them while living in Winston-Salem.

He'd liked the town he and Allison had shared just after he'd graduated from college. He'd had a good job teaching high school English, and they'd had a house with a nice backyard for AJ to play in. They'd also been close to his parents, who had moved back after his father's retirement. Winston-Salem was where his mother had grown up. But it was hot—just beyond the reach of the mountains and more susceptible to the scorching summer temperatures that typically graced the Southern states. If Henry *had* to find a silver lining to his divorce and subsequent move to the mountains, cooler temperatures might be it.

Checking his watch again, he thought about pulling out his laptop to see if he could get a few pages of writing in before the start of the meeting, but his mind wasn't clear enough to write—not after his conversation with

Dr. Adler. He agreed he was struggling with his students. Some were doing fine, but others? Sometimes he couldn't sleep for the worry they caused.

Because Rockbridge was so small, never more than sixty students at a time, the circumstances of Henry's teaching were a little different. He taught English to all sixty, from grade seven all the way to twelve. Henry had five groups with seven to fifteen kids in each, divided by age and curriculum. The rest of his students he met with on an individual basis.

His mind turned to Daniel—a fifteen-year-old student who was having a particularly difficult time. Daniel had been at Rockbridge six full weeks and had yet to make any real progress in Henry's class. It wasn't that he wasn't smart. The conversations Henry had had with the other teachers and with Daniel's counselor had assured him the boy was bright, even exceptionally so. But for Henry, Daniel would not work, preferring instead to sit for hours in sullen silence if it meant not having to pick up a pencil. In a way, Henry felt as if Daniel were his challenge—the determining factor as to whether or not he was really cut out for working at Rockbridge. He sensed his fellow faculty might feel the same way.

It was Lila who had called to tell him about the teaching position at Rockbridge nine months before. She'd read it in Rose Creek's local newspaper and thought he might be interested. Henry had readily applied for the job, thinking less about the unique challenges Rockbridge might bring and more about his desire to be close to AJ. Within a week, he'd made the drive over to meet the Adlers and had accepted the position. It wasn't like him to be so impulsive. In retrospect, he questioned his decision, his willingness to make such a drastic move without more careful thought and consideration. Despite his doubts, Henry knew he would have made the same choice over and over again. He'd moved for AJ. And for AJ, he would have to find a way to get through to his students.

Henry glanced behind him when he heard the sound of voices drifting toward the porch. His vantage point allowed a full view of the parking lot and staff apartments so he was able to quickly see Flip and the new counselor walking toward the building. Henry watched the woman, her face animated as she talked with Flip. She must have related something funny because Flip leaned his head back in robust laughter. The woman's laugh joined his, and Henry noted how comfortable the two looked, how at ease they seemed, even having met just short of a week prior. But that was Flip. Flip got along with everyone, made everyone feel at ease. It was why he was so good at what he did. People like Flip were made for places like Rockbridge.

Henry remembered the woman's name—Eliza Redding—from the last staff meeting, when Dr. Adler had spoken of her forthcoming arrival. She was younger than he had expected, though he thought perhaps her braided pigtails made her look younger than she actually was. To be a licensed counselor, he knew she had to have at least a master's degree, and those didn't happen overnight. He continued to watch her as she and Flip climbed the stairs to the administration building and looked his way.

She was attractive, yes, but there was something more than that. Everything about her seemed to sparkle with energy. From her red hair to her fair, freckled skin and the vibrant colors of her clothing, she seemed more alive than anyone Henry had ever seen.

"Henry! How are you, man? Have you had the chance to meet—"

Before Flip could finish his sentence, Natalie Porter, one of Rockbridge's counselors, stuck her head out the front door and called to Eliza. "Eliza, I'm glad you're here early. Can you come inside? We're trying to work out our schedule for next week and need your input."

"Of course." She glanced at Henry. "If you'll excuse me."

"Oh, and Flip," Natalie said. "Frank was asking about you. Something about missing tent stakes?"

Flip nodded his head. "Ah, the tent stakes. I'll go explain." He looked back at Henry. "See you inside."

As quickly as everyone had appeared, they were gone again, leaving Henry alone once more. With nothing else to do, he picked up his bag from the bench beside him and followed the others inside.

Chapter 1

ELIZA REALIZED SHE WAS GAMBLING. All she knew for certain was that Flip said Henry was a Mormon. She had no idea if he was planning to attend church that morning or if he even attended regularly at all. Still, she decided to wait a few more minutes.

She sat on the stairs just in front of her apartment and glanced at her watch one more time. If Henry didn't appear in the next five minutes, she'd have to go ahead and leave if she wanted to find the chapel in Rose Creek before the meeting started. She looked at the directions she'd printed out the night before. It wasn't complicated—she was sure she could find the building without any trouble—but it felt silly to drive all that way if Henry was going to make the same drive.

The previous Sunday, weary from her long trip, Eliza had inadvertently overslept. It wasn't in her nature to skip church, but she must have needed the extra sleep. She had no recollection of even hearing the buzz of her alarm. By the time she'd awakened, the late morning sun had been streaming in through her bedroom window and sacrament meeting had been completely over. She wondered whether Henry would have made more of an effort to meet her and say hello if she'd been able to attend church.

He was the only one on campus she hadn't officially met. She'd even gotten to know Gerald, the maintenance man. He wasn't nearly as bad as Flip had described. But, then, she'd taken him cookies when she'd gone to say hello. Cookies made everything easier.

It seemed only natural that she and Henry should be friends. She couldn't be certain they were the only members on campus, but she felt it a pretty safe assumption.

Yet she was nervous. By all descriptions, Henry was never anything but kind—polite, even to a fault. But everyone at Rockbridge agreed that socially, he was a lost cause. He continually turned down invitations to join staff members for dinner or trips into Rose Creek. Instead, he was known to retreat quickly, appearing to prefer the solitude and simplicity of his own space. With so little to say to others, he might think a car ride all the way to church in Eliza's company would be pure torture.

Three, then four minutes passed, and Henry had yet to appear. Eliza stood and gathered her things. She would have to find the church on her own. When she reached the foot of her porch steps, she saw Henry locking the door to his apartment. He turned and moved quickly toward his car. Eliza hurried to catch him before he left.

"Henry," she called.

He looked up. "Good morning." He was obviously dressed for church. He wore a navy suit and a light blue tie that complemented the blue of his eyes, and he held his scriptures and a Gospel Doctrine manual under his arm.

"If you don't mind," Eliza began, "I thought we could ride together."

Henry looked at her quizzically. "I don't understand."

"You're going to church, aren't you?"

"Well, yes, but . . . it's a Mormon Church."

His hesitance made Eliza smile. She held up her bag. Her leather-bound scriptures were just barely visible at the top, and her old missionary name tag was clipped to the side. It was hard for any set of scriptures to look more Mormon than hers.

"Um, I'm pretty much okay with that."

"Oh," Henry said. "I'm sorry, I didn't realize . . . didn't expect . . ."

"To ever see another Mormon around this place?" Eliza finished his sentence. "I know. Neither did I."

Henry still looked confused, and Eliza started to feel awkward. "I'm sorry," she said quickly. "I'm being presumptuous. Flip mentioned that you were a member, and since I've never been to the meetinghouse, I just hoped . . . Well, I thought since we were leaving from the same place, it only made sense . . ."

"No, of course," Henry said. "Please." He crossed to the passenger side of the car and opened the door for Eliza.

She climbed into the front seat of Henry's sedan, placing her purse and scriptures on the floor in front of her. After Henry settled into the driver's seat, he buckled up, gave Eliza a nod of acknowledgment, then eased the car out of the parking lot and onto the windy, narrow road that led into Rose Creek.

Eliza had seen Henry at staff meeting and around campus a handful of times. But here in his car, close enough to smell his aftershave and notice the detail of the print on his tie, she felt like she was getting her first good look.

Flip had implied that Henry was a bookish type who kept to himself. Eliza had to admit he looked the part. But Eliza had a feeling there was more to Henry than just a pair of glasses and a conservative suit. There was a depth to his blue-gray eyes that drew her in, and she found herself staring, studying his jawline, the thick lashes that framed his eyes. When he glanced away from the road and they made brief eye contact, she felt utterly exposed. Henry might *look* the part of a studious professor, but Eliza had never had an English teacher who looked as good as he did.

Eliza cleared her throat and willed her thoughts to behave. "I appreciate the ride," she said. "I'm sure you weren't expecting someone to bulldoze into your morning."

"It's no trouble. Now you'll know how to get to the building next week."

Eliza quickly turned her head so Henry wouldn't see the blush that flooded her cheeks. Not five minutes in the car together and he'd already made it clear how he really felt about her tagging along. He was too much of a gentleman to refuse her, but clearly, this was not something he desired as a regular arrangement. Momentarily puzzled by his dismissal, Eliza swallowed hard, took a deep breath, and decided to give it another go.

"I made you some cookies." She tripped over her words as they tumbled out. "I wanted to introduce myself and thought cookies would be a nice way to do that. But then, when I took a plate over to Gerald, he talked for quite a while, and I ran out of time. I tried to find you the following day, but I got distracted with work, and before I knew it, I'd eaten all your cookies myself." Eliza couldn't decide if her nerves were making her yammer on or if she was simply trying to make up for Henry's reticence with an excess of her own words.

"You made me cookies?" Henry asked. Before Eliza could respond, Henry added, "You took cookies to Gerald?"

Eliza realized she'd been holding her breath and finally exhaled with relief. Henry's tone was just light enough to ease her discomfort. "He's not that bad a guy. He was very polite to me."

"After you gave him the cookies, I'm sure. Maybe your efforts will soften him for all of us."

"I do make a mean chocolate chip cookie. They've been known to soften hearts before."

"I'll have to take your word for it," Henry said, "since you ate all of my cookies."

Eliza smiled. "They're better fresh anyway. I'll make you another batch this afternoon."

"That's kind of you to offer," Henry said. "Another time though. My Sunday afternoons are generally pretty occupied."

Snubbed. Again.

Maybe it was just as well she'd eaten his cookies.

Henry turned his full attention to the road as the car approached a dizzying series of switchbacks that wound down the mountain into town. Eliza leaned her head back on the seat and closed her eyes, trying to avoid a threatening wave of carsickness.

"Ugghh, these roads are terrible," she said. "They don't make them like this where I'm from."

"Try rolling the window down. I've heard that helps."

Eliza cracked the window and leaned into the cool air that whipped across her face.

"That does help," she said. "A little."

"Where *are* you from?"

Eliza wasn't sure if Henry thought distracting her might help or if he was unaware of just how desperately she was trying to *not* throw up in his car. She paused a moment before answering, breathing slowly, deeply. They rounded the last bend, and the road straightened, at last giving Eliza a slight reprieve.

"Ashland City," she said. "It's just west of Nashville."

Eliza released her grip on the door and tried to relax into her seat. Henry was a good driver, taking the curves at a reasonable speed, but this was the first time Eliza had ever made the trip into town as a passenger. She thought the worst was over, but just in case, she kept her head back and her eyes closed.

"Are you all right?" Henry said. "You look . . . pale."

She opened her eyes, only slightly, and looked in his direction. "I always look pale. It comes with the red hair." She tried to smile, though she guessed it looked more like a grimace. "Are we getting close?"

Most of Rose Creek was still unfamiliar to Eliza. She didn't recognize where they were, but it appeared they were approaching civilization. The endless trees and mountains were giving way to scattered homes and mailboxes.

"Just a few more miles," Henry said. Eliza was surprised when Henry pulled onto a narrow gravel drive just moments later. He parked the car in front of a redbrick, ranch-style home with a narrow porch and rickety white railings on either side of a set of concrete steps.

"I'll just be a minute," he said.

Eliza nodded. She watched as he hurried up the cement walkway of the house and rang the bell. A small blonde woman answered the ring and smiled briefly through the screen door. She turned behind her and gestured to someone inside the house. As she ushered a small boy out onto the porch, she must have noticed Eliza's presence. She called to Henry as he and the boy walked to the car. He turned and answered her question, giving her a dismissive wave and a shake of the head. Eliza was sure the woman was asking about her.

"This is my son, AJ," he said to Eliza as he helped the boy into the backseat. "AJ, this is Sister Redding. She works with me at Rockbridge and needed a ride to church this morning."

"It's nice to meet you," AJ said. The boy looked much like his father. His hair was lighter than Henry's, but his eyes looked like a mirror reflection. He wore a neatly pressed white shirt and tie, polished shoes, and a tailored suit coat. With his hair neatly slicked to the side, AJ looked like a man in miniature. In his hands, he reverently carried a set of scriptures that looked brand-new. The gold lettering on the front bearing AJ's name was still shiny.

Henry placed AJ's backpack on the floor of the backseat. "Are you all set?"

"Yeah, I'm good."

Of all the things she'd speculated about Henry, casting him as a divorced father had never been one of them. It occurred to her why he might be less than willing to shuttle her to and from church every Sunday or spend an afternoon eating her chocolate chip cookies. Henry lived alone at Rockbridge during the week, which meant he probably spent his weekends with AJ. She felt foolish for having so brazenly forced her way into Henry's Sunday plans.

Eliza willed herself to be silent, listening instead as Henry asked AJ about soccer, about his dog, about his grandparents. The short, lifeless tone of AJ's answers surprised her. He was trying to say the right answers, but both father and son seemed uncomfortable. For a moment, Eliza thought the tension might be because of her presence, but the routine of Henry's questions and AJ's answers wasn't new. It seemed a familiar pattern—one she guessed played out over and over again. Whatever the history of their relationship, something was amiss.

Eliza wondered if anyone at Rockbridge knew Henry had a son. Flip most certainly didn't know. Surely Henry's coworkers wouldn't poke fun at his lack of social interactions if they realized he was turning down dinner with them to attend soccer games or Cub Scout pack meetings. Of course, fatherhood itself wasn't generally an excuse for social exclusion and solitude, but broken marriages and strained parental relationships could go a long way toward damaging a man. Perhaps Henry was simply too preoccupied to invest in friendships.

He pulled into the church parking lot, giving Eliza her first view of the chapel. It was a small building situated on a nicely wooded lot with a large green lawn. Henry pulled his keys from the ignition and glanced at AJ in the rearview mirror.

"You ready to go?"

AJ nodded and unbuckled his seat belt. Henry turned to Eliza. "Are you feeling any better?"

"I think so, though I think I'll sit here for another minute or two, just to make sure the nausea has passed." Eliza had a suspicion that for Henry—a single father—to show up to church with a woman no one had ever met might turn a few heads. Sparing him the task of explaining who she was, where she came from, and why she happened to show up to church with him seemed the very least she could do.

As Henry got out of the car, he glanced back and gave Eliza a small smile of acknowledgment. She couldn't be certain, but she thought she saw gratitude in his eyes.

* * *

Just after sacrament meeting, an attractive brunette approached Eliza as she stood at the back of the chapel. The woman was young—probably not much older than Eliza—and appeared to be very, very pregnant. She smiled. "You look lost. Can I help you find Sunday School?"

"That would be wonderful," Eliza said. "I've just moved into the branch, and—"

"Moved in? Here? That's wonderful!" The woman's enthusiasm took Eliza by surprise. She must have noticed because she quickly explained. "A lot of people vacation in the mountains, but nobody ever stays. I'm sorry," the woman continued. "I didn't introduce myself. I'm Kate Porterfield."

"It's nice to meet you. I'm Eliza Redding."

Kate waved at a man heading toward the rear door of the chapel. He smiled and came over to join them.

"Andrew," Kate said. "Come meet the newest member of our branch. This is Eliza Redding. Eliza, this is my husband, Andrew."

Eliza recognized his name from the sacrament program. He was the branch president and had addressed the congregation at the close of the meeting. He smiled and extended his hand. "Eliza, welcome. What brings you to Rose Creek?"

"I've started a new job at Rockbridge Academy," Eliza said. "I'm a counselor there."

"Ah, so you must know Henry Jacobson."

Eliza nodded. "I do. Henry was actually kind enough to give me a ride to church this morning."

"Henry's a good guy." Andrew glanced across the room at another man, gesturing toward the hallway. "I've got to see what Brother Phelps needs. It was nice to meet you, Eliza, and welcome."

"Brother Phelps *always* needs something," Kate said. "He's the nicest man you'll ever know, but don't start a conversation with him when you're on the way to the bathroom. You'll never make it in time!" She took Eliza by the arm. "Come on. I'll take you to Sunday School."

Later, in Relief Society, Eliza stood and introduced herself at the start of the meeting. When she mentioned her work at Rockbridge, a ripple of excitement seemed to pass from one woman to the next until the entire room was filled with an audible buzz.

Eliza sat back down and looked at Kate, her eyebrows raised in question. "It's Henry," Kate whispered. "He grew up here, and everyone loves him. You're young and pretty, and you work with him. The mere possibility of romance has them excited."

Eliza's cheeks flushed with warmth at the thought. "I hardly know him."

Kate smiled. "That doesn't matter with this crowd. There aren't many prospects around this place—they feel obligated to consider every eligible female when it comes to their beloved Henry."

While the Relief Society president continued with the announcements, an elderly woman sitting to Eliza's left leaned over and whispered, "Do you like working with Henry Jacobson? Did you know he was divorced? His wife left him—that foolish girl. I never did care for her, but Henry is one of the finest men I know. Perhaps you're getting to know him already?" The woman raised her eyebrows and smiled, nodding her head conspiratorially.

Eliza hardly knew what to say. She looked back at Kate, disbelief all over her face.

Kate shrugged her shoulders. "It was the same way when Andrew brought me to church for the first time. It'll pass."

* * *

After church, Eliza found Henry leaning against his car, his hands thrust into his pockets.

"I hope you weren't waiting for me," she said.

Henry shook his head. "AJ will be right out. He just ran back in to get his scriptures." He stifled a laugh. "He's probably too young to have his own set. He leaves them inside almost every single Sunday."

"I don't know; he seemed pretty proud of them this morning," Eliza said. "And I overheard him telling Sister Porterfield all about how you got his name printed on the front so people would always know who they belonged to. He seems like a sweet kid."

Henry smiled the first real smile Eliza had seen on him. It changed his face in a way that made her breath catch. She'd found him handsome from the start, but his smile definitely took things to a different level.

"He is," he said.

"A sharp dresser too," she continued. "He must feel some pride in coming to church dressed like you."

Henry looked surprised. "Do you think so?"

"Of course. Most boys want to look like their fathers, don't they?"

She couldn't be certain, but a shadow of doubt seemed to cross Henry's face. He cleared his throat. "Maybe so."

"Henry, I'm sorry if I've ruined your plans with AJ today. I feel awful thinking that now you have to take me home instead of spending time with him."

"Actually, AJ is coming up to Rockbridge this afternoon, so it works out. I think I'll take him up into the forest, maybe drive on the parkway." There was an entrance to the Blue Ridge Parkway just a few miles away from Rockbridge.

"Oh, well, that's good, then," Eliza said. "Do you only get to see him on the weekends?" she asked tentatively, hoping it wasn't too personal a question.

"I can see him anytime," Henry responded. "But with my schedule at Rockbridge and the drive being what it is, it's mostly on the weekends, maybe once or twice during the week."

"That must be hard."

Henry looked at Eliza, locking his eyes with hers. "It's the hardest thing I've ever done."

* * *

Over the next several weeks, Eliza settled into the routines and rhythms of life at Rockbridge. She loved her job, loved getting to know the students and working with them through the ups and downs of their therapy. Occasionally, she struggled with the constant demands of being on call even when she wasn't working, but each week that passed made her unusual schedule feel a little more normal.

Sometimes there was no rhyme or reason for when one of the students needed her help. She'd been called upon early in the morning, after dinner, even in the middle of the night. Though she was far from city life, from the noise and people and demands of her previous job, she actually felt busier at Rockbridge. At the same time, when she did have time off, the beauty of the mountains around her made it that much easier to find peace.

The deep colors of the forest and the constant hum of wildlife infused Eliza when she felt her own strength diminishing. She loved the mountains for that reason. They filled her. Even though she was stretched and challenged far more than she ever had been before, everything about Eliza's life at Rockbridge seemed richer, from her work to her time alone to the time she spent getting to know her fellow staff members and friends.

Six weeks after she started at Rockbridge, Eliza and Jeff, along with Flip, Natalie, and several level four and level five students hiked to the top of Silar Bald, a mountaintop that boasted spectacular 360-degree views. Not all students were allowed off campus. Day trips were only for those who earned them through good behavior and positive attitude.

Eliza enjoyed the opportunities to get off campus with the kids. Sometimes she felt like she learned more about them as individuals during day trips than she did in a solid week of regular therapy.

She turned and looked down the slope of the mountain behind her. It was well worth the two and a half miles they'd hiked to reach the top. For the most part, the trail had meandered along the side of the mountain, switching back and forth as it climbed through the dense forest. But the last quarter mile opened into a large field that climbed steeply to the top of the bald.

Others might find it disheartening to see so clearly how far they had to go to make it to the summit, but Eliza found it invigorating to see the finish. Excited to take in the view for the first time, she had plowed ahead of the group, reaching the crest ahead of her companions. She waved at Flip, who was still several hundred feet down the hill at the back of the group. He waved back, then motioned for several students directly in front of him to pick up speed. From Eliza's vantage point, they looked less than enthusiastic about the remaining uphill stretch.

When everyone had finally made it, they stood together in silence and soaked up the view. The sky was a vibrant, summer blue directly overhead, then blended softly into the smokier blues and greens of the mountains at the horizon.

"It's beautiful, isn't it?" Flip moved up so he and Eliza stood side by side.

"I've never seen anything like it. It looks like the mountains go on forever."

"Not quite forever," Flip said, "but far enough that we could explore them for months and not come close to seeing everything."

"I want to see it all," Eliza said. "I don't think I could ever grow tired of living here."

"You're turning into a true mountain girl. I like that about you."

"I suppose. I'm happier here than I was in Tennessee, that's for sure. It's everything though, not just the mountains. I love the job too, and the people."

"I'm sure the feeling is mutual, Eliza. I know I'm happier now that you're here."

Eliza looked at Flip, trying to make eye contact, but he'd already turned his attention back to the group. She followed his gaze and watched as the kids settled onto the ground, forming small groups, pulling out their lunches from their day packs. She made sure everyone had someone to sit with, hoping to get a sense that all were happy and included.

Momentarily satisfied, she pulled out her own lunch and sat down next to Flip, who was already halfway through his sandwich. Natalie and Jeff joined them, forming a row so it was easier to keep an eye on the students while they ate. It wasn't likely that this far into the mountains, with nothing but a day pack, a student would try to break away from the group, but stranger things had happened in the past. The counselors couldn't be too careful.

Handling themselves responsibly on several day trips was necessary before kids were approved for one of Flip's lengthier ten-day wilderness excursions. The outings were tremendously therapeutic, but if a student posed a flight risk, they could also be very dangerous. Sending a student on excursion was never a decision anyone took lightly.

"I remember when I hiked Silar for the first time." Flip finished his last bite and wiped his fingers clean before continuing his story. "I was fourteen, down for a visit with my parents, and we went on a night hike sponsored by the outdoor center in Rose Creek."

"A night hike?" Eliza was incredulous. "Doesn't that defeat the purpose if you can't see the view?"

"Well, sure, if hiking is only about the view. We had a good time though. It felt like an adventure to hike by moonlight, and they had a big bonfire at the top."

Eliza still didn't get it. The view was her favorite part.

"I was a teenager the first time I hiked up here too." Natalie paused. "I was a student at Rockbridge."

Eliza turned and looked at Natalie. "How did I not know this about you?"

She shrugged. "I don't know. I guess it never came up."

"Eliza, the next time you see Frank, ask him to tell you the story of when Natalie found a stray dog on campus," Jeff said with a mischievous grin.

Natalie's eyes went wide with shock, but she never lost her smile, so she must not have been too upset. "Oh, you did not just bring that up." She gave Jeff a playful push. "Eliza, as a woman and a friend, I expect your full loyalty in this matter."

"I don't know," Eliza said. "Flip, have you heard the story? Is it a good one?"

Flip laughed under his breath. "One of the best I've heard."

"Oh, fine," Natalie said. "I found a dog. He was really sweet, and it was cold outside, and he was wet, so I decided to save him. He could have died out there in the woods! So I snuck him into the admin building to get him something to eat, and then he . . . well, he sort of . . . got away."

Flip and Jeff were already laughing.

"That's it?" Eliza asked. "He just got away?"

"Well, he might have . . . maybe . . . sort of . . . run into the board room and jumped onto the table and eaten Dr. Adler's sandwich." Natalie's voice was full of feigned innocence.

"Don't forget the shaking," Jeff said. "That dog stood right in the center of the table and flung dirty, hairy water all over the entire room, including on Dr. Adler."

Natalie was finally laughing herself. "I'm lucky she was such a good sport about it."

A few minutes later, when the laughing had died down and everyone was finished with their lunches, Eliza moved so she and Natalie were sitting side by side. "How long were you at Rockbridge?"

"Eighteen months. I was pretty much a total mess *until* Rockbridge."

"Is that why you wanted to come back?"

"You know, it's funny. It was something like six months, maybe nine months later, after I left. I was just starting college, and Dr. Adler sent me a Christmas card. When I saw the picture of the school on the front, everything just sort of clicked, and I realized what I wanted to do with my life. So here I am."

Eliza smiled. "I think it's really amazing that—" She paused. Natalie's focus had been pulled elsewhere. Eliza followed her gaze and saw, several feet away, a single student—Chloe—sitting alone, her arms wrapped around her legs, knees pulled up. Behind her, three other girls were sitting together tossing small pebbles at Chloe's back. The stones weren't large enough to do any physical harm, to even inflict a sliver of pain through the layers of Chloe's clothing, but they were plenty large enough to leave an emotional scar.

Eliza watched as Chloe lightly flinched each time a pebble made contact. This was not the kind of behavior Eliza would tolerate. She motioned to Natalie, and the two counselors stood, Eliza heading for Chloe and Natalie approaching the offending threesome behind her. Eliza lowered herself next to Chloe, sitting cross-legged, and waited for Natalie to move the other girls farther up the hill. Eliza sensed that Chloe wanted to speak, so she waited silently, patiently.

"You didn't have to stop them," Chloe finally said. "I'm strong enough to take it."

"I have no doubt that you're strong enough," Eliza said. "Why were they throwing rocks at you?"

Chloe shrugged. "Because they can. It's just a game to them."

"Do things like this happen often?"

She shrugged again. "Not really. I mean, sometimes, but it's not a big deal. Like I said—I can take it."

"Chloe," Eliza said gently, "you are not a punching bag—or a game to entertain a pack of disrespectful girls. You're a person with the right to be treated at all times with dignity and respect. You are worthy of love, of true friendship, of mutually uplifting relationships with others."

Chloe rolled her eyes. "Do you say that to everyone?"

"If I did," Eliza said, "it would only be because it's true of everyone."

"Yeah, well, it's not true of me," Chloe said defensively. "If it were true about me, I wouldn't be here. I'd be with my family because we would have '*mutually uplifting relationships*.'" She raised her fingers in the air and made mock quotation marks around the last three words of her sentence.

Eliza heard the rest of the group gathering their things behind her. "We'll talk more about this in our next session," she told Chloe. "Would you like to hike out with me?"

Chloe looked at her, her eyes distant. "Yeah. Because that will solve all my problems."

"Chloe, watch your tone, please," Eliza said calmly, "or you won't be leaving campus next week."

With another eye roll, Chloe picked up her bag and threw it over her shoulders. "Whatever," she mumbled under her breath. Considering the circumstances, Eliza chose to ignore the girl's disrespect. She wanted Chloe to be willing to open up to her in their next counseling session. Her gut told her that for now, it was best to leave well enough alone. She looked at Natalie as she moved up beside her.

"Is she all right?" Natalie asked.

"I think so."

"And you?"

Eliza looked at Natalie. The question felt deeper, as if it was referencing more than just the exchange she'd had with Chloe. The last month had been harder in many ways than Eliza had expected, but she still knew how she would answer Natalie's question. She smiled. "I'm good," she said simply. "I've got this."

Chapter 5

HENRY STOOD AT THE WINDOW of his classroom, his arms folded tensely across his chest, his jaw tight. The room was empty, save one other person. Daniel, Henry's student who had been causing him the most grief, was slouched down in his seat with his legs extended in front of him, staring idly at the ceiling.

It had been more than a month since Henry's meeting with Dr. Adler regarding his performance and progress at Rockbridge. Circumstances with a few of his other students had improved, but with Daniel, things were just as difficult as ever. Most of the time, the two of them were at complete odds. Daniel barely did enough to scrape by in Henry's class— so much so that Henry had yet to assign him to a group class and was still meeting with him one-on-one. While Daniel had completed a handful of assignments for Henry, he never offered more than a few disjointed sentences when answering questions.

Henry tried to relax his jaw and shake the tension out of his shoulders. The assignment sheet sitting on Daniel's desk was still blank. For close to twenty minutes, Daniel had been sitting sullen and silent and hadn't so much as reached for his pencil.

"Daniel, I don't want to waste your time, and I certainly don't want to waste mine," Henry said. "I'm not sure I understand why you simply can't write a few paragraphs in response to the essay prompt. It isn't a big deal. I just want you to tell me about yourself, tell me about the books you like to read, the music you like to listen to."

"What does any of that have to do with English?" Daniel didn't even turn his head to look at Henry. "Can't you just assign me some book to read and let me get out of here?"

Henry closed his eyes and took a deep breath. Daniel's assignment was simple. It was generally something he had students complete on the first day of class—basic questions about books they'd enjoyed in the past or subjects they liked to study. It was an easy way to identify a student's interests while also giving Henry a little bit of insight into where each student stood in their writing and reading skills. It *should* have been simple, but for Daniel, it was anything but.

"It has everything to do with English," Henry said. "I'm asking you about books you like to read. What interests you? What doesn't? These aren't hard questions."

"All right, whatever," Daniel said. "But what if I just don't like to read at all? Can't exactly write about that, can I?"

"I've seen you reading, multiple times, all over campus. You can't tell me you don't like to read. Just write about the last book you read. Tell me why you liked it or didn't."

"I don't feel like writing anything. Not for you."

"Daniel, this is an English class. You're going to have to write things down."

"Or maybe I'll just sit here and stare at your ceiling."

Henry walked to the front of the room and stood with his back to Daniel. He suddenly felt tired, annoyed that day after day the two of them seemed to be stuck in the same place. "Look. Right now my class load isn't very heavy. There are fewer students here over the summer, but in August, it will pick up. Classes will be bigger, and I will have more students who need my time and attention. I won't have time to sit here watching you refuse to complete a simple assignment. I don't know what you feel like you have to prove, but quite frankly, I don't have the patience for it anymore."

Henry was frustrated, almost angry, but his warning to Daniel sounded hollow. The truth was he didn't know what the consequence would be if Daniel *did* simply stare at his ceiling for the rest of the summer.

"Whatever," Daniel said again. "Why does it matter so much? Why can't you just give me a grade and be done with it? Why do you even care?" He shoved his notebook forward on his desk, sending his pencil flying to the floor.

"This isn't a regular high school," Henry said, trying to infuse calm into his voice. "You want to be where people don't care? Then you're in the wrong place. Everyone here cares. You won't do the assignment for me? Then we'll get Jeff in here to talk about why not. If you won't do the assignment for Jeff, then we'll get Eliza and Natalie and James in to let them have a go. We'll even call the director down. Maybe she will be able to figure out why you don't want to do the work."

Henry knew he needed to stop. He was letting anger dictate his words—an approach that surely wouldn't accomplish anything.

Daniel slouched over onto his desk, his head resting on his arms.

Henry blew out his breath in a weary sigh. "That's enough for today, Daniel. We'll meet again Wednesday afternoon."

The boy was silent as he stood, retrieved his fallen pencil, and slung his backpack over his shoulder. Henry watched him leave, then sank into his chair and pressed his forehead into his hand, massaging his temples with his thumb and forefinger. This wasn't a problem he could tackle on his own. He simply lacked the experience and discernment to know what approach might get through to Daniel. He'd tried on his own, and nothing was working. It was time to ask for help.

Daniel was Henry's last student of the day, and as he walked toward his apartment, he noticed Eliza and Flip sitting at a picnic table outside the administration building with two girls he recognized from his morning class. On the table, there was a large basket that appeared to be full of peaches. From Henry's viewpoint, it was hard to tell. Eliza looked up and waved him over.

It *was* peaches—one basket on the table and another on the porch beside Eliza. Two large silver bowls also sat on the table, one full of sliced fruit, the other full of discarded peels and pits. The group had obviously been working hard. The growing pile of fruit in the center of the table was impressive.

"Flip brought them up from South Carolina this morning," Eliza said by way of explanation. "And they're glorious—perfectly ripe. Do you want one?" Eliza motioned with her paring knife to the basket on the porch. "Take as many as you like."

"Thank you," Henry said. "I love peaches." He bent down to the basket and picked out several peaches, slipping them into the outside pocket of his leather school bag.

"Belinda says if we get them all sliced, she'll make cobbler for the Fourth of July picnic tomorrow." Henry looked at the girl who spoke. She was a new student; she had only been at Rockbridge a couple of weeks. He waited for her name to come to him. *Janie.* He smiled.

"Cobbler will be wonderful."

"Mr. Jacobson, I just finished reading *The Book Thief.*" This time, it was the other student who spoke—Brooke.

"And what did you think of it?"

"I thought it was terrible and sad and beautiful and brilliant all at the same time."

Henry nodded. "I felt the same way the first time I read it. We'll have a class discussion at the end of the week. But if you'd like to start thinking about your essay, remind me in class tomorrow, and I'll give you the prompts. There are four you can choose from."

"All right," Brooke said. "Ms. Redding, are we almost done? My fingers are numb."

"Mine too," Janie said.

"I think we're just about finished up. Girls, take this bowl in to Belinda and see if she thinks it's enough for cobbler."

The pair scrambled off the picnic bench and hefted the large silver bowl between them.

"Careful," Flip said. "Here, I'll come with you to open the door." He rose and moved ahead of the girls. "Later, Liza," he called over his shoulder.

Eliza cut one last peach in half and removed the pit, then offered half to Henry. "Want to sit awhile? You look tired."

"It's been a long afternoon." He took the peach from her hand. It really was perfectly ripe. It tasted like summer, and a wave of nostalgia washed over him. Suddenly, Henry was back at his mother's kitchen table with a fresh tomato sandwich and a large bowl of sliced peaches drizzled with cream and sprinkled with cinnamon. Eliza passed him a paper towel, which he used to wipe up the juice dripping down the side of his hand.

"Want to talk about it?"

He didn't, really. At least, normally he wouldn't. But he needed help, and Dr. Adler had suggested Eliza as a useful resource. He felt surprisingly comfortable sitting across from her. Her look of hopeful expectance put him at ease and he knew he could trust her capabilities as a counselor. She was the perfect person to ask for advice.

"It's one of my students—Daniel. He and I aren't exactly seeing eye to eye." Henry went on to tell her about their struggles and the frustrations he felt over their lack of progress.

"Is he doing well in his other classes?" Eliza asked.

"He's doing the work, which is a far cry better than what he's doing for me. I feel utterly powerless to get through to him. We can't keep sitting in silence; I know that much. But he seems so determined to ignore me, so . . ." Henry struggled to find the right word. "So *indifferent*."

"I don't think I've met Daniel," Eliza said. "What's he like?"

Henry paused. Even with firsthand experience, he didn't know much about Daniel's personality. In Henry's classroom, Daniel was stubbornly silent, generally short-tempered, and completely unwilling to comply with even a little of what Henry requested. "I wish I could say. He won't give me anything to go on in the classroom. What is it about my class, about *me*, that rubs him the wrong way?"

"With these kids, Henry, it's so hard to know. What does he say when you ask him to complete an assignment?"

"That he doesn't feel like writing anything down. It's mostly the writing he refuses to do. Grammar, short-answer stuff—he'll do it. But he won't write."

"He doesn't feel like it," Eliza repeated. "That hardly seems like a good enough reason."

"It's not," Henry said. "But he won't budge. I keep telling him we're all required to do unpleasant things. That's what life is about sometimes. But it's an argument that hasn't gotten me anywhere."

"If Daniel is doing the work in his other classes, there must be some particular reason, something specific that's causing him to withdraw. I don't think it's you, Henry. What if it's the subject material?"

"In what respect? Why would an English class make someone withdraw?"

"What if Daniel doesn't hate writing at all? What if he really loves it and that's the problem?"

Henry looked at her quizzically. "I'm not sure I follow."

"I'm just theorizing here, but what if he's holding back because he doesn't want to share a part of himself that he feels so passionately about? Could it be possible that Daniel is afraid that if he writes for you, he'll be giving you a window into the one part of him he feels is his own? When kids come here, they often feel like their entire life has been taken away from them. It takes them awhile to see how much Rockbridge can help. I imagine Daniel isn't there yet. In his eyes, we're still the bad guys trying to rob him of his freedom and his happiness and every other good thing."

Henry was starting to understand. "So maybe he's resisting because writing feels too personal."

Eliza shrugged. "It's a possibility. Or maybe he's just a punk kid who likes to see your ears turn red when he gets under your skin."

Henry's hands reflexively flew to his ears. "Are they red?"

Eliza laughed. "Not so much anymore, but I could tell you'd been through something when you first sat down."

Henry knew it was the added pressure he felt to succeed that made it so easy for Daniel to irritate him. Of course he wanted Daniel to progress for his own benefit, but he was invested for personal reasons as well. "I wish I knew what to do," he said more to himself than to Eliza.

"Henry, whatever the reason for Daniel's defiance, I don't think he's going to respond until he decides he can trust you."

"How can he trust me when he won't speak to me?" Henry couldn't help but feel defensive. The longer they discussed his dilemma, the less he felt capable of handling it. "I'm not his counselor. I'm just an English teacher. Building trust, forging relationships—that's your department. I do grammar. I talk books and poetry. That's what I'm good at."

"If that's all you're good at, you're working at the wrong school."

Henry tensed. She couldn't know about his conversation with Dr. Adler. She couldn't know about the pressure he felt looming over him, threatening his position at Rockbridge and his ability to stay close to AJ. Her comment wasn't based on anything but her own observations, which perhaps made it sting even more. He stood. "I think I'm going to head home now."

Eliza stood up too. "Henry, wait. That came out sounding harsher than I intended. I don't think you're working at the wrong school. I think you *can* do this. You can get Daniel to trust you. You just can't limit yourself. If you're going to reach these kids, you have to stretch, to try to see things in a different way. It isn't all black and white, right and wrong. You might just have to be inventive, creative, *intuitive*. That's all I was trying to say."

"It's fine," Henry said curtly. He reached down and picked up his bag. "I'm sorry, Eliza. You haven't said anything wrong. I think I'm just tired." He turned to walk away, then turned back. Eliza still stood at the table, her arms folded, her eyes full of concern. "Thank you for your help," he said.

As he walked to his apartment, Henry was embarrassed by how much Eliza's words had impacted him. She hadn't said anything that wasn't right, but her inadvertent reminder that, yes, it was a very real possibility he wasn't cut out to work at Rockbridge shook him, and it caused him to be more defensive than Eliza had deserved. Once inside, Henry crossed through his kitchen and collapsed on his living room sofa.

Trust.

How could he get a boy he hardly knew, who seemed set on keeping his distance, to trust him? Lowering his head into his hands, he offered a silent prayer, a plea for guidance and understanding. Before he'd even concluded his prayer, a thought came over him with such gut-wrenching force he dared not question its source.

Not that. There has to be another way.

It wasn't a possibility, no matter the prompting or the good it might do. There simply wasn't a way he would *ever* share something so personal with Daniel, with anyone.

Chapter 6

ELIZA HADN'T MEANT TO INSULT Henry. He was a good teacher. Many of the students she worked with had good things to say about him and his classes, but he was being too careful with Daniel. She suspected that nothing would happen until Henry decided to give of himself a little, to reach out in some way.

Eliza glanced at her watch. She wanted to think more about Henry's situation, perhaps even talk with Jeff about Daniel's individual counseling sessions, but it would have to wait until later. She had one last group-therapy session before dinner. If she didn't hurry, she wouldn't make it on time.

Her schedule followed a fairly predictable routine. She had fifteen students she met with on a weekly basis, assessing individual growth and discussing any issues or difficulties they were experiencing. Meeting one-on-one was Eliza's favorite part of the job. She loved having the opportunity to really talk to the kids and get to the center of what it was they needed.

In addition to providing individual counseling, Rockbridge had several group-therapy sessions, covering everything from substance abuse to dealing with family upheaval, such as divorce. The session Eliza was nearly late for focused on self-injury. It was the hardest session of Eliza's week. It pained her to see kids who were in such a dark place emotionally that inflicting personal pain actually brought them some relief. Because of Rockbridge's thorough supervision, it was difficult for such behavior to continue once kids were enrolled, but therapy wasn't just about preventing poor behavior. The key was to teach kids coping mechanisms that empowered them to take control of their lives—to feel capable of choosing a different behavior.

Eliza gathered the knives and bowls still sitting on the picnic table in front of her and made a stack of supplies to drop off in the kitchen on the way to her session. Realizing she had more than she could carry on her own, she was happy to see Flip coming toward her.

"I've been sent to retrieve Belinda's knives," he said with a good-natured grin. "That woman doesn't like her kitchen meddled with, does she?"

Eliza laughed. "I had to beg her to let me bring everything outside, but it was such a nice day, it seemed a crime not to enjoy it." Once Flip's arms were full of Belinda's bowls and knives, Eliza hurried to gather her personal belongings.

"Where are you off to now that I'm handling Belinda?"

"Group therapy," Eliza said. "I'll be late if I don't hurry."

"Mind if I hurry with you? I was hoping I could ask you a question."

"I'm not sure Belinda will appreciate the detour."

"Don't you worry about Belinda," Flip said. "I'll sweet-talk her into forgiveness. She's always had a thing for the Irish."

Eliza laughed again. It was hard to imagine a circumstance where sweet-talking from Flip wouldn't be effective.

"All right, then," Eliza said. "What's up?"

"Nothing, really. It's only . . . Well, I was hoping you might be interested in having dinner with me Friday night."

Eliza paused. "Flip," she said playfully, "are you asking me out on a date?"

"Something like it, I think. It's only dinner. That's not a big deal, is it?"

Eliza thought of a conversation she'd had with Natalie earlier in the week.

"Is it getting serious with you and Flip?" Natalie had asked.

Natalie hadn't believed her when Eliza had insisted they were only good friends. "Eliza, don't be stupid," she had said. "You and Flip spend a lot of time together. When he isn't on excursion, he's with you. If you aren't more than friends in your eyes, you better take a look at his. 'Cause I think you mean more to him than you realize."

Eliza suspected Natalie was right. The question, then, was how did Eliza feel about it? She liked Flip. It was impossible *not* to like Flip. He was funny, charming, and handsome. Her only hesitation stemmed from the fact that Flip wasn't LDS. But it *was* only dinner, and Flip was such a good friend. What harm could there be?

"I'm not scheduled off this weekend," Eliza finally responded. "I'll have to ask Natalie if she can cover for me. If she can, dinner on Friday sounds great."

"So I'll check with you tomorrow?"

"Sounds good." Eliza paused outside the door of the group-therapy room and shifted her bag higher onto her shoulder. She gave Flip one last smile and whispered a hasty "See you later" before ducking into the room.

* * *

Friday evening, Eliza stood inside her apartment listening to the messages on her answering machine. It had been an adjustment for her to once again rely on a landline telephone and answering machine. She often wondered why she still had a cell phone. Of course, she used it when she drove into Rose Creek, but at Rockbridge, it was completely useless.

She had three messages on the answering machine. The first was from her mother. Everything was fine. Gina was fine. She'd just wanted to hear Eliza's voice. Eliza smiled. She missed her mom. She would have to plan a weekend home to see her soon.

The second message was someone on the activities committee at church. Was she planning on attending the Pioneer Day celebration later in the month? Could she come early to help decorate? Eliza hurried to the counter and grabbed a pen just in time to jot the woman's telephone number down on the message board she had hanging in her kitchen. She didn't think she'd be able to get away that weekend. She was almost positive Natalie already had that weekend scheduled off.

The third message was Kate Porterfield inviting her to dinner Sunday evening.

"Dinner is at seven," Kate's message said. "We've invited Henry and AJ too, and they've already confirmed they'll be there. Maybe you can catch a ride down the mountain with Henry?"

Eliza reached for her phone to call Kate back. She would love to have dinner with the Porterfields.

"So you'll come?" Kate said once Eliza had her on the line. "Please tell me you'll come."

It was hard to refuse Kate's enthusiasm. "I can't believe you're still cooking for people, but yes, I'll come. I'd love to."

"Cooking is a distraction," Kate said. "Everything has been ready for this baby for weeks. If I'm not cooking for people, I'm sitting around waiting, and that's far too stressful. Besides, Henry's coming, and Andrew really wants to get the two of you together."

"Why is that?"

"Haven't you heard? It's the latest trend—branch presidents turned matchmakers."

"Kate, I don't know how I feel about matchmaking—"

"Okay, okay, I'm kidding. He just wants Henry to socialize more, you know? Get his feet under him again. I promise it's nothing more than that."

Eliza wasn't so sure.

A sharp knock sounded on her door, and she glanced at the clock. Flip was already there to pick her up for dinner, and she had yet to even glance at her reflection in the mirror. She ended her call with Kate and ran back to her bedroom to change clothes.

"Just a minute," she called to Flip. "I'll be right out!"

* * *

Flip took Eliza to a small café situated, of all places, in the corner of a building that also housed a gas station. At first Eliza questioned his choice, but once their food arrived, her doubts quickly dissolved. The food rivaled anything she'd ever eaten at even the fanciest of restaurants in the city.

"With food this good, why not change locations?" she asked Flip. "Build a restaurant somewhere that doesn't happen to share a parking lot with the Hot Spot?"

"It doesn't seem to be hurting their business."

Flip was right. The restaurant was packed, every table full and lines of people waiting out the door.

"Gas station chic," Eliza joked. "I wonder if it will catch on."

Over dinner, the conversation was light and funny. Eliza had expected to enjoy Flip's company. She always enjoyed being around him and hadn't doubted they would continue to get along on a date. But for the first time, she allowed herself to push past her reservations and actually consider the possibility of a relationship with Flip. It surprised her how quickly the idea crystallized into something desirable.

"I can't believe I haven't asked you this before now, but is Flip really your name?"

Flip shook his head. "I've been Flip since I was kid. My real name is Frederick."

"Middle name?"

"Finnegan. It was my mother's maiden name. I wish there was a funny story about a younger sister saying my name wrong or something else that makes sense about why they called me Flip, but my mother said she always felt like Frederick was too serious for me."

As they ate dessert—a huge slab of house-made chocolate cake—Eliza told Flip about the time her mother had dragged the garden hose into the house, pulling it all the way into the bathroom where Eliza's dad was taking a shower.

"We all crept into the bathroom, trying so hard to be quiet, which was really hard, considering the obnoxiously heavy garden hose we were hauling through the house. The hose kept getting tangled around corners and on chair legs, and we laughed every time it did. It was totally ridiculous. But the timing was perfect. Just as we made it into the bathroom, Dad turned off the water and reached for his towel. Then Mom snaked the hose over the top of the shower curtain and doused him in icy water. I'll never forget the sound he made—for years, my sister called it the shriek heard 'round the world."

"That's a great story. It sounds like your parents were a lot of fun."

Eliza only reflected for a moment. "Yeah, we had some pretty good times." The air between them suddenly felt thick with the words Eliza *wasn't* saying. She was having *fun*. Flip was fun. If she were to unleash her history, crack into the hardened, calloused shell that was her family, it would do nothing more than spoil the party.

Instead, she licked the crumbs off the back of her dessert fork and changed the subject. "I'm so full!" she said. "I don't think I've eaten that much in months."

"I always feel that way after I come here. What do you say we go for a walk. That'll make us feel better."

"You walk; I'll roll."

They left the restaurant, and Flip drove across the street to Rose Creek's Greenway Park.

"If there's one thing Rose Creek doesn't have," Flip said as he opened Eliza's door, "it's a night life. Instead, we're left on our own to commune with the birds and the bees."

"And the flowers and the trees," Eliza said.

Flip immediately started to laugh. "You just quoted a Dean Martin song."

"You started it." Eliza joined him in laughter as they walked down the paved path that hugged the bank of the Little Tennessee River.

"It's beautiful here," Eliza said.

Flip stopped walking and reached for her arm, turning her to face him. "There's a part of me that wants to say it's not as beautiful as you, but I'm afraid it might sound a little corny."

Eliza blushed. "Maybe a little."

Flip was leaning closer, looking at her in a way that could only mean one thing. When his lips were just inches from hers, Eliza couldn't help but feel herself surrendering to the moment. Flip moved his hand to the small of her back and pulled her a little closer, closing the distance between their lips. He was good at this—*very good*. But it wasn't right. As quickly as she had felt herself surrendering, Eliza felt a need to retreat. She dug her fingernails into her palm, willing the pain to snap her back into reality. She pulled away from the kiss.

"I can't do this."

"You can't do what?" Flip asked. "Are you all right?"

Eliza took a slow breath and looked at Flip. There was one particular thought desperately working its way to the front of her mind. All night she'd been pushing it back, losing herself in the pleasure of his company. It was only dinner, after all; she had no reason to stress. But a kiss like that? It was too much for Eliza to ignore. She had to be honest with herself, and more importantly, she had to be honest with Flip. She walked to a nearby bench and sat down, motioning for him to join her.

"Here's the thing. Flip, I really like you. You're fun and easy to be around, and I enjoy your company."

"I sense there's a 'but' to that sentence."

Eliza sighed. "For me to let this happen wouldn't be fair, not to me and not to you."

"Eliza, let what happen? What are you getting at? It was just a kiss."

"When is a kiss ever just a kiss? People kiss because they like each other. And when people like each other, they wind up in relationships together, and even if they aren't serious at the start, they often end up serious, which leads to even more serious things like marriage and families and little mini Flips running around."

Eliza paused. Flip was looking at her quizzically, his eyes wide with surprise.

"You just jumped from a first kiss all the way to marriage and family in one breath. Don't you think you're getting a little ahead of yourself?"

"But am I really? I realize I'm running the risk of sounding like every guy's first-date nightmare, but I like you too much not to be honest. The trouble is when you kiss me like that . . . I just . . . I can't ignore how easy it is for me to imagine myself in a relationship with you."

"Then that's a good thing, isn't it?" Flip reached for her hand. "I'm not sure I understand the trouble."

Eliza kept her eyes down. "Flip, my faith is the most important part of who I am. It's everything. It's the biggest part of what I want my future to be, specifically when it comes to my marriage and my future family."

"Ah, now I see. The trouble is that I'm not a Mormon."

"It probably makes me sound awful. I'm just past wanting to date around and have fun, you know? I can see myself falling for you, and I can't risk that. Not when I know in the end things couldn't work out."

Flip leaned forward and propped his elbows on his knees, letting his chin rest in his hands. "It doesn't make you sound awful, Eliza. This isn't exactly what I expected, but I can't say I don't understand where you're coming from."

"I probably should have said something sooner."

"Nah, if you'd said something sooner, I might not have gotten in that kiss." Flip gave her a good-natured grin, but Eliza could still see the disappointment in his eyes.

"I'm sorry," she said softly.

He stood and extended his hand, pulling her up from the bench. She didn't mind when he didn't let go. As they walked back toward the car, Flip asked Eliza what made marriage for Mormons so different. She gave a brief overview of the doctrine but focused mostly on her desire to have a marriage where her faith could be central to the relationship.

They arrived at the car, and Flip walked Eliza to the passenger side, where he unlocked her door. Before he opened it, he leaned in, his face just inches from hers once more. "So, what if I decided to become a Mormon?" Flip asked. "Would you kiss me then?"

It was tempting to kiss him again right then. Eliza swallowed and took a very intentional breath. "Well, you'd have to do it for the right reasons. No insincere church joining allowed."

"I'll seriously consider it," Flip said. "Otherwise, you might wind up with Henry. Imagine how boring your life would be then."

Chapter 7

WHEN HENRY WOKE UP ON Saturday morning, he found a note and a small basket of peaches on his front porch.

"I can't eat them all myself—Enjoy! P.S. Want to ride to the Porterfields' together tomorrow?"

He took the peaches inside and set them on the kitchen counter. He appreciated Eliza's thoughtfulness. It had been another hard day. His morning classes had gone well, but several students in his afternoon group were struggling, and Daniel was *still* refusing to cooperate.

Henry tried to push aside the idea that had immediately sprung to the forefront of his mind when he first prayed about Daniel. He knew God was trying to tell him something. Every time he thought of Daniel, the very next thought was of his book.

With growing frustration, he walked to his desk and opened the left bottom drawer. There, under a stack of manila envelopes and a stapler, sat his first finished manuscript. He pulled it out and read the title page—*One Day in Ten by Henry Jacobson*. It had taken him six months to write it, and no one, not even his family, knew it existed.

When Henry was thirteen, he'd read *To Kill a Mockingbird* for his eighth grade English class. The following summer, he'd read the novel three more times. Somehow, the words had changed him. It wasn't just the story, compelling as it was. It was the words—the ability the author had to weave simple lines and phrases into a piece of profoundly moving literature. It was still his favorite novel—still the one he turned to when he felt worn or weathered or in need of inspiration.

He looked up at the now-tattered copy of the book sitting on the corner of his desk. More than one friend or family member had since purchased him a newer copy, but he still held on to the old one. To throw it away would be to throw away a very real part of him. It was that copy of the book he'd been reading all those years ago when Allison had first approached him in the park and plucked it out of his hands to casually flip through its pages.

"I've seen you read this thing a thousand different times," she'd said. "What makes it so special?" A grade behind him in school, she hadn't yet had the pleasure of reading it for eighth grade English. He snatched it back from her protectively. "You'll have to read it next year," he said. "Then you'll understand."

"What if I want to read it now? If it's good enough for you to read so many times, it must be worth it."

He'd loved her almost instantly. They'd bonded over the book that summer. She hadn't even laughed when he told her he planned to name his first son after Atticus. That summer was also the season of Henry's budding desire to become a writer himself. His mind was constantly filled with possibilities, with stories he longed to tell.

But writing wasn't a very predictable career. There was such risk involved and a real, even likely possibility of failure. An older, wiser Henry had easily decided teaching was a safer, more reliable route. Still, he'd never been able to stop the stories from coming. All through high school and college, he'd filled notebook after notebook with short stories and ideas.

It was only after finishing his English degree that Henry had started writing a novel—a story about a boy and his father and a girl whom no one was supposed to love. It was finished now, and Henry felt a tremendous sense of accomplishment. It was enough to know it was there. There was no need for anyone else to know about it, for anyone to read it—not yet anyway.

Except, letting someone read it—letting *Daniel* read it—was precisely what Henry felt he was supposed to do. Even the thought made his palms sweat and his throat feel tight. It was a risk. And Henry didn't like risks.

He dropped his manuscript back in place and slammed the drawer shut with a final, definitive thud.

* * *

Because Henry had plans to spend Sunday afternoon with AJ, he turned down Eliza's invitation to ride together to the Porterfields'. Still, he found he was glad that she would be there. He and AJ had joined Kate and Andrew for dinner before. Kate's niece Emily was in AJ's class at school, and the two were good friends. Henry expected that since AJ had been included in the invitation, it was likely that Emily would be there for dinner as well.

Eliza was talking to Andrew in the driveway when Henry and AJ pulled up. Andrew was pointing at the massive white farmhouse situated behind them, gesturing expressively with his hands.

Henry smiled. Andrew had never been good at dampening his enthusiasm when he talked about his wife's house. With a large wrap-around porch filled with rocking chairs and large whiskey barrels overflowing with flowers, the house definitely had a welcoming charm. To the right of the front door, Henry saw Emily sitting cross-legged on the porch swing, a large book open in her lap.

"Why don't you go see what Emily is up to," he said to AJ as he climbed out of the car.

AJ was up the steps in a flash, pausing only briefly to say hello to Eliza and Andrew. "Hi, Sister Redding. Hi, President Porterfield."

The two laughed as he darted past.

"I hope you aren't offended that AJ seems to prefer Emily's company to either of yours." Henry extended his hand to Andrew. "Thanks for having us over, President. We appreciate it very much."

"Henry, you call me 'President' like you and I didn't grow up together." Andrew turned to Eliza. "I spent my summers in Rose Creek as a kid. I knew this guy when he was a scrawny teenager with his nose stuck in a book, and yet, he still won't call me Andrew."

"I won't dispute the scrawny," Henry said jokingly, "but I did put my books down on occasion. To eat or sleep, for example." Everyone laughed.

"It's nice to see you, Eliza," Henry said.

"Likewise." She held his gaze just long enough to make Henry's heart quicken, leaving him momentarily befuddled. He wasn't sure what had just happened, but he shook the feeling away, focusing on Eliza's words, now addressed to Andrew. "How's Kate feeling? She's got what, a month left now?"

"Less than that. The due date is just over three weeks away, though her doctor says it could happen sooner."

"Which is why I think she's crazy for fixing us dinner."

"It wasn't my idea." Andrew held his hands up in mock surrender. "She insists it gives her something to do to keep her mind busy rather than just sitting around the house waiting all day."

"She told me as much," Eliza said. "But I still think she's crazy."

As they talked, they climbed the stairs to the porch, where Andrew held open the front door and invited them into the living room. Before they could sit down, Kate called from the dining room that dinner was ready.

After they ate, the four adults moved to the sunroom off the back of the kitchen, where Kate served peach slab pie for dessert.

"This tastes like my childhood," Kate said. "My aunt Mary used to make it every summer. We'd eat it sitting right here in the sunroom, waiting for it to get dark so we could go catch the fireflies."

"You grew up here?" Eliza asked.

"In this very house."

"Then you must have known Henry growing up, and Andrew too."

"I remember Henry," Kate said. "He was a year or two ahead of me in school, but I knew who he was. And I was on swim team with Andrew's cousins. Andrew and I didn't meet, though, until much later."

"You didn't know him from church?"

"Oh!" Kate said, realization dawning. "I wasn't a member of the Church growing up. I was baptized just a couple of years ago."

Henry watched Eliza's face light up. "I was baptized when I was seventeen," she said. "I didn't grow up in the Church either."

Henry turned to Eliza. He'd never thought to ask about her membership in the Church and was curious to hear how it came about. "Seventeen—that's not very old."

Eliza paused just long enough to make Henry wonder if he'd asked something wrong, but then she looked up, her eyes bright. "When I was fourteen, I was living in a foster home, and the family happened to be LDS. Their home life was so completely different from anything I had ever experienced before. They were the most wonderful people—kind and thoughtful and respectful. And I was hungry to know everything they could teach me. I didn't come from a religious family, but I was overwhelmed by the purpose and the joy that obviously came from living a godly life. I knew in a matter of weeks I wanted to be baptized."

Andrew shook his head. "To know so young is pretty amazing. Did you ever have any doubts?"

"Not once," Eliza said. "The gospel made sense. Everything seemed so clear. It was as if, suddenly, I was looking at life through a high-definition lens. My foster family worried that they had pushed, that I might feel pressure living in a house full of Mormons, so they suggested I wait until I was back living with my mother before I made the decision to be baptized. It was a good idea, for my mother's sake as well. But that's the only reason I waited until I was seventeen."

Henry was quiet as the conversation continued. He was curious about the details of Eliza's circumstances that would have landed her in foster care but felt it too invasive to ask. Regardless of how she got there, he enjoyed hearing her speak of her faith in general. Her passion was beautifully applied to the gospel, and he found her testimony rich and inspiring.

When Eliza and Kate retreated to the kitchen, Andrew leaned closer to Henry, a conspiratorial look on his face. "Eliza's nice."

Henry looked up. "Yes, she is." He had an idea where this line of conversation was going.

"Have you thought about asking her out?"

Henry almost laughed. "You don't waste any time getting to the point, do you?"

Andrew smiled. "Don't tell me you haven't thought about it. She's pretty; she's smart. Why wouldn't you?"

Henry kept his eyes down, his hands fiddling with his watchband.

"Henry, it's been two years. It's all right for you to think about moving on."

"It's not that easy." Henry struggled to turn his thoughts into words. "I can't . . . I mean, how do I . . . ?" He took a frustrated breath. "I can't even keep up a good relationship with my kid. Besides that, why would someone like her ever be interested in someone like me?"

"Someone like you? What's that supposed to mean?"

"It means that emotionally crippled, divorced fathers aren't typically at the top of the list of what women want." He stood. "I've got to go check on AJ."

Henry headed to the back porch, where he'd last heard the children playing. From the door of the screened-in porch, he was able to see them swinging from the low branches of a sugar maple in the corner of the backyard. He watched as AJ swung his legs up over the lowest branch, then hefted himself higher into the tree. At first, his climbing seemed innocent enough, but as he moved higher and higher, Henry grew concerned. He pushed through the screen door and walked across the yard.

"AJ," he called. The boy seemed to climb even faster. "That's too high, son. I don't want you to fall." Henry's heart quickened as he approached the tree. AJ was far enough up in the branches that it would be difficult for a man of Henry's size to follow him. He took a breath, willed his heart to slow, and tried again. "Atticus James, it's time to come down right now. You're too high. You're going to get hurt if you go any farther."

"Atticus?"

Henry turned at the sound of Eliza's voice. She stood just behind him, her eyes focused on AJ.

"He's not coming down," Henry said. "Every time I call him, he goes up a little higher."

"Emily?" Eliza asked. "Do you know why AJ is climbing so high?"

Emily looked a little sheepish. "It's my fault," she said from her position at the base of the tree. "He dared *me* to climb to the top, and I said I wouldn't do it, so he called me a wimp. So I called *him* a wimp and told him to prove he wasn't."

"AJ, you're not a wimp, son. But it's dangerous up there."

"Do you think he'll make it down?" Emily asked.

"Of course he'll make it down," Eliza said cheerfully. "Emily, have you had any of Aunt Kate's peach pie yet? There's homemade vanilla ice cream too." Eliza's voice was louder than necessary, and Henry immediately realized what she was trying to do. "I think there's just two pieces left, so you better hurry before Andrew eats the last of it."

A flicker of movement up above turned Henry's gaze back to AJ.

"Henry, did you enjoy your pie?" Her voice was still loud and overly enthusiastic.

Henry cleared his throat, not sure if Eliza's tactic would work, but no harm could come from trying.

"I sure did." He matched the volume of Eliza's voice. "It might just be the best peach pie I've ever had, even better than Grandma Lila's." The conversation continued for a few more moments before AJ, with a soft thud, landed on the spongy ground beneath the tall tree. Without a word, he ran off in the direction of the house but then stopped and turned back to his father. Henry watched as he ran back and stopped directly in front of him.

"I just want you to know I didn't get out of the tree 'cause you asked me to. I *just* wanted pie." Without another word, he turned and raced into the house.

Henry looked at Eliza. He could tell she wanted to laugh. Of course AJ's rudely expressed opinion would be entertaining to an outsider, but to Henry, it was a measure of his inadequacy as a parent. His son had had no intention of listening to him, no desire to show him even a sliver of respect. He tried to keep the dejection out of his voice. "Thanks for your help," he said as he and Eliza walked back to the house. "I guess I should have thought of that."

Eliza shook her head. "No, you were thinking like a concerned parent. I was thinking like someone who'd just finished off a third piece of pie."

Henry smiled. "And yet, your way of thinking was far more successful than mine."

As they climbed the steps to the back porch, Henry remembered the questioning tone in Eliza's voice when she'd repeated AJ's name.

"It's from *To Kill a Mockingbird*," he said by way of explanation.

Eliza stood just in front of him on the stairs. She turned to face him but didn't say anything.

"His name," Henry continued. "I named him after Atticus—one of the main characters in *To Kill a Mockingbird*."

"I know the book."

"Atticus James, so we call him AJ. Allison thought Atticus alone was too much to saddle a kid with, so we compromised. I'm not sure he really likes the Atticus part, but when he's old enough to read the book, I hope he'll appreciate more where the name came from and why I chose it for him." Henry paused. "I'm rambling, aren't I?"

"Not at all." Eliza held the door open for Henry. "I think Atticus James is a very nice name."

Chapter 8

AFTER HER LAST THERAPY SESSION, Eliza walked slowly back to her apartment, enjoying the cooler temperatures of evening. When she passed the admin building, she saw Flip sitting on the front porch.

"Hey, Eliza," he called. "You got a minute?"

She headed over to see what he needed. Things between them had been good, if a little strained, since their dinner a week prior. Flip was keeping a little more distance than usual, but Eliza couldn't really blame him for that. At least he was still being kind.

She found him sitting on the split-log bench beside the front door, in a sea of supplies for his next wilderness excursion. Clearly, there was a lot of gear involved when taking twelve teenagers into the mountains for ten days.

Eliza loved this part of Rockbridge's therapy. These were not cushy camping trips with campfires, s'mores, and ghost stories. These were difficult treks that included challenging hikes, shelter construction, food preparation, and navigation. She'd only seen one group go and return since she'd arrived, but the successes of that one group alone were enough to convince her the program had merit.

"Hey." Eliza stepped over a coil of rope and a string of carabiners hooked end to end. "What's up?"

"Nothing too much; just making sure everything's ready."

"Who's going with you this trip?"

"Adler is going, of course, and Jeff is coming too, I think."

Adler—a casual reference to Frank Adler, Dr. Adler's husband and the cofounder of Rockbridge. He didn't spend a great deal of time on campus, but he went on every single wilderness excursion. It was the part of the program he considered the most beneficial to the teens.

"Is Leslie not going, then?" Leslie was Flip's female counterpart—the wilderness leader for the girls on campus. The excursions were often coed, requiring separate camps and separate leaders.

Flip shook his head. "No girls going this time, so it's just us men."

Eliza had a sudden thought. "Is there a Daniel in the group this time?"

"Don't know right offhand," Flip said. "I generally don't know till we're leaving, unless I seek out the list. Why? Is he one of yours?"

"No, if he were one of mine, I wouldn't have to ask. He's in Jeff's therapy group, but he's also in Henry's English class. I was just curious."

"How is Henry?" Flip asked. "I haven't seen him around lately."

Eliza raised her eyebrows at Flip's sudden interest in Henry. "He's good, I guess. I haven't seen him much either." She was quiet for a moment, watching Flip fiddle with the straps of his pack.

"I was wondering," he finally said, his eyes still locked on his bag. "I was thinking about asking you if I could maybe have a copy of the Book of Mormon."

Eliza tried to hide her surprise.

"After our date last weekend, I did a little research. I went to the website . . . and it seemed . . . nice. I don't know. If you feel so strongly about something, it can't hurt for me to learn a little more, can it?"

"Not at all," Eliza said. "I can definitely get you a copy of the Book of Mormon."

"I don't suppose you have one handy, do you? I might have a bit of time this week to do some reading."

Eliza quickly cataloged what she knew was on her bookshelf in the corner of her apartment. No extra Book of Mormon. Nothing but her own scriptures. *Sheesh. Whatever happened to every member a missionary?* Suddenly, it occurred to her that Henry might have a spare copy.

"I might," she said to Flip. "Will you be here a minute? I'll be right back."

On her way back to the apartments, Eliza ran into Jeff. He confirmed that Daniel was going on the excursion, but Jeff had little insight as to why he might be struggling in Henry's class specifically.

"I'm not sure if it's a character clash or what," Jeff said. "But for whatever reason, Daniel has simply decided not to participate. I hope the wilderness excursion will be good for him. I'll try to see if I can talk to him, find out what's behind his obstinacy."

"Let me know if there's anything I can do to help," Eliza offered. "And I hope you have a nice trip."

"Oh, it'll be all right. I'll be ready for some of Belinda's cooking by the time we return, for sure. Flip's a great guy, but he's no chef."

"I can't see a survival experience lending itself well to gourmet cooking, can you?" They laughed together before Eliza said good-bye.

She bypassed her own apartment and headed straight to Henry's, not doubting her decision until she was climbing his porch steps. It was late in the afternoon, and she knew classes were over for the day, but that didn't mean Henry would be home. She knocked on his door twice, but he didn't answer. She saw his car in the parking lot, so he had to be around somewhere. Hopefully it wouldn't take long to track him down.

"Are you looking for me?" The sight of Henry striding down the sidewalk in her direction, shirt sleeves rolled up to his elbows and sunglasses perched on his head, made such an impression that for a moment, she forgot what she was doing there.

"I, um . . . I *was* looking for you," she finally sputtered out. "I was wondering if you had a spare copy of the Book of Mormon."

Henry pulled his keys out of his pocket and moved past her on the porch. "I think I do. What for?"

"It's funny, really. Flip just asked me if he could have one."

"Flip? Really?" Henry pushed on the screen door and held it open, ushering Eliza inside. "I never would have guessed."

"I know. I said the same thing. He said he was hoping to read some while he's on excursion." Eliza stood by the front door and waited while Henry went into his bedroom to retrieve the book. The inside of his apartment was similar to Eliza's, but her eyes were quickly drawn to those things that made the room uniquely Henry's. His desk was neat and orderly—no surprise there—and his bookshelf was crammed with books. She crossed the short distance to the shelf so she could study the titles.

She first noticed the titles she knew and loved herself—*The Good Earth*, *East of Eden*, *The Adventures of Huckleberry Finn*, among others. Of course, she wasn't surprised when she noticed not one but four different copies of *To Kill a Mockingbird*. Henry had mentioned it was his favorite. She turned at the sound of his voice.

"Here you go." He handed her the Book of Mormon. "I keep meaning to get a bigger shelf. I've still got boxes of books in the bedroom that I don't have room for out here."

"Forget the library," Eliza said. "I think you might actually have a more impressive collection right here."

Henry smiled. "Do you like to read?"

"Yes," Eliza answered a little wistfully. "I wish I had more time for it now, but books really meant something when I was a kid. They helped me through a lot of tough times, you know?"

She watched as Henry's eyes scanned his shelves. "Here." He reached for a title. "Have you read this one? It's one of my favorites."

She read the title: *How Green Was My Valley* by Richard Llewellyn. "No, I haven't read it."

"It's a simple story, but the writing is beautiful. I think you'll like it."

Eliza liked this Henry—the relaxed, comfortable, talking-about-books Henry. She smiled. "Thank you. I'm sure I'll like it if it's one of your favorites. And thanks for this too," she added, holding up the Book of Mormon.

"Don't mention it."

Eliza knew she needed to get back to Flip but was surprised to realize how much she wished she had a reason to stay with Henry a little longer.

After leaving, she stopped by her own apartment long enough to drop off the book Henry had loaned her and give herself a quick glance in the mirror. Not because she wondered how she would look when she got back to Flip but because, suddenly, she was worried about how she *had* looked when she was with Henry.

She couldn't help but compare the two men. She liked them both, but there was something different about Henry. Flip was fun, and there was a spark of chemistry between them, but when Eliza was around Henry, she felt more than just flirty chemistry. She felt *connection*.

Get a hold of yourself, Eliza. Shaking off her distractions, she hurried back to the admin building, where, fortunately, Flip was still sitting on the porch. He was leaning against the wall behind him, his arms behind his head and his legs stretched out. His gear was completely packed at his feet.

"Sorry it took so long," she said. "I had to track a copy down for you."

"I hope you didn't go to any trouble."

"No, I didn't have a spare copy, but Henry did. You can keep this one." She handed him the book.

"Thanks." He slipped it into the outside pocket of his pack.

"So, I guess let me know if you have any questions. Between Henry and me, I'm sure we can help with anything you want to know."

"Between you and Henry," Flip said lightly. "What if I only want answers to come from you?"

"Then I'd question your motives and maybe even take that book back right now." Eliza kept her voice light, even though she meant every single word of what she said.

Flip laughed. "Don't question my motives. I really am interested. You're just so much prettier than Henry."

Eliza rolled her eyes and punched Flip gently on the arm. "You're terrible."

"Nope, just honest."

She said good-bye and headed back to her apartment. It was close to dinnertime, but she wasn't in the mood for the cafeteria. It was hard to give up Belinda's cooking, but living where she worked provided few moments for solitude. As much as she loved being with everyone at Rockbridge, sometimes it felt good to spend an evening on her own.

As she climbed the steps to her apartment, she heard the phone ring inside and hurried to unlock her door. She answered the phone just in time.

"Hello?" she said breathlessly.

"Eliza? Is that you?"

Eliza recognized her Aunt Barbara's voice and immediately sensed the trepidation of those first four words. "Barbara? What's wrong? Is everything okay?"

Eliza heard Barbara sigh. "It's Gina. She's come here again, and I just didn't know who else to call. It's bad this time, Liza. She's real bad."

Eliza sank onto the bar stool next to her kitchen counter.

"How long has she been there?"

"Three days. Showed up in the middle of the night saying your mother locked her out and she'd only stay the night, but then she just never left. Liza, I love your sister, but she can't stay here. My kids—they're still so young. They don't know what to make of her, how to understand what she's going through. And I just can't have her drinking in this house. Not with my babies around."

"Barbara, you have nothing to explain. Of course she can't stay at your house. No one would ever expect you to endure such a thing. Have you spoken to Mom?"

"I've tried, but I figure she knows Gina's here. She won't return any of my calls. They must have had some sort of blowup for your mother to act this way. Gina won't tell me anything either. I hate to bother you, being so far away, but I just didn't know who else to call."

"She's drinking?"

"She was at first. Her friend, that dark-haired man that's always coming around, he came by the second day she was here and must have brought her something. But then I told him he wasn't welcome in my home, and well, I don't keep any liquor in the house. If she wants to drink anything else, she'll have to leave to find it. But she's not even getting out of bed. She just sleeps all day. I can hardly get her to eat. I just . . ." Eliza heard her aunt's voice crack, could almost see the tears running down her cheek. "Eliza, I'm so sorry."

Eliza leaned forward, pressing her forehead into the heel of her hand. It was time for this to stop. Gina was hurting too many people, taking advantage of too many family members. She needed someone to step in and stop her before it was too late. Eliza felt small—weak and completely incapable—as she looked at the mounting task before her. She wanted to hang up, to run away from her sister's problems and never look back. But then what? Leave Barbara to deal with the mess? Eliza knew she could never do such a thing. This wasn't Barbara's mess. This was Gina's mess. And Eliza was her sister.

"Barbara, I want you to listen to me. It will take me just under five hours to drive to your house. I'll leave as soon as I can and drive straight there, okay? If you can keep Gina from knowing that you've called and that I'm coming, that really would be better. Otherwise, I expect she'll leave before I get there."

"I won't tell her," Barbara said. "I'm sorry you have to come so far."

"Please don't apologize. She's my sister. I can't let her do this to herself. Not anymore." Eliza hung up and ran into her bedroom, where she started throwing a few changes of clothes into her overnight bag. She couldn't think. How long would she be gone? What would she need? With increasing intensity, she shoved random blue jeans and shirts into her bag.

She was struggling to keep her anger and frustration under control. She was angry that she was leaving, that it was her responsibility to clean up her sister's life—again. But more than that, she was angry at herself for resenting the fact that she had to be involved.

She'd been fooling herself the past couple of months, thinking she could leave Nashville and leave her family struggles behind. This was her cross to bear. No matter where she lived, she was still Gina's sister. That wasn't something Eliza thought she should ever resent. Fiery hot tears dripped onto her bag as she finally zipped it closed.

The tears continued to fall as she carried her bags outside. After loading them into the backseat, she leaned on the side of her car and begged the Lord for strength, for the patience and tolerance and love she knew she would need but doubted she would have.

Chapter 9

"ELIZA, ARE YOU ALL RIGHT?" Henry found Eliza sitting on the curb beside her car, her face damp with tears and her eyes strained with worry. She wiped at her cheeks when she saw him approaching.

"I'm fine," she said quickly, rising to her feet. "I just . . ." She hesitated. Her shoulders dropped as she closed her eyes. She was a picture of discouragement. "I'm not fine," she said softly. "My sister's in trouble, and I have to go get her. I'm leaving right now."

Henry was concerned. It was obvious Eliza was in no condition to drive herself anywhere. "Is there anything I can do?"

She shook her head. "I'll be fine, I think. I do need to get going though. It's a five-hour drive, and I really should have left by now." She glanced at her watch as if to confirm.

Five hours? Surely she didn't intend to make the trip alone in such an emotional state. "Eliza, you can't drive five hours alone. Are you sure you're even okay to drive at all?"

She shrugged. "It doesn't matter if I am or not. I have to go. My sister needs me, and she needs me right now." She moved to the driver's side door, but he stopped her, placing both hands on her shoulders.

"Eliza, stop for just a minute. You can't get in the car this upset. Let me get you some water. You can sit for a few minutes. I'll sit with you."

"You don't understand, Henry. I've wasted enough time as it is, and I'm the only one who can do this. It has to be me. I have to be the one to go . . ." She seemed agitated, almost frantic, and tried to push Henry away, but he held firm until she collapsed against his chest, her angry sobs soaking his shirt front with tears. He hardly knew what else he could do but wrap his arms around her and let her cry.

After several moments, she finally raised her head, and he released his grip. "I'm sorry, Henry. This whole thing . . . It's just my family . . . I guess my emotions are running pretty high."

"Eliza, does anyone know you're leaving?"

She looked momentarily confused. "I didn't even think . . . No, I haven't talked to anyone."

"Listen. Go find Natalie. With Jeff on excursion, she and James will have to stay on campus the entire time you're gone. You need to make sure she knows you're leaving. While you're doing that, I'm going to get a few things together, and then I'll drive you wherever it is you need to go."

Eliza looked at him, her eyes wide with surprise. "You would do that? What about work and AJ? You're sweet to offer, but I can't ask that of you."

"I really don't want you to make such a long trip on your own, not when you're feeling this way. Work will be fine, and AJ is out of town with his mom. Besides, you didn't ask. I volunteered."

Eliza wiped the last of her tears off her cheeks and gave Henry a hug. "Are you sure?"

"I'm sure."

"Thank you, Henry. That might be the nicest thing anyone has ever done for me."

He watched her as she walked up the sidewalk to find Natalie. As he headed to his own apartment to pack a bag and gather a few things he'd need for the trip, he wondered if he hadn't just jumped into a deep end he was ill equipped to swim in. He had no idea what was wrong with Eliza's sister or why Eliza had such a desperate need to go get her. All he knew was that he had known without a moment's hesitation he couldn't let her make the trip on her own. Whatever the reason, he felt she needed him somehow. He hoped he wouldn't let her down.

* * *

"What did you do about your classes?" Eliza asked.

"Russ is going to cover them."

"Russ, the creative arts director?"

"It was either him or Gerald."

Henry was happy to hear Eliza laugh. They'd been driving for nearly two hours. At first she had been quiet, speaking only enough to tell him where they were going. Once he'd started down the right interstate, heading west into Tennessee, she'd leaned her head back on the seat and closed her eyes. She'd quickly fallen asleep and slept long enough for Henry to grow used to the quiet. When Eliza asked him about his classes, it startled him to hear her speak.

"Has Russ covered your classes before?"

"A few times," Henry said. "He does a good job."

Eliza glanced at her watch and yawned.

"You slept for over an hour."

"I'm surprised. I don't normally sleep well in the car. I didn't snore, did I?"

Henry smiled. "Only a little."

"Well, that's extremely embarrassing," she said. "Let's move on. Are you hungry? I'm hungry."

"Sure. Do you want to stop or just pick something up to eat in the car?"

He watched as the light in Eliza's eyes went dim. It was as if she'd momentarily forgotten the ominous reason for their journey and his question brought the weight of it onto her shoulders tenfold.

"Let's do something quick," Eliza said. "Something we can eat in the car. Is that okay?"

"Of course. Whatever we need to do."

Eliza was quiet for a few moments, then spoke quite suddenly, her voice calm but thick with emotion. "My mother was an alcoholic." Henry waited for her to continue, a knot of dread growing in his stomach. "My dad died from cancer when I was eleven, and my mother had a terrible time getting over it. She'd always struggled with depression, and my dad had been her lifeline—her anchor. When he died, her depression became all-consuming, worse than it had ever been before, and she started drinking. It was like her grief was choking all of us—slowly, you know? It was draining the light out of everyone in the house, and we didn't realize how dark it was getting until it was almost too late. When I was fourteen, I came home from school one day to a quiet house. My mother was drunk, still in bed, with her curtains drawn and her door closed. I went into her room to tell her I was hungry."

Eliza shifted in her seat, pulling her feet up and wrapping her arms around her knees in a way that made it easy for Henry to see her as a child suffering under the indignities of her mother's illness. "There wasn't anything to eat in the house. She didn't respond the first time I asked, so

I went to her, shook her, told her there was nothing to eat." Eliza let out a muffled, scornful laugh. "She rolled over, told me there was cash on her dresser and I could take the car into town and buy myself whatever I wanted." Eliza turned to face Henry. "I remember standing there, looking at this poor woman, completely broken, utterly incapable of taking care of me, and I knew I had to get out. I needed help; we both did. So I took the car. I drove myself to the police station and turned myself in to social services."

Henry was surprised. "Can kids even do that?"

"Not technically," Eliza said. "Not without a pretty thorough investigation as to why a kid would want to leave in the first place. It took a couple of months, but that day was when the process started. I was assigned a case worker, who visited my mother and our home to see what needed to be done and to determine how desperate our situation actually was. They wanted to make sure I wasn't just a disgruntled teenager looking to get back at my parents. Finally, my mother went to rehab, and I went into foster care. Gina—she's four years older than me—she was already eighteen, and there was little they could do for her. So it was just me."

"How is your mother now?"

Eliza finally smiled. "She's been sober for eleven years. She's an artist and has a studio right in her home. She's doing pretty well selling her own work and is really making a name for herself. I'm proud of her."

"That's great," Henry said. "I imagine it doesn't always work out so well." He scratched his chin and gave Eliza a sideways glance. "It seems a little out of character for a teenage girl to *want* to end up in foster care. Weren't you scared?"

"I wasn't at the time. Though, in hindsight, especially now that I've worked so much in the system, I realize how terribly wrong it could have gone. Foster care isn't always the best care, you know? But I got lucky. I was placed in the best possible home. And my mom? Rehab worked." Eliza sighed. "But my sister wasn't so lucky."

"It must have been really hard on her, losing her dad during such a critical time of her youth. And then to endure your mom's drinking. I'm sure it was tough."

"I think she just felt like there wasn't anyone who really cared. She managed to graduate from high school, but she never went to college and hasn't ever had a steady job. Drinking, drugs, she's done it all. She's an artist just like Mom, or at least, she could be if she could stay sober long enough to try." Eliza wearily pressed her face into her hands. "I don't know what I'm going to do when we get there, Henry. I just don't know what to do."

With Eliza's story now out in the open, Henry didn't hesitate to ask a few questions. "Where exactly *are* we going?"

"Gina's at my Aunt Barbara's house in Hendersonville, just outside of Nashville. She's been there for three days because my mother kicked her out and she didn't have anywhere else to go. But she can't stay with Barbara because Barbara has young children. She's in no position to have a drug-addicted alcoholic living under her roof. So we're going to get her. I just hope we get there before she leaves on her own. If that happens, who knows where she'll end up."

"So . . . this is basically an intervention?"

"Minus the huge support network and all the advanced planning, I guess it is. I maybe should've told you that before I let you come along, huh?"

Henry swallowed hard. An intervention *was* a little more than what he was expecting, but Eliza had enough doubts. She certainly didn't need to deal with his too. "How do you think she's going to take it?"

"If I can't figure out some sort of plan before I get there, she'll probably run. I need to present things in a way that gives her little choice but to come with me. She needs rehab, I know that much. But the trouble is she's *been* in rehab in Nashville—fulfilled her court-appointed obligations, then fell right back into her old habits and ways. I feel like she needs to get out of town—away from her friends, from everything—but I don't have a clue where I could take her."

Henry could tell Eliza was growing frustrated.

"I don't know, Henry. I don't even know if she'll be willing to talk to me, much less leave with me. I don't know if she'll be drunk or high or both, if she'll be reasonable, remorseful. I'm terrified of how this is all going to go."

Instinctively, Henry reached over and put his hand on Eliza's arm. "We'll figure something out, all right? It's going to work out."

"But I should already *have* it figured out. I'm a social worker. This is what I do for a living, and yet I feel paralyzed by this entire situation. I can't seem to think straight about it."

"This isn't work, Eliza. It's your family. Of course it's going to be harder for you to think straight. Let's just back up and talk about the things we know, and then we'll come up with a plan on how to move forward."

Eliza looked at him long enough and with enough intensity that his pulse stuttered and then restarted twice as fast. "I'm really glad you're here, Henry."

"Tell me about your mom. Is there any chance she'll want to be involved?"

Eliza shook her head. "I'm afraid to ask her, only because she's been enabling Gina for so many years already. If she's finally turned tough and kicked her out, I don't want to give Gina the opportunity to wear her down. I guarantee that's what Gina is waiting for: for Mom to change her mind and let her come home."

"Does your mom know you're coming?"

"If she knew, she'd already be at Barbara's house waiting for me, and that's why I haven't told her. For Gina's sake, Mom needs to be out of the picture. I think her absence will actually send a stronger message than her presence, if that makes sense. Because then Gina will realize she has no other option but the one I'm giving her."

"And that option is going to be what?"

Eliza's shoulders fell. "I guess it's going to be state-funded rehab. I can't afford anything else. I just have to hope this time it sticks."

Henry wished he knew what to say to make her feel better, but nothing came to him.

Her next words tumbled out, a jumble of thoughts and emotions he could tell she'd been struggling with for a long time. "I was so stupid," she said. "I left. And for a while it felt so easy, like I could have this new life without having to worry. But I should have been thinking about this—planning for this sooner. I was foolish to think I could escape without this part of my life coming back to haunt me."

Before Henry could answer, Eliza pointed up ahead. "There, look," she said, her voice still dejected. "There's a Chick-fil-A. Let's stop to get something to eat."

Henry pulled through the drive-thru lane and ordered their meals while Eliza used her phone to look up information on rehab centers that might work for Gina.

"Did you find anything that looks promising?" Henry passed the bag of food across to her, letting her divvy everything up while he turned back onto the interstate. He noticed as they ate how much of an effort Eliza made to make it easier for him to eat while he drove. She held his french fry container, handed him his drink, even put mayonnaise on his sandwich.

Despite the stress she was surely feeling, she still focused on Henry's comfort. It was a small kindness, but one that was not lost on him.

"There are a couple of places that might work," Eliza said. "Nothing seems ideal, but it might be the best I can do. Once I'm done eating, I'll make some calls and see who has room for her."

A thought suddenly occurred to Henry. "Listen—I've got an uncle who manages a large hospital in Raleigh. He knows a lot of people and has a lot of connections in the hospital network. It's probably a long shot, but I could give him a call too. Maybe he knows of a place that would work well for Gina—someplace different, and away from Nashville."

"I'll take long shots," Eliza said. "At this point, I'll take *any* kind of shot. That would be great if you don't mind calling."

Henry was pleased to see the hope his suggestion had given her. He realized how much he wanted her to be happy, how much he wanted to ease the burden she carried. A part of him wanted those desires to mean something. When he thought about how it had felt to hold her as she'd cried—solid and real in his arms, the warmth that lingered on his fingers after he touched her—he wondered if it *could* mean something, if it would ever mean something to *her.*

After two years of believing no one could ever replace Allison, to realize he could even consider the possibility was thrilling. And utterly terrifying all at the same time.

* * *

Two hours later, Eliza and Henry sat outside Barbara's house. It was a modest home, well kept, but smaller than the others lining the suburban street. It was older as well and had a bigger yard, giving the impression that it existed long before the cookie-cutter houses surrounding it had popped up. The street light at the corner filtered light down through the sprawling branches of a large maple tree in the front yard, casting eerie shadows across the grass. The house itself was mostly dark. Only the dim light of a lamp shone in a corner window.

Eliza was quiet. Henry knew she was simply trying to prepare herself for the conversation that was to follow.

"It's going to be all right, Eliza," he said gently.

She took a deep breath. "Will you pray with me? Pray that I can do this?"

Henry took her hands in his and offered a prayer on her behalf. When he finished, Eliza looked up with tears in her eyes.

"Thank you . . . I hope you're right. I just have to trust that everything is going to be all right." She leaned over and kissed him on the cheek.

"I'm going to stay here in the car, okay?" Henry said.

A brief flash of panic crossed Eliza's face, but then she softened, nodding her head as if in resignation. "It probably would be better. I don't want to give Gina any reason to feel uncomfortable, and since she doesn't know you . . ."

Henry nodded. "I'll be right here if you need me. I'm right here."

Chapter 10

ELIZA FOUND GINA MINDLESSLY FLIPPING channels on an old television set in the back bedroom of Barbara's home. The bed was unmade, the floor littered with Gina's clothes and several stacks of used dishes. A dark-blue bath towel had been draped over the closed curtains, most certainly to diminish the light that filtered into the room during daylight hours.

It was a dismal sight. Gina herself was hardly an improvement. Eliza thought she looked thinner than she had the last time she'd seen her. Her cheeks were sunken, her eyes rimmed with red. She looked awful—awful and completely surprised to see her younger sister walk into the room.

"What are you doing here?" She was instantly accusatory, her voice edgy and strained. Eliza didn't say anything. She simply sat down on the bed across from Gina and waited for her to figure things out. Anger flared as soon as she did. "Wait, did Barbara call you? I don't believe this. Barbara!" she yelled. "You called my baby sister to come and check up on me?" She turned back to Eliza. "Really, Eliza, you didn't have to come all this way. I'm fine. I don't need anything from you."

"Gina, you can't stay here. It's not fair to Barbara. She has kids to take care of; she has a life. She can't have you lounging around, eating her food, getting drunk in her back bedroom."

"I'm not drunk." Gina tossed the TV remote onto the bed beside her and crossed her arms defensively.

"Not right now," Eliza agreed. "But for how long? This isn't your home. Barbara loves you, but you aren't welcome here anymore." Eliza watched as Gina stood and paced nervously around the room.

"What, and she had to have you drive all the way here just to tell me I'm not welcome? Why didn't she just tell me herself?"

"She didn't want to turn you out, Gina. She loves you. She wants you to be safe. It just can't be *here*."

"So I'll leave, then." Gina started to pick up the clothing strewn about the room.

"Where will you go?" Instinctively, Eliza moved to the door. She didn't think her sister would try to flee. Her only mode of transportation was her own two feet, but Eliza felt better blocking the doorway just the same.

"What's it matter to you where I go? Just go home. I'll figure something out."

Eliza took a deep breath. "I didn't come here just to deliver a message and then leave again. I'm going to stay a few days." She paused to gauge her sister's reaction. Gina stopped moving about the room and turned to face her but didn't say anything in response, so Eliza continued.

"I want to take you to rehab, Gina. You can't do this anymore—not to Mom, not to Barbara, and most importantly, not to yourself. I want you to let me help you."

"You think it's that easy? That you can just waltz in here and say, 'Hey, sis, time to quit life and go to rehab because baby sister says so'? Well, here's a news flash for you: I don't need your help."

"Yes, you do," Eliza said evenly. "Where are you going to go? Mom has locked you out; Barbara is kicking you out. Where does that leave you?"

"I have friends. I'll . . . stay with them." Her voice faltered just enough for Eliza to know Gina's welcome among her friends must have been wearing thin.

"For how long? Until Mom comes around? She changed the locks, Gina. She doesn't want you to come home." The rough exterior of Gina's reserve was starting to crack. She turned away from Eliza and sank onto the bed.

"Have you talked to Mom?"

Eliza thought about lying to her sister. She wanted Gina to believe her family was unified—that they were all serious about her making a change right *now*. She believed her mom would stand beside her, but she couldn't be certain, and she wasn't willing to test her mother's mettle when Gina was at such a critical point. But she couldn't bring herself to lie. Trust was more important. "No. She doesn't know I'm here. I was afraid if she thought I was coming, she'd try to talk me out of it. Or come and get you herself."

"She won't come for me—not this time. Do you know what I did? Do you want to know why Mom kicked me out?"

Eliza sat on the bed next to her sister.

"I came home in the middle of an art class. She was teaching, and I was drunk. She asked me to stay out of the living room, to just stay away until everyone had gone, but I couldn't do it. She was just so . . . happy. She was happy because I wasn't there to ruin things."

Eliza closed her eyes. She could only imagine where this was going.

"I ruined the painting she was working on. Just walked into the room, picked up a cup of black paint, and tossed it onto the canvas—hers and then her student's." Gina shook her head. "You know what's sad? I don't remember doing any of it."

"Gina, don't you see?" Eliza said. "It's time to stop. It's time to get help, to make things right with Mom again." They sat quietly, Eliza holding her breath as she waited for her sister's response.

"No," Gina finally said. "Maybe I need to change some things, but I'm not doing rehab." She stood and shoved the last of the clothes she'd been gathering into a worn blue duffel bag she'd pulled out from under the chair in the corner.

"Why won't you let me help you? You don't have to do this on your own," Eliza pled. "Please, Gina. Just let me help." Gina pulled a pair of tall black boots over her faded jeans, then hoisted her bag over her shoulder.

She stopped in the doorway of the bedroom. "That's just it, Liza. I don't *want* your help." Eliza followed her to the front door and watched her sister slip silently into the darkness.

Gina was smaller than Eliza—a few inches shorter with a narrower frame. Eliza could have physically restrained her sister had she tried. But she couldn't force her to get help. If Gina wasn't even willing to have the conversation, what else could Eliza do? Still, to simply let her walk into the darkness alone, to wind up who knows where?

"You okay?"

Barbara stood in the hallway, worry and concern evident in everything from the look on her face to the way she kept threading a dish towel through her fingers.

Eliza sniffed and wiped a stray tear from the corner of her eye. "I don't know what happened. She got up to leave, and I just . . . I let her go."

"We're only a few blocks away from the bus station," Barbara said. "I expect that's where she's headed. Where she'll go after that is anybody's guess." Both women turned when a knock sounded on the front door. Eliza opened the door and found Henry standing there looking a little sheepish.

"I'm so sorry," he said. "I don't mean to intrude, only I saw your sister leaving. I just wanted to make sure everything was all right."

Eliza shook her head. "I wish it were, Henry."

"Do you want to follow her in the car? Should we try to bring her back?"

Eliza was quiet for a moment. "No," she finally said. "I don't know why, but I think we need to let her go."

"I don't understand," Barbara said. "If kicking her out was all she needed, I could have done that on my own. Did you really come all this way just to let her walk out after one conversation?"

Eliza looked resolutely at her aunt. "She's going to come back. I have to believe she's going to come back."

Barbara looked doubtful. "I know you want to hope for the best, but Gina's track record isn't very good, Liza. I wouldn't hang your hopes on that thought."

"It's not just a hope. It's a feeling. Gina doesn't have anywhere to go. Her pride made her leave tonight, but . . . she'll come back. Just wait and see."

* * *

The following morning, Eliza and Henry sat at opposite ends of Barbara's round kitchen table. Barbara was off delivering her children to summer day camp, so for the moment, Eliza and Henry were alone. Eliza had slept in the bedroom where Gina had been staying, and though her sleep had been fitful, she still guessed she'd fared better than Henry, who'd done his best to be comfortable sleeping on the small sofa in the living room. It couldn't have been easy squeezing his six-foot frame onto four and a half feet of sofa. He didn't complain, but he didn't exactly look rested either.

Eliza pushed the last of her scrambled eggs around on her plate. Barbara had fixed a lovely breakfast, and Eliza had forced herself to eat, knowing she needed it. But her stomach was too tied in knots for her to really enjoy her food.

"Your aunt is very nice," Henry said, breaking the silence.

Eliza smiled. "She's a lot like my dad. For a while after he died, it was hard to be around her because they're similar in so many ways. But now I find it comforting. I figure if there are parts of him in his sister, then there must be parts of him in me too."

"That's a nice thought." Henry cleared his throat. "So, uh, what are we going to do if Gina doesn't come back?"

Eliza looked up. "She *is* going to come back."

"Well, but what if—"

"Have you heard back from your uncle in Raleigh?" she interrupted him. "I'm going to follow up with a few of the places I called last night. Maybe you could check with your uncle again too?"

Eliza was being stubborn, but it was too painful to think about what might happen if Gina continued down her current path. This had to be it. This had to be the beginning of Gina's recovery. Still, Henry was right. Eliza didn't want to admit it, but he had asked a very valid question. What if this time Gina really did disappear for good?

* * *

Barbara took her role as host to Eliza and Henry quite seriously. At every turn, she was offering them something to eat. After a lunch of fried chicken, potatoes, and coleslaw, Eliza thought she'd keel over if she tried to eat the key lime pie Barbara pulled from the refrigerator.

"Barbara, you shouldn't have gone to all this trouble. You've been in the kitchen all morning."

"Oh, it's nothing. I never get to see you, so it feels right I should spoil you while you're here. Besides, you look thin. I'm going to send you home with the leftover fried chicken."

If only Barbara had been around when Eliza had been in foster care; she would have taken Eliza in without a second thought. But she'd been living across the country, teaching in California while her husband, Dave, finished his degree. She'd done what she could—phone calls had been frequent, and she'd made sure she visited Eliza every time she was home.

Eliza remembered how wonderful it felt to have Barbara move back to Tennessee just after she had moved back in with her mom. The extra measure of support was something they had both needed as they'd worked to rebuild their relationship.

After Eliza and Henry finished their pie, they moved to Barbara's living room and continued their day-long discussion regarding the various options available for Gina's treatment. Eliza had found a state-funded program that was willing to admit Gina, but it was the same facility Gina had attended for court-mandated rehab when she'd been arrested for drunken and disorderly conduct. She'd stayed for the required twenty-eight days and had made baby steps of progress, but she hadn't stayed sober for more than two weeks after leaving the facility.

Another program Eliza felt better about had a wait list of several months, which obviously wouldn't do for Gina's immediate needs, though it couldn't hurt to get her name on the list assuming she decided to come back. Insurance for the future, perhaps?

Henry had a promising conversation with his uncle, who had an old friend who ran Hazelwood Therapy, a posh, privately funded rehab center in the suburbs of Raleigh. He was waiting to hear back about availability, but Eliza felt that in the end, it wouldn't matter even if there *was* a bed available. She would never be able to afford a residential program of that caliber.

She sighed and rubbed her temples with the heels of her hands. She was beginning to doubt that anything was going to work out. When Henry's cell phone rang, they all jumped. He glanced at his phone and gave Eliza a slight nod. It was his uncle returning his call. He excused himself to the front porch to answer.

Eliza sat impatiently in the living room, picking at her nails. It was a nervous habit, one she thought she'd overcome, but as she looked at the mangled mess that graced the ends of her fingers, she realized it was clearly still an issue. She sighed and glanced at Barbara, who sat benignly at the kitchen table, folding a load of clean towels.

"Barbara, give me something to do. If I have to sit here waiting for something to happen for one minute longer, I'm liable to pick my fingernails off."

Barbara smiled. "Here, take these towels down to the linen closet in between the kids' bedrooms."

Eliza took the towels and headed down the hall. She paused to look at the rows and rows of family pictures Barbara had crammed into every square inch of available wall space in the hallway. Most of the pictures were of Barbara's own three children, but scattered amongst the more recent snapshots, Eliza recognized a photo of her father and Barbara as children.

Her father looked to be about ten, Barbara a few years younger. They were standing in front of a swimming pool, their lanky arms tangled around each other's necks and childish grins gazing out from squinted, sun-kissed faces. Right beside it hung another photo of Eliza's family when she was just a baby. Her parents sat on a park bench with four-year-old Gina between them and baby Eliza squished contentedly on her mother's hip. Of course, she had no recollection of the photo, but she did remember how happy they'd been before her dad had gotten sick.

She often wondered how different her life might have turned out had her dad never had cancer, had her mom not spiraled into such a debilitating depression. She took a deep breath and shook the thought away. There was no sense in feeling sorry over her past.

"Is that you there?"

Eliza jumped. She hadn't heard Henry approach her. "Yes." Henry was pointing at the picture of her family sitting together in the park. "And that's Gina right there." She pointed to her sister.

"Your red hair came from your dad," Henry said. "And those eyes too."

"I was young when he first started chemotherapy for his cancer. Maybe seven or eight years old. I remember being so devastated when his hair started falling out. The red hair was kind of our thing, you know? I told him once I was going to grow my hair out extra long so I could cut it and have a wig made just for him."

"He was sick for a long time, then," Henry said. "He died when you were eleven?"

"He went into remission once, but it didn't even last a year. We found out the cancer was back just after my eleventh birthday. He only lived a couple more months."

"I'm sorry, Eliza," Henry said gently.

"It was a long time ago." She turned and walked to the linen closet, where she hastily stacked the towels on an empty shelf. "What did you find out from your uncle? Good news?"

Henry smiled. "Yes, as a matter of fact, very good news."

They rejoined Barbara in the living room.

"My uncle put me in touch directly with his friend, who is the director of Hazelwood. They *do* have availability and would be happy to see Gina admitted. Of course, this place is wildly expensive. But they have some scholarship funding. We can thank my uncle for this one. The director said he owed a favor to my uncle, and he'd be happy to help work something out."

"What does that mean? There might be money available for Gina?"

"He made it sound very promising. But there's a catch. Scholarship funds can't just go to anyone. They don't, for example, want to fund rehabilitation for someone family members bring in kicking and screaming all the way. Scholarship funds are for those serious about succeeding at Hazelwood. Patients must go willingly and commit to making their very best effort at succeeding in their treatment."

Eliza's face fell. "That's not Gina."

"What if it is me?"

Everyone turned at the sound of Gina's voice. She stood in the living room entry just off the foyer. No one had heard her come in the front door. Eliza stood and took a few steps toward her sister.

"It's a good place, Gina. Much nicer than the last one you tried." Eliza tried to keep her voice steady in an effort to mask the emotion bubbling inside. It almost seemed too good to be true. Gina *had* come back. She was there, so close to saying yes. "Will you go?"

Gina looked over Eliza's shoulder at Henry. "Who's he?"

"This is my friend Henry. We work together. It was his uncle who put us in touch with the director of Hazelwood."

"How do we know I'd get the scholarship?" She directed her question at Henry.

"We don't know for certain. You would still have to apply, but it was the director himself whom I spoke with. He seemed very confident it wouldn't be an issue."

Gina looked at the floor for what seemed like an interminable amount of time. "I'll go," she finally said. She looked up at Eliza, tears welling in her eyes. "I'll go."

* * *

Just after 11:00 p.m., Eliza left her sister sleeping in the guest bedroom and padded down the hall in her bare feet to get something to drink from the kitchen. The kitchen opened into the living room, where Henry was sleeping for the night, so she treaded extra softly, not wanting to disturb him if he'd already gone to bed. She was surprised to find him sitting at the kitchen table, his laptop open in front of him.

"Hi." She smiled. "What are you working on?"

He looked up and shrugged his shoulders. "Nothing, really. Just reading over some notes."

"What, like lesson-plan notes?" She pulled a bottled water from the refrigerator and sat down beside him at the table.

"No, more like story-idea notes."

Eliza's eyebrows shot up. "Henry, are you a writer?" She hardly knew why she was surprised. Writing certainly fit with everything else she knew about him. "What do you write?"

"Don't go jumping to conclusions yet," Henry said good-naturedly. "I like to write, but I don't think I can call myself a writer. I've never been published or anything. It's more just a hobby."

"Surely you don't have to be published to call yourself a writer," Eliza said. "What do you write?" she asked again. "Fiction? Nonfiction? Catalog product descriptions?"

Henry looked at her quizzically. "Catalog descriptions?"

She waved her hand dismissively. "I had a roommate once who wrote for a clothing store. That was her job . . . to write descriptions for the catalog. She didn't love it, but it paid the bills."

Henry shook his head and laughed. "Well, that's more than can be said for my writing. It hasn't ever paid a single bill." He hesitated for a moment. "I write fiction. I wrote a book a couple of years ago. I don't know. I don't even really know if it's any good." He seemed self-aware, even uncomfortable talking about his writing. She could tell it wasn't something he frequently discussed.

"Have you ever had anyone read it?"

"No. And I don't intend to, at least not anytime soon."

"But you have to. How will you ever know if it *is* good if you don't let anyone read it?"

"Precisely." Henry folded his arms across his chest. "Ignorance is bliss." His tone was playful, but Eliza could tell there was a measure of seriousness to his claim. True, she couldn't imagine all that went into creating a novel. She could hardly manage to write down a page-long journal entry. To write something so extensive, then risk the criticism and rejection that inevitably accompanied putting it out there? The thought made *her* nervous, and she wasn't even the one who had written the book.

"Well, if you ever decide to let it see the light of day," Eliza said, "I'd love to read it."

He smiled. "I'll remember that." She watched him as he removed his glasses and rubbed his eyes before placing them back on again. "I should get some sleep." He stood from the table.

"Wait." Eliza reached out and touched his arm. She stood up beside him, her hand still resting just below his elbow. She was standing close to him—closer than she had intended—and it made her mouth go dry and her pulse quicken.

Henry had been her rock the past forty-eight hours. He'd kept her calm and focused. He'd been encouraging and helpful and kind. But nothing that she was suddenly feeling had anything to do with him being kind. She pulled her hand away as if breaking their physical connection would keep him from knowing the thoughts racing through her mind— thoughts she was certain would embarrass Henry to the point of never wanting to speak to her again.

How would it make him feel to know she was busy wondering what it would be like to touch the stubble along the edge of his jawline or run her fingers through his hair? She quickly pushed the thoughts from her mind. This was no time to distract herself from Gina, from the job she had to do the following day. Still, there was no denying the appeal Henry suddenly had or the intensity of the feelings that had so quickly overwhelmed her. *Focus, Eliza!*

"I just wanted to say thank you," she finally said. "I don't think there's a way I could adequately describe how grateful I am for all your help the past few days. Your kindness means a great deal."

The words felt clumsy as they came out of her mouth. It seemed impossible for her to really convey the depth and sincerity of her gratitude. Everything that was happening with Gina was happening only because Henry had been there for her. He had surprised her in so many ways over the past couple of days—dropping everything to help her when it would have been so easy to send her on her way without a second thought.

"You're most welcome," Henry said. "I'm happy to help any way I can."

"You're a good man, Henry," Eliza whispered. Their eyes met for a brief moment before, seized by sudden impulse, Eliza closed the distance between them, stood on her tiptoes, and kissed him full on the lips. When she pulled away, Henry stood there, his eyes wide with surprise. He'd kissed back. She was certain of that. He could have pushed her away, and he hadn't. But the stupefied look on his face didn't exactly make it easy for her to know what to do next.

"Oh, gosh," she said. "I'm so sorry. I don't know what I was . . . I was just . . ." She shook her head. Henry didn't move, the shocked look on his face frozen in place. "I don't know what I was thinking. I'm just going to go to bed. I'll, um, I'll just see you in the morning." She backed out of the kitchen, then turned and hurried down the hall. She was fairly certain Henry still hadn't moved when she closed her bedroom door.

Chapter 11

HENRY AND ELIZA DECIDED HE would drive for the first half of the trip so she could spend time with Gina and then she'd take the wheel when they drove from Raleigh back to Rockbridge.

He was intrigued as he listened to the sisters' conversation. Things had been tense at first, but with Eliza's careful attention, Gina had eventually started to relax. Henry, on the other hand, couldn't relax at all. He was mesmerized by Eliza's ability to communicate with Gina, to put her at ease when the situation had the potential to be such a stressful one.

She was in her element with her sister; she was gentle, supportive, and steadfast. Whenever Gina's resolve started to waver, Eliza was ready with the encouragement she needed. "This is the right thing," she would say over and over again.

Henry wanted to believe Eliza was right, but he wasn't so sure. He would never admit it out loud, but it almost seemed too easy.

They'd been driving for three hours when Henry stopped for gas in Knoxville. He stopped the car next to the gas pump and reached for his wallet.

"Here, Henry, use this," Eliza said, reaching up to hand him her debit card. He shook his head. "It's all right. I've got it this time."

"Can I get you something to drink, then?" Eliza unbuckled her seat belt. "I need a Coke."

"Just some water would be great."

The air was hot and muggy outside the car, thick with humidity. It felt like a wet blanket draped over Henry's shoulders, and it left him longing for the cooler temperatures at Rockbridge. When the tank was full, Eliza hadn't yet returned from inside the gas station. He glanced into the back of the SUV, where Gina was leaned back in her seat, her head turned so she was staring out the window in the opposite direction. He opened the door and stuck his head inside.

"Can I get you anything?"

When she looked his way, he could see the tired desperation in her eyes. He realized that what her body was likely telling her she needed she'd just committed not to have.

"A shot of vodka would be nice," she said idly, confirming his impression.

Henry wished there were something he could do to help her. Reassurance was all he had to offer. "You're going to be okay, Gina."

Gina shrugged her shoulders. "Maybe."

"I'm going to go find Eliza. Are you sure you don't need anything?" When she shook her head, he closed the car door and went inside.

Eliza was standing in the chip aisle, a bottle of Coke in her hand and a water bottle under her arm. She was on her cell phone, her back to Henry. He approached her slowly, not wanting to startle her, and touched her gently on the elbow. She turned and smiled, rolling her eyes as if to say, *This conversation is taking longer than I thought it would.* Henry shook his head, hoping she knew he was telling her not to worry. He reached for the drinks, eyebrows raised in question. She handed them over, and he took them to the counter to pay for them, realizing only when he got there that he'd left his wallet in the car.

"There, finished," Eliza said, coming up beside him.

"That's good 'cause my wallet is in the car."

"I'm supposed to buy the drinks anyway." Eliza pulled a couple dollars out of her purse and handed them to the cashier. "I finally talked to my mom," she said.

Before leaving Nashville, they'd debated whether it would be prudent to drive forty-five minutes backward to go see Beverly in Ashland City. Eliza had wanted to see her mom but worried that the potential conflict of the visit might change Gina's mind about rehab. In the end, they'd decided to head straight for Raleigh instead.

"How's she doing?"

"I think she's okay. She feels guilty I'm the one having to do all this, you know? There's a lot of things my mom still struggles with that she can't seem to forgive herself for. I wish she would though. I don't think anyone blames her for what happened."

Henry opened the door for Eliza, and they stepped back out into the steamy summer heat.

"But not everyone would feel that way. A lot of people *would* blame her for all that's happened. I think it's really wonderful that you don't."

Eliza only shrugged. "I buried the blame a long time ago. That doesn't mean sometimes I don't resent the way things are. I mean, I definitely have my selfish moments."

Henry shook his head. "I have a hard time imagining that."

Back at the car, Eliza turned to Henry, a questioning look on her face. "Where's Gina?"

"I don't know. She was here when I went inside to find you."

Eliza was already walking back into the gas station. "I'll check the bathroom. Maybe she snuck past us inside."

Henry turned back to the car and opened the driver's side door. His heart sank. His wallet was sitting on the seat, open and dismantled. He sighed.

"She's not there," Eliza said when she returned. "She's not anywhere inside."

Henry slowly turned. "Wherever she is, she's got $120 with her."

Eliza's face fell. She let out an angry laugh. "Ugh. I should have known this would happen. Did she take anything else? Any credit cards?"

"No, just the cash." Henry felt terrible. If he hadn't left Gina alone in the car, with his wallet sitting in plain sight, no less, this might not have happened. "Eliza, I'm so sorry. I shouldn't have left her alone."

"It's not your fault. She would have found another way," Eliza said. "If not here, then the next stop. She would have climbed out a bathroom window or even stolen the car if given the chance."

Henry was silently grateful he'd kept Eliza's keys in his pocket while he'd gone inside. "Do you think she ever had any intention of going to rehab?" Henry asked. "Or was she just using us for a ride?"

"I don't know." Eliza's reply was halfhearted. "I thought she seemed sincere . . . but she hasn't had a drink in a couple of days. As soon as the craving came on, she probably lost her nerve. I don't think I overestimated Gina's sincerity. I think I underestimated the power of her drug." Eliza leaned against the car, visibly frustrated. "I'll pay you back for the cash she took."

"That's the least of my concerns." Henry repeated the same question he'd asked at Barbara's house the night he and Eliza had arrived. "Should we go look for her? She couldn't have gotten far." Henry looked around the gas station parking lot and down the road in both directions. She couldn't have gotten *anywhere*. There wasn't anywhere to go.

"She's not here," Eliza said. "Gina knows how to hide. She jumped into the cab of some truck and hitched a ride going the opposite direction, I'm sure."

"What do we do now?"

Eliza looked at him, her eyes full of a distant sadness Henry realized he couldn't ever touch. "We go home," she said simply. "What choice do we have?"

* * *

Knoxville was just over an hour away from Rose Creek. When they made it into town, it was just past 8:00 p.m.

"Hey," Henry said. It was the first either of them had spoken in quite some time. "We've missed dinner at Rockbridge. Do you want to pick something up here in town before we go up?"

Eliza nodded. "Dinner would be good."

They picked a Japanese place right in the heart of downtown. Even though it was a Saturday evening, the restaurant was mostly cleared out.

"I bet they were busy three hours ago," Eliza said jokingly.

"You've learned Rose Creek well." It was nice to see her smile again. Conversation over dinner was pleasant, but Henry couldn't help feeling like there was a giant elephant in the room—something they both wanted to talk about but wouldn't.

He didn't want to seem shallow, considering the worry Eliza surely felt over her sister's whereabouts, but he also didn't want things to remain awkward forever. He could hardly bear the thought of wondering every time he and Eliza were together if she would mention what had happened between them.

"Eliza," he began quickly so as not to lose his nerve. "About the other night—"

"You don't have to say anything," Eliza cut him off. "It was impulsive and crazy and clearly not something you were expecting."

"It's not that," Henry said. "I mean, I wasn't expecting it, but that's not what . . . I just . . . agh, this is hard." He took a deep breath and tried to focus his words. "I met Allison when I was fifteen. She was the first girl I ever kissed, and then I married her. After the divorce, I haven't really . . . That is to say, I just haven't done any . . . dating." He watched Eliza's expression change and knew she understood what he was trying to tell her. He'd never kissed anyone but Allison. Until now.

What he couldn't tell Eliza was the internal turmoil she had awakened within him. It wasn't that he hadn't enjoyed the kiss. He could still conjure up the smell of her hair and the softness of her lips, both sensations he had enjoyed. But what he wasn't prepared for was the raw realization that Allison, in any role except AJ's mother, was no longer a part of his life. Of course, he'd already known this. He'd been divorced for nearly two years. But until he'd felt another woman's lips touching his, he'd never really let himself think about what that meant. For two years, he'd been living in denial. And then Eliza had woken him up.

"I shouldn't have been so forward, Henry. I'm sorry."

"Please don't apologize. It's just that I'm still a little broken. Everything about my past, my relationship with Allison, with AJ . . . It's complicated."

"You don't have to explain," Eliza said. "I understand. We're friends, and I don't want to lose that. What do you say we just pretend like it never happened?"

It wasn't a likely prospect. Henry would never be able to forget what had happened. But he also couldn't, in his right mind, expect someone like Eliza to jump into his angst-filled, confusing life without fair and sufficient warning. For her sake, it was probably better if she *did* forget.

"It's a deal." He regretted the words the moment he said them.

"So where did AJ and Allison go?"

Henry tried to hide his grimace. While he appreciated Eliza's efforts to change the subject, AJ's current whereabouts was only slightly lower than Eliza's kiss on his list of things most difficult to talk about.

"They went to Disney World," he said. "With Robert." A surge of frustration filled Henry as he thought of them all vacationing together. Of course, he trusted Allison and knew if Robert was going to be a part of her life, he would have to be a part of AJ's life too. But it still felt wrong. For all he did to build a relationship with AJ, for all the thought and care and effort he put forth, it was completely disheartening to feel so easily replaced.

"Robert?" Eliza asked. "He's a friend of Allison's?"

"Yeah." *Please don't make me talk about this further.*

"Vacationing together . . . It's serious, then." Eliza must have sensed his distress. "I'm sorry. That seems like a really awful thing to have to get used to."

"It's fine," Henry said. "I mean, it's not fine. I hate it, but they didn't really ask how I felt about it, so, what can I do?"

"I'm sorry, Henry. I don't envy the position you're in. Are you ready to go?"

Henry breathed a sigh of relief. "Yeah," he said. "I'll get the check."

* * *

"So tell me more about your family." She was driving slowly, handling the roads that wound up the mountain to Rockbridge as best she could in the dark. "We've spent all this time together, and all we did was talk about *my* family. It's not fair."

"It's true. Your family did a good job of stealing the spotlight the past few days."

"Shut up." Henry could tell she was joking by her tone. "I'm still emotional over the whole thing. You're not allowed to make jokes for at least another week."

"Fine, fine. We can talk about me the rest of the way home. What do you want to know?"

"Siblings? Are your parents still together? Do you look like your mom? Your dad?"

"You want me to tell you my shoe size and my little league batting average while I'm at it?"

Eliza laughed. "Yes, please."

"Let's see. I have three younger siblings, one brother, and two little sisters. They're all great—not anything like me. My brother—he's fun and outgoing, the life of every party. He's a pharmacist in Winston-Salem, not far from my parents. My sisters are both in college out at BYU. My parents just celebrated their twenty-fifth anniversary last month. What else? People say I look like my mom. I wear a size eleven shoe. And I don't remember my batting average, but I'm sure it was terrible. I think I hit the ball three times the entire season."

Eliza laughed again, a sound Henry was growing particularly fond of.

"The trouble," he went on, "is I would have had to actually *look up* from my book to see the ball coming. I was doomed from the start, really."

"I bet you were an interesting kid."

"Are you kidding? I was an utterly boring kid. I lived in books."

The conversation waned for a moment, and then Eliza asked, "Wait. Back up. Your parents have been married for twenty-five years? Where do you fit in?"

Henry's shoulders tensed, and Eliza must have noticed.

"Oh, Henry, I'm sorry. That was terribly rude. It's not any of my business."

It was a question Henry was used to avoiding. He'd done it countless times when people had mentioned the stark contrast between his own looks and his father's. His father had fair skin and green eyes, while Henry had a more olive complexion and darker hair. "I look like my mom," he always said. And it was the truth. He *did* look like his mom.

His family history wasn't something he generally shared, but he'd involuntarily made it a point of conversation when he'd mentioned how long his parents had been married—twenty-five years—not long enough to have a son who was thirty.

It might have been the closeness he'd developed with Eliza over the past couple of days or the amount of trust she had placed in him. Maybe it was simply that he was weary of the walls and fences he constantly and quite diligently built around himself. Whatever the reason, he decided the easiest answer was the truth. "It's okay," Henry said. "I was adopted. I'm my mother's biological son but was adopted by her second husband."

"Oh, now I see."

"You know what's funny? People often tell me I sound like my dad— my stepdad. I guess that happens when you grow up with someone. You pick up mannerisms, expressions, that sort of thing."

"How old were you when he adopted you?"

"I was five."

"What happened to your biological father?"

Henry was silent. Discussing adoption was one thing, but Eliza's questions were venturing into dangerous territory. He only had one memory of his biological father, and it wasn't one he cared to relive.

"I'm sorry, Henry," Eliza said suddenly, apologizing for the second time. "You don't have to talk about this with me."

He shook his head. "No, I don't mind. I don't know what happened to him. We didn't keep in touch."

Eliza didn't say anything in response. He was grateful she wasn't pushing the issue, but she didn't have to speak her questions for him to know they were there. The questions were always there.

"I have a father," Henry began. "He's a good man. He adopted me, took me to the temple, raised me as his own son. I *am* his son. I have no reason to seek out a man who can't claim to be anything other than a biological relation."

"You're right," Eliza said, her tone gentle.

Henry glanced in her direction. She was keeping her eyes on the road, both hands firmly holding the steering wheel.

"Why do I feel like there's something you aren't saying?"

Eliza shook her head. "It's nothing," she said. "I don't know . . . I guess I'm just wondering if you ever wonder about him. Is it strange to know nothing? Where he is? Who he is? Whether or not he ever wonders about you?"

"Eliza, he gave me up." Henry's voice was controlled but still emotional. "My mother took me to see him, in prison, of all places, and he gave me up—signed the adoption papers while I stood there and watched. He didn't want me then; I imagine he has little regard for what I'm doing with my life now."

"Oh, Henry," Eliza said. "I was being thoughtless to even suggest such a thing. I'm sure that's a difficult memory for you."

"It's not difficult," Henry said quickly. "He told my mother it was the only way he'd sign the papers—that she had to bring me to see him one last time. He'd been in prison for years though. I can't remember anything but that one conversation. William Harrison"—he paused for a moment, hesitating over the man's name—"he wasn't a father. Signing those papers—it was the best thing he could have done for me. I don't doubt that at all."

And yet Henry knew the edge in his voice indicated otherwise. True, he didn't doubt his adoption was the best thing that could have ever happened. But it was a lie that the memory of his last confrontation with his biological father hadn't been difficult.

As a child, he'd spent years wondering what he could have ever done that would make a man sign away rights to his own kid. Now, with the wisdom and perspective of a man who *had* his own son, it was easy to understand why someone might reasonably make such a choice. Sometimes it was necessary for logic and reason to dictate matters that couldn't be trusted to the heart. The right choice was often the most painful one. But logic and reason aside, the scars of Henry's suffering as a child were still part of him.

"It would still make me sad," Eliza said.

"Sad? What do you mean?"

"I mean, I'm sure it was the best thing for you to be adopted, but it would still feel painful to have a parent say they don't want you . . ." Her words trailed off. "Good grief, Henry. How many times am I going to feel like I need to apologize? I don't know what's wrong with me today. It seems like I keep saying the wrong thing."

Except she hadn't said the wrong thing. No one had ever been willing to voice what Henry had felt his entire life. He didn't want things to change; he would never give up the relationship he'd developed with his adoptive father, but it still hurt to feel cast aside. It hurt, and it felt amazing to have someone else acknowledge that fact. "You didn't say the wrong thing, Eliza. You're right. It does hurt."

A minute, then two passed before she reached over and touched his arm. When she spoke, her voice was soft. "Henry, I'm glad you told me."

* * *

They arrived back at Rockbridge just after 10:00 p.m. They said good night before Henry turned and walked down the sidewalk to his own apartment. Despite the length of time he'd just spent sitting in a car and the emotional context of many of his conversations with Eliza, he found himself in a good mood. Eliza's company was encouraging, even uplifting.

He had tremendous respect for her—for the way she'd handled the difficult circumstances she'd dealt with over the weekend. She'd shown fortitude and faith and hadn't let discouragement get the best of her when things hadn't worked out. She was optimistic and trusting, and she wasn't afraid. That might have been what he admired about her most of all. She didn't live her life in fear.

Suddenly, Henry knew what he needed to do. He hurried into his apartment, dropped his things in the kitchen, then walked over to his desk. He glanced at his watch, then hastily reached for his manuscript. If he hurried, he'd make it to Daniel's room before Cooper went to bed.

The dorm building was already locked, so Henry knocked lightly on the dorm manager's window. "Cooper! Are you awake? Can you let me in?"

Cooper opened the window. "Hey, Henry. You're back. You and Eliza have a nice weekend?" He raised his eyebrows and grinned.

"What? It wasn't like that. I was just helping out with some family trouble."

"Oh. Well, that sounds way more boring than what everyone around here has been speculating. Good thing Flip's off in the woods. He might have been hanging out in the parking lot ready to meet you for a duel."

"Cooper, what are you talking about?"

"Flip. He's got a thing for Eliza. You haven't noticed?"

Henry hadn't noticed, though he wasn't surprised. What did surprise him was the tightening he felt under his ribs when he thought of the two of them together. He shrugged it off. Hadn't he just told Eliza his life was too complicated for them to be anything more than friends? "I guess not," he finally said. "I don't know why I would have. Look, can you just let me in? I need to give this to Daniel."

"Sure thing." A moment later, he was at the door, holding it open for Henry. "It just occurred to me that Daniel is out on excursion. They won't be back until Sunday. Do you want to leave it in his room?"

Henry nodded. "Yeah. I'd like him to see it as soon as he returns."

"Cool. Down the hall and to the left, room 204—his name's on the door."

Henry hurried to Daniel's room, fearing he might lose his nerve if he didn't follow through in the moment. When he opened the door, he noted that half of Daniel's room was stripped bare—no sheets on the bed, no personal belongings on the desk. The thought brought him comfort. Daniel didn't presently have a roommate, which meant there wasn't anyone else who would see Henry's manuscript. Pulling a sticky note off a pad on Daniel's desk, he paused, not sure what to write. Finally, he wrote, "Hope it's good enough you make it all the way to the end."

He scribbled his name at the bottom of the note but hesitated before sticking it to the front of his manuscript. He hardly knew Daniel. How could he trust him with something that quite literally felt like a part of his soul? Henry shook away his doubts. If Daniel was ever going to trust Henry, Henry had to trust him too. *Don't let me regret this*, he silently prayed. With a final deep breath, Henry left the manuscript on Daniel's desk and returned to his own apartment.

Chapter 12

ELIZA SANK ONTO THE SMALL couch in the corner of her living room, too tired to unpack—too tired, really, to do much of anything. Adrenaline and sheer force of will had kept her going for the past three days. Now that she was home, the exhaustion of it all was finally catching up with her. And it wasn't over. She still had to call her mom to tell her about Gina. It wasn't a conversation she was looking forward to. But, then, she guessed her mom would probably handle the news the same way Eliza had. She had been disappointed when Gina had run away, but in her heart, she hadn't been all that surprised.

Stretching her tired muscles, she stood and retrieved her phone from the kitchen. She moved back to the couch, grabbing her laptop off the desk on her way. She opened her e-mail while she waited for her mom to answer the phone.

When Eliza told her what had happened, Beverly breathed a heavy sigh. "The only thing that surprises me is you made it all the way to Knoxville before she fled. I'm sorry, Eliza. I'll let you know if I hear anything from her. I'm sure she'll turn up eventually."

An outside observer might have been surprised by her mother's casual response, but Eliza knew how many times she'd been through a similar routine with her sister. Gina had disappeared for weeks, even months on end in the past. They'd both learned a long time ago that where Gina was concerned, they couldn't count on anything to go as planned.

After hanging up with her mom, Eliza scrolled through her inbox, starring messages she'd have to address tomorrow. There were requests for progress reports from Dr. Adler and next week's schedule from Natalie still waiting for Eliza's approval. There was an e-mail from Lexie—details for the wedding and a plea to make sure Eliza had worked out her schedule and would *absolutely* be attending the following month. She would be there, but messaging Lexie to let her know could wait.

Eliza slid her computer off her lap and leaned her head against the couch cushions.

Her thoughts turned to Henry. She wasn't sure why he had offered to drive her to Tennessee, and she wasn't exactly sure why she had agreed, but she was grateful he had been there. Over and over again, he had proved to be exactly what she'd needed. He'd been calm when she had needed calm. He had been encouraging when she had needed encouragement. He had been . . . Well, he had been perfect.

She thought of Flip's off-the-cuff comment about how boring her life would be if she married Henry. Just thinking about it made her heart race. Would she be bored with someone like Henry? She didn't think Flip gave him enough credit. There was much more to Henry than Flip realized. And it wasn't just his personal life that made him interesting, though that certainly qualified as complex. Eliza thought if she was willing to peel back the layers, she'd find many things about Henry to admire.

For one, he was fun to kiss. Clearly, he was struggling to move past his divorce and find his footing as a part-time dad. Either that or she completely repulsed him, and the baggage of his life was an easy way to let her down gently and make sure she knew she better not try to kiss him again—ever.

But he didn't push me away.

It hadn't been a fly-to-the-moon, pop-your-foot-up kind of kiss, but she'd felt something. And all her feminine intuition told her he had felt something too. Eliza groaned, grabbed a throw pillow, and pressed it firmly into her face. Her brain was too tired for this. She reached for the remote control. Maybe thoughtless television would provide the distraction she needed. But it was no use. No matter how hard she tried to turn off her brain, she couldn't get Henry off her mind.

She thought again of what he'd told her regarding his biological father. If she put on her counselor hat, it was easy to recognize the ways Henry's early childhood experiences could have influenced his ability to open up to people or how they had hindered his ease at developing close relationships. Eliza understood firsthand the emotional scarring that occurred when children felt abandoned or forgotten by one or both of their parents. It had taken her mother a long time to earn back Eliza's trust. Their relationship was in a good place now, but it hadn't happened overnight.

Henry had seemed certain he wanted nothing to do with his biological father, but Eliza couldn't help but wonder if the feeling was mutual. Had William Harrison simply signed off, removing himself completely from Henry's life, or was it possible that he still thought of the son he'd once had? There was no way for Eliza to know the man's thoughts or feelings, but maybe there was a way for her to know *something* about him. At the very least, she could probably find out if he was still in prison.

She reached for her laptop once more and navigated her browser to the North Carolina Inmate Enquiry page of the Department of Corrections. She filled out the search fields, and her search yielded seventeen results. She clicked through each listing, looking for dates that corresponded with a visit from a five-year-old Henry. When she found him, it wasn't the dates that gave him away. Eliza gasped when the picture pulled up. She was staring into the face of an older, sadder version of Henry—William Grant Harrison.

Her heart started racing as she read the details of his history. His crimes weren't insignificant, though she was at least comforted to know the charges against him were not as serious as they could have been. She would have hated to learn Henry's father was guilty of assault or even murder. He'd served time for grand theft and possession of a firearm, as well as drug possession and distribution.

Because of North Carolina's "three strike" policy, his third conviction had landed him in prison with a life sentence. But there, at the very bottom of his profile, were the words *Released on parole for good behavior*. It was dated nearly two years prior. Next to his release date was an address, presumably the address he would go home to upon release. It was in a town called Lawsonville, a suburb, Google told her, of Winston-Salem. If Eliza remembered correctly, Henry's mother had lived in Winston-Salem before she'd remarried and moved to Rose Creek.

As Eliza read through the details of the page one more time, she began to feel uncomfortable. Who was she to intrude on Henry's privacy? He hadn't asked her to search for his father. It was only impulsivity that had led her to do so. Now that she'd actually found something, she wasn't sure how she should process the information. Should she tell Henry? It didn't feel right to keep it a secret.

She pulled up Gmail, hoping that if Henry was online, she could send him an instant message. She was relieved to see him under her list of available contacts. She clicked on his name to send him a message.

Eliza: Please don't hate me . . .

Henry: I could never hate you. Why?

Eliza: I just Googled your biological father.

Eliza held her breath, waiting for his response. When, after a moment, he didn't respond, she sent him another message.

Eliza: I'm sorry, Henry. I was only curious. I probably shouldn't have, but once I found something, I felt like it would be wrong for me not to tell you.

Henry: It's okay. I've searched for him before too. Is he still in prison?

Eliza: He was released on parole two years ago.

. . .

. . .

. . .

Eliza: Henry?

Henry: Yes?

Eliza: Are you all right?

Henry: Yes. Good night, Eliza.

Eliza: Good night.

* * *

Eliza caught up with Henry in the parking lot after church the following day.

"Henry," she said as she approached him. "You got a minute?"

He turned. "Sure."

She tried to read his expression. She had been worrying all morning about how he *really* felt about her digging into his past.

"Listen, about last night . . ." She watched Henry stiffen. He placed his scriptures on the roof of his car and slid his hands into his pockets. "I just wanted to apologize in person. I don't know why I felt like it was my place to meddle in your private affairs. I hope I didn't make you uncomfortable."

"It's really fine." She was relieved to hear the sincerity in his voice. "You didn't do any harm by running a search for his name. Why were you so curious though? Why does it even matter?"

"I don't know," Eliza answered. "I guess it just made me sad thinking about the possibility of this man existing out there somewhere without a single clue about who you are, how amazing you are. I remember feeling awful, completely worthless when my mother let social services walk me out of her house. She didn't even try to stop them, and I was heartbroken. But it wasn't that she didn't care. I know your father gave you up, but he must have loved you at some point—enough that he would get a tattoo of your name—"

"Tattoo?" Henry looked surprised.

"It was listed as a part of his physical description."

Henry shook his head. "I must have missed that part."

"I saw his picture, Henry. He . . ." She hesitated. "He looks just like you."

Henry took a deep breath. "I don't really know what to say. I mean, what do I do with information like that? Call him up? Invite him to dinner?" He sighed. "He's not my family."

"You're right," Eliza said. "He isn't your family. But what if there is some small chance that he cares? Maybe he's thought about you, wondered how you turned out. He spent your whole life in prison. Maybe he would appreciate knowing that not everything he contributed to this world was bad. Maybe it would feel good for him to know you're happy, successful."

Henry stifled a laugh. "Or maybe he was happy to be rid of a living, breathing burden of responsibility. Don't you see? It could go either way. Sure, looking this guy up might prove to be a cathartic experience of some sort, but it could also open old scars and hurts, even create new ones on top of the old. And I don't have just me to think about. How would it affect AJ? Is this the kind of man I would want my son to know? I mean, let's be real. It's not as if a life full of convictions and prison sentences gives him much of a positive track record."

Henry made a very valid point. He *did* have to think about AJ, and that was reason enough to be extremely cautious. "You're right. I hadn't thought of it that way, but you're completely right. I don't know what I was thinking."

"You're thinking like Eliza—who believes that hearts are good and intentions always kind. I like that about you, but this time, I can't do it. I'm just not willing to see the best in William Harrison."

Chapter 13

HENRY SAT ALONE IN HIS classroom on Monday afternoon and stared at his laptop, William Harrison's photo filling the screen. He'd been sitting there far too long; his last class had ended well over an hour ago. But he couldn't get up. He felt frozen—the tired eyes of William Harrison locking him into place behind his computer screen.

He didn't blame Eliza for looking him up. Her intentions were pure, if not a little meddlesome. And it wasn't as if she'd found out information he didn't already know. He'd been eighteen the first time he'd used the Internet to try to find his father. Though his mother had offered to talk about him a time or two, it was never a conversation Henry wanted to have with her. It felt wrong somehow to make her relive past hurts just to satisfy his need to have more answers. But the Internet felt safe, just detached enough for him to gain information without the risk of anyone getting hurt.

And he hadn't gotten hurt. He'd learned the man was still in prison, confirming Henry's opinion that he really was better off without him. And Henry hadn't looked for him since, not until Eliza had mentioned that she'd found him.

The mug shot with his file was newer than the one Henry had seen previously. His hair was gray, and the lines surrounding his eyes and mouth were more pronounced. Eliza said she thought Henry looked like him, but Henry wasn't so sure. The eyes were the same; he could at least see that much.

It was particularly unsettling because they weren't just Henry's eyes—they were AJ's eyes too.

Henry shook his head in frustration. He didn't want to think about this man. He didn't want to think about William Harrison's blood coursing through AJ's veins, making his eyes that distinct shade of blue that people always noticed. He didn't want to think about a tattoo of his name etched onto the chest of the man who wasn't supposed to love him, who wasn't supposed to have ever cared. Eliza's questions from the previous afternoon played over and over in his head.

What if he did care? What if he *would* like to know that Henry had turned out okay?

Henry scrolled to the bottom of the screen and saw the home address, a route number in Lawsonville. With just a few simple clicks, he entered the address into a search engine and was able to find a telephone number.

The name registered to the number was Paul Harrison. A brother, maybe?

Oh, what the heck, Henry thought to himself. Impulsively, he reached for his office phone and quickly dialed the number. His heart raced, sweat dripping down his brow as he listened to one ring, then two. On the third ring, a man answered the phone.

"Hello?" The voice was older and gruff.

Henry was silent, paralyzed by fear.

"Hello?" the voice said again.

This was madness. Henry didn't want to have a phone conversation with William Harrison. He didn't want to know what his voice sounded like or know if he'd had a nice day. He didn't want to know the man at all. What had he been thinking?

He hung up the phone and shoved it forcefully across his desk, sending a cup of pencils careening onto the floor.

Henry leaned his head into his hands and tried to slow his breathing. Even on the off chance that Eliza was right, a conversation with William Harrison simply wasn't something he was ready for—not now, maybe not ever.

* * *

Wednesday, a week later, Henry sat at the same desk in his classroom, waiting for his two o'clock appointment with Daniel. He was nervous and anxious to discover if he'd read his book. The thought of someone else turning the pages of his manuscript and reading the words he had so carefully crafted nearly made him sick. What if Daniel hadn't liked it? What if he'd read four chapters in and decided it wasn't even worth his time?

Henry stood and shoved his hands into his pockets, breathing out an agitated sigh. His head was in the wrong place. He knew his focus shouldn't be on his book. He should be thinking about Daniel, about what he was trying to accomplish with *him*. He hoped his effort to reach out would work—that his leap of faith would pay off in the form of a stronger relationship. Of course, it wouldn't hurt if, in the process, he was able to hear Daniel's opinion of *One Day in Ten*.

At the sound of footsteps approaching, Henry picked up a stack of papers from his desk and tried to look busy. Daniel shuffled into the room and, per his usual routine, dropped his backpack on the floor and slumped into the middle desk of the front row, just across from Henry's desk. Henry looked up, waiting for Daniel to speak. When he didn't, he moved around his desk and leaned against it, sitting lightly on the edge.

"How was your stay in the wilderness?"

Daniel gave a halfhearted shrug. "The food stunk."

Henry laughed. "I've heard Flip's not much of a cook." More silence passed before Henry said, "Right, well, I guess we should get started."

"It was good." Daniel interrupted him. "Your book—it was good."

Henry breathed a quiet sigh of relief. "Thank you."

"Are you going to publish it?"

"Maybe someday."

"Why not now?" Daniel asked. "People should read it."

Henry folded his arms across his chest. "Daniel, can I tell you something man to man?"

Daniel looked skeptical. "I guess."

"Besides me, you're the only person in the world who's read that book."

"Dude, you're kidding, right?"

"I'm not kidding. I've never shown it to anyone."

"Why not?"

"The honest, naked truth," Henry said, "is that I'm too much of a chicken. It's hard to let others read your words. It feels like it's me on those pages, you know? It's personal."

"So why'd you let *me* read it, then?"

Henry moved to the desk beside Daniel's and sat down, leaning back and extending his legs out in front of him. "I was hoping since I showed you a little bit of what I like to write, you'd tell me a little bit about what *you* like to write."

Daniel was silent for a moment. "What makes you think I like to write?"

"Call it a hunch."

Daniel didn't respond.

"Listen," Henry said. "We're going to skip all this extra stuff, and I'm going to move you into a curriculum I think will work well for you. If you decide you don't like it, we'll figure out something else. You'll be doing a lot of reading, but I'd like to give you the opportunity to write as well. I'm not putting you in with another English class. It'll just be you and me, one-on-one. If you're up to it, I thought we might work together, maybe form our own critique group, so to speak. What do you think?"

Daniel looked at him out of the corner of his eye. "So, what, like you read my stuff, and I read yours?"

"Among other things, yes."

Daniel was quiet. He rolled his pencil up and down his desk for what seemed like an eternity to Henry. "Science fiction," he finally said. "That's what I like to write—science fiction, maybe a little fantasy."

Henry felt the tension in his shoulders ease. This was what he had been waiting for—for Daniel to let him in.

Daniel reached into his bag and pulled out Henry's manuscript. "Here. You probably want this back. And also . . ." He placed a stack of loose-leaf paper filled with the tiny scrawl of his handwriting on top of Henry's heftier work. "It's just four chapters, but . . . I don't know. You can read it if you want."

"I'd really like that," Henry said. "How about we break for today, and I'll see if I can't have this read before our next class. If you'd like to move forward, I'll have an outline of your new curriculum and your reading assignments ready for you Friday afternoon. Sound good?"

"Sounds good," Daniel echoed. He stood and headed toward the door, turning before he walked out. "Thanks, Mr. Jacobson. See you Friday."

As he watched Daniel walk away, Henry said a silent prayer of gratitude for the progress he had just made. But God wasn't the only person he needed to thank. Henry knew he needed to find Eliza.

* * *

Henry had one more class after his session with Daniel. After his students left, he hurried through the last of his paperwork, anxious to find Eliza to tell her about his progress with Daniel.

On his way out of his classroom, he ran into Natalie. "Hey, have you seen Eliza?" he asked.

"She had group counseling until four. You might check her office. She normally heads there to write her reports after her sessions."

"Thanks, Natalie. If you see her, can you tell her I'm looking for her?"

Eliza wasn't in her office, but Henry found her on the front porch of the old building, sitting on one of the long cedar benches with Flip. They were leaning forward, obviously deep in conversation. For a moment, Henry waffled back and forth between feeling like he shouldn't interrupt because they seemed so lost in conversation and feeling like he *had* to interrupt . . . because they were so lost in conversation. In the end, good manners won, and he turned to walk away, but then Eliza must have glanced up and seen him.

"Henry," she called.

"Sorry," Henry said. "I didn't want to interrupt."

Eliza shook her head. "It's fine. What's up?"

Henry felt awkward and self-conscious talking to Eliza with Flip close by and watching. Flip was good with people, good at communicating—a skill Henry knew he often lacked. As a contrast to Eliza's conversation with Flip, she was sure to find Henry foolish and clumsy. "It's nothing. We can just talk another time."

Eliza got up and walked over to where he stood. "Are you all right?"

"Oh, I'm fine," Henry said. "I just . . . I had a good class session with Daniel today. I just wanted to thank you for your advice."

Eliza's face lit up. "That's wonderful! I'm so glad to hear it. What finally worked?"

"I took a risk," he said. "Reached out in a different way. I think it's going to work."

"I'd love to hear all about it. Can I come find you after dinner?"

"Sure. Hey, have you heard anything about Gina?"

Eliza frowned. "I just talked to my mom this morning. She hasn't seen her or heard from her yet."

"I'm sorry to hear it." He watched as Eliza glanced back at Flip, still sitting on the bench behind her. Following her gaze, Henry noticed the book Flip was holding in his hands. It was the Book of Mormon he'd given her a couple of weeks before. "How's that going?"

"It's good, I guess. He says he read a lot of it while he was gone. He has a lot of questions."

"Wow," Henry said. "I mean, that's really great." He never would have expected it of Flip. He wanted to be genuinely happy that he was expressing interest in learning more about the Church, but after what Cooper had told him about Flip having a thing for Eliza, Henry couldn't help but question Flip's motives.

Still, he could see the excitement in Eliza's eyes. He didn't have it in him to squelch it. "I'll let you get back to him, then." He turned and started down the main stairs of the admin building.

"See you later?" Eliza called.

He nodded his head and waved, then turned the corner to head to his apartment.

Henry considered himself a pretty good missionary. He'd served well in Brazil, broken through a lot of his initial discomfort and pushed through a lot of his own personal boundaries. And yet he'd known Flip a lot longer than Eliza had, and not once had he even considered the possibility of giving him a Book of Mormon.

But, then, Flip had *asked* Eliza for the book. Henry was sure it didn't have anything to do with the fact that she was a beautiful redhead with an engaging smile and incredible eyes.

Right. Nothing at all.

Henry realized what was bothering him wasn't the possibility of Flip's misplaced motives, though that was definitely cause for concern. What bothered him was the idea of Flip and Eliza having a relationship in the first place. He was annoyed to realize how much it made perfect sense. They were similar in personality, had the same energy and passion for life. Flip was everything Henry wasn't.

But Eliza had kissed *him*. In that moment, there had been something real between them, something . . .

Something Henry had promptly told Eliza to forget ever happened.

When he reached his apartment, he swung his door open with a little more force than necessary, and it banged against the wall before falling back into place with an angry thud. The sound still echoed in his ears when he collapsed onto his couch, frustrated and annoyed by his own thoughts.

Of course Eliza would choose Flip. Henry had taken away her ability to choose him.

Chapter 19

ELIZA TRIED TO FOCUS ON her conversation with Flip, but her heart was no longer in it. She had watched Henry leave the porch and head toward his apartment and wished she'd had the courage to follow him. She would love to hear the details of his success with Daniel and was touched that he'd been anxious to share it with her.

But Flip had been waiting for her, and if she was truly honest with herself, she wasn't sure how she was supposed to act around Henry anymore. They had talked about the kiss, and Henry had made it clear that it would be better if they forgot about it, but that didn't mean they could simply go back to being friends. At least, Eliza knew *she* couldn't.

Every time she was around Henry, she felt herself drawn to him more and more. Trying to forget they had ever kissed was impossible when even just seeing him made her think about how much she wished they could kiss *again*. How was that a normal friendship?

Still, if she wanted to hear about Daniel, she'd have to find Henry later, no matter how flustered it made her feel.

"Eliza, are you in there?" Flip leaned forward and tried to make eye contact.

Eliza realized he'd been talking, and she had no idea what he had said. "Sorry, I was just thinking about Henry."

"What's up with Henry? He looked a bit serious." Flip tightened his brows and frowned in lighthearted mockery.

Eliza rolled her eyes and smiled. "Everything is fine. He's just made a breakthrough with one of his students. I'm going to find him later so he can tell me about it."

"I guess sometimes the tough ones require a more concentrated team effort. I'm glad Henry's making progress."

"Yeah, me too."

Flip was quiet for a moment. "I'll be honest, I wasn't sure Henry had what it took to make it at Rockbridge—all collars and ties and buttoned-up politeness. I worried the kids would look at him like nothing more than a stuffed shirt. But I guess he's doing all right. Wonders never cease, do they?"

"You don't give him enough credit, Flip. There's a lot more to Henry than you might think."

"I'm not saying he isn't a nice guy, but it takes a special type to do well in a place like this. Some of these kids—they're brutal, you know? You've got to be the kind of person they can relate to, that they *want* to relate to."

Flip was right. It was crucial to be able to develop relationships that were based on trust and mutual respect with the students at Rockbridge. It was something Flip was good at. All of the students liked him. He was firm, unrelenting when it came to expectation and performance, but he had enough "cool" factor that most kids wanted to follow his example and do as he asked. For Flip, Rockbridge was a perfect fit. But that didn't mean Henry couldn't also be successful.

"Henry is exactly the kind of person the kids need to be around," she countered. "He is steady and honest and generous to a fault. He's . . ." She searched for the right word. "Henry is just good. The kids need to be around that too—to be around goodness."

Flip looked at Eliza quizzically. "You got a thing for Henry, do you?"

She rolled her eyes for the second time in their conversation. "It's not like that. I just think people around here are selling him short. You can almost feel everyone's anticipation, wondering how long it's going to take him to fail. Sure, this job may be a little outside his comfort zone, but he can do it. I know he can."

"Well, you don't have to convince me." Flip held his hands up, palms open in surrender. "I don't write the guy's paycheck."

Eliza took a deep breath and leaned back onto the outside wall of the admin building. "We just spent a long time talking about Henry," she finally said.

"I noticed," Flip said. "He came right up on the porch and completely stole my thunder."

Eliza smiled. "Well, take it back, then, why don't you?" She gestured to the Book of Mormon still sitting on Flip's lap. "Do you have any more questions?"

"I guess I just wonder what happens now. I like what I've read, but what does that mean, really?"

Eliza considered her answer. "I guess that's up to you. The next step would probably be to meet with the missionaries in Rose Creek. They can teach you more and answer your questions."

"Missionaries?" Flip said. "You mean white shirts and name tags and bicycle-riding missionaries?"

Eliza laughed. "The very ones; I promise they're completely harmless."

"What about you? Can you be there too?"

The sudden shift in Flip's tone made Eliza uncomfortable. She looked down, hesitant to make eye contact. "Of course I can. If you want me to be."

Flip reached for her hand. "What if I say I always like it when I get to be where you are?"

No, no, no!

Things could get muddled very quickly if she wasn't careful. She pulled her hand from Flip's grasp and stood.

"Don't make this confusing, Flip. This can't be about me." She turned and leaned across the porch railing directly across from where he sat.

"What, this?" He held up the Book of Mormon. "Of course it's about you, Eliza. I told you I was interested in you. You told me it wouldn't work if I wasn't a Mormon. How am I supposed to separate one issue from the other? True, I wouldn't just become a Mormon because a pretty girl wanted me to, but that doesn't mean I'm not considering the possibility of learning more because of how I feel about you."

"I wish you wouldn't say that. We're friends. Let's just be friends right now, okay? If we were anything else, all of this"—she motioned to the Book of Mormon—"it would just get too complicated."

"Why is it complicated?"

"Because this church isn't just something you do on Sunday. It's everything—your entire life. You have to know that if I were never a part of it, if I married Henry or anybody else, you'd still want to go to church because it's what you believe for you, *just* for you."

"If you married Henry, huh?"

Eliza's cheeks flamed red. "I was just making a point," she said defensively. "He's the only Mormon guy you know that I could use as an example."

Flip let out a slow, genial laugh. "I'm sure you were just making a point." Eliza chided herself for making such a huge blunder. What sort of impression was she trying to give Flip? She chewed on the corner of her lip and kept her gaze down. At this point, she felt like a follow-up comment would only get her into more trouble.

"Look"—Flip stood and leaned on the railing beside her—"I understand what you're saying, but remember I'm a grown man. Yes, I like you, and it was your introduction to the Book of Mormon that urged me to give it a read in the first place. But I'm not a twitterpated teenager that's going to rush into a life-altering decision because I can't resist the green of your eyes. If I were to join your church, it would be for the right reasons. I promise."

Eliza tried to relax. Maybe she wasn't giving him enough credit.

"So," Flip continued. "You'll come with me if I meet your missionaries?"

"Yes, I will. But just . . ."

"Just as friends," Flip finished for her. "I get it, I get it."

* * *

After dinner, Eliza found Henry sitting on the steps of his apartment, reading a book.

"What are you reading?" she asked.

"*Peace Like a River* by Leif Enger." He held up the book so she could see the cover.

She lowered herself to the stair below him. "Is it any good?"

"It's very good, but I'm having a hard time focusing." He motioned to his laptop sitting beside him on the porch. "I was trying to write, but . . . I don't know. I'm three chapters in, and I'm not sure I even like my main character enough to keep going. I'm tempted to just trash the entire thing and start over."

"Would you like a second opinion? I promise I'll be honest and tell you right out if you've written something that deserves the trash bin." She gave him a hopeful smile, even though she knew full well there was no way Henry would ever accept her offer.

"Hmm. Maybe next time."

"You know, you'll have to let someone read your stuff eventually, Henry. Why not now? With a trusted friend?" She hoped he could tell she was teasing him, though she'd read his book in a second if he'd let her.

"Someday I'll let you read it. I'll send you a copy of my manuscript via e-mail and make you promise you won't utter a word about it in person ever again. You can only send me your opinion via instant message. Smiley faces for good or frowns for bad."

"Henry Jacobson, I had no idea you were funny."

He smiled. "Besides, oh, you who thinks I have no courage, I *did* let someone read my book."

"What?" Eliza exclaimed. "Who?"

"Daniel read it. He read it, and he liked it."

Understanding flooded Eliza's mind as she realized what Henry must have done.

"So he *is* a writer! Oh, Henry, I'm so glad you were able to reach him. Tell me all about it."

She sat and listened as Henry outlined his impulsive decision to leave his manuscript for Daniel to read and then the subsequent conversation they'd had because of it. She could tell he was genuinely happy to have made progress and was looking forward to working with Daniel on a personal level. In a way, it seemed like it had been a breakthrough for them both. For Daniel, opening up to Henry was huge, but for Henry to share something he'd never shared with anyone before? That was pretty huge too.

"I'm really happy for you," Eliza said when he'd finished his explanation. "I think you'll be exactly what Daniel needs."

"It felt good," he said. "I could tell he really heard me, that the words actually sank in. It was like he was a different kid. He's always been so closed off in the past, but today he looked me in the eye. We actually . . . talked."

Eliza smiled. "Ah, the impenetrable wall that is a teenager. Sometimes you just have to find the one thing that will make them open up a little. And you have to open up a little too. I'm sure it wasn't easy, what with that iron grip you keep around everything you ever write." She playfully nudged his knee and smiled.

"No, it wasn't easy," he agreed. "But I had a feeling it would be worth it. It wasn't exactly my idea." His words had a certain humility about them, and Eliza immediately understood his meaning.

"God knows Daniel better than anyone, that's for sure. Good on you for listening."

"It took me long enough," Henry said. "You know what finally convinced me to just get over myself and take the risk?" He didn't wait for her to respond. "It was you."

Eliza turned to face him and shook her head. "I just gave you a little push. You're the one who decided what to do."

"No, it wasn't just your advice. You were right when you told me I might need to get out of my comfort zone, but it was . . ." He kept his eyes down and was fidgeting with his book, turning it over, running his fingers up and down the spine. "I tend to like my comfort zone just the way it is, but you, it's like you're comfortable everywhere, talking to everyone. I just decided maybe I needed to be a little more like you."

Eliza thought to reach out to him, to touch his hand or his arm, create some sort of physical connection, but she held herself back. He told her it wasn't what he wanted—*she* wasn't what he wanted. Instead, she held her hands in her lap and leaned her head against the porch rail beside her.

"Thank you," she said simply. She finally looked up. He was looking at her, a deep intensity in his eyes that completely disagreed with the sentiments he'd expressed about their kiss. She returned his gaze, a question in her eyes.

What are you thinking, Henry?

"I, uh, I should . . ." He closed his eyes and she watched his Adam's apple bob in his throat as he swallowed. "I think I'm going to get back to my writing."

Eliza sighed. *Of course you are.*

"Sure." She stood from the steps, feeling completely deflated. "Good night, Henry."

* * *

Eliza covered the short distance to her own apartment and went inside. She slumped onto her sofa and crossed her arms over her chest. She needed to call her mother but wasn't in the mood. For her mom, she had to be happy. She had to keep herself together, never have a bad day.

It was silly, really. Her mother knew Eliza was human. But with all of Gina's struggles, Eliza had somehow adopted the role of the easy one—the independent, reliable one who never gave cause for concern. She didn't want to worry her mom simply because she was in an off mood.

But why am I in an off mood?

There was something under the surface that was keeping her from settling down. It wasn't work. Her counseling sessions were going well, and her work relationships were getting stronger with both the Adlers and her fellow counselors.

She fit at Rockbridge. She had no doubt about that. No, Eliza didn't feel off because work wasn't going well. She felt off because no matter how hard she tried, she couldn't figure out how to keep herself from falling in love with Henry.

Chapter 15

HENRY TURNED ON HIS LIVING room light and set his laptop and book down on the desk. He was too distracted to write, even though he told Eliza that was what he planned to do. He couldn't stop thinking about her eyes. They looked like they held an invitation, a beckoning. And for whatever misguided reason, Henry felt like the invitation was for *him*.

Or maybe he was crazy—imagining things, seeing things, pretending things actually mattered, when, even if he *was* reading Eliza right, things couldn't work out between them anyway.

He pushed his thoughts aside and pulled Daniel's handwritten chapters out of his bag. Much to Henry's surprise, the writing was good enough that he immediately forgot his own struggles.

The story was a bit disjointed and rough in a few spots, but overall, Daniel had a natural storytelling ability. His narrative was compelling, his characters unique. Henry pulled out a sheet of paper to make a few notes.

In an hour's time, he'd worked through all four chapters, notating what he liked and making a few suggestions he hoped would be helpful. In the morning, he would sit down to write out Daniel's curriculum.

One of the things that made Rockbridge so wonderful was that it accommodated so many different learning styles. But this was the first time Henry had thrown aside existing lesson plans and started completely from scratch. It would take time and effort to come up with something he felt would work for Daniel, but his writing was far above grade level. He was the kind of student who would benefit from specialized curriculum. Henry couldn't help but wonder what Daniel's life *before* Rockbridge had been. No two students at Rockbridge ever came to the school with the same story. Many came from families that were well off—easily able to handle the tuition for a dually therapeutic and educational experience. Still other families, desperate for help for their teenager, did the best they could to cover expenses.

Henry knew the Adlers had significant scholarship and funding programs in place so few children ever had to be turned away, but he imagined many families still sacrificed a great deal to make the situation work for their kids. He made a mental note to ask Jeff for a little more of Daniel's background. It might offer some additional insight as he worked to personalize Daniel's writing assignments.

* * *

At the end of Monday's staff meeting a few days later, Henry gathered his notes from the conference room table and headed toward the door. He was a few paces behind Eliza and Flip, and though he wasn't trying to eavesdrop, it wasn't difficult to follow their conversation.

"We'll leave at six thirty, then," he heard Flip say. "I'm glad you're coming with me. See you in a bit."

Henry watched Flip gently touch Eliza's arm before leaving her and heading out the back door of the admin building. Henry stood still for a moment, his emotions morphing from jealousy to disappointment, then quickly to resignation. He had done this. He had pushed Eliza away. It was only natural she would grow closer to Flip.

He shook his head as if to physically dislodge the jumble of feelings from his mind. This was ridiculous. While Eliza stopped to talk to Natalie, he snuck past her and moved to the front door, stepping into the dimming sunshine of the late afternoon.

Outside, Henry saw a man standing at the bottom of the porch's large front steps, facing away from the building. There was something in his body language that Henry thought seemed hesitant. Parents of prospective students didn't often drive out to Rockbridge, but it wouldn't be the first time someone had shown up without an invitation. Henry approached him to see if he needed help.

The man stood as tall as Henry, nearly six feet. His hair was dark, speckled with gray.

"Excuse me," Henry said. "You look lost. Can I help you find someone?"

The man turned, his eyes searching Henry's face before speaking. "Henry?"

It took only a moment for Henry to recognize the eyes and jawline that mirrored his own reflection. His heart raced as his mind traveled back twenty-five years to the prison where he'd last seen his father. And now he was here, standing not two feet in front of him, a look of hopeful expectance on his face.

"It's you." Eliza spoke from where she stood at the top of the steps.

The man looked at Eliza and raised his eyebrows in question. "Have we met?" He looked back at Henry and ran his hand through his hair, leaving it messy and askew.

Henry felt like he was having an out-of-body experience as he watched Eliza descend the remaining stairs and walk toward the man standing before him. He had to fight the urge to flee, to run like a frightened boy into the woods and never look back.

He felt sick.

He needed to breathe, to think, to calm himself down somehow, but his world was spinning, and the only emotion he could latch on to was anger. Turning back to the admin building, he climbed the steps and walked to the end of the porch, where he gripped the railing to steady himself. He took slow, deliberate breaths and closed his eyes, hoping to find some sense of control.

He felt Eliza approach behind him.

"Are you all right?" she softly whispered.

He turned and looked at her. "You don't talk to me." His voice was cold and distant. "I told you . . . I . . . ." He paused and took another deep breath, trying his best not to yell. "You knew I didn't want any contact with him. You knew, and you meddled anyway."

"Henry, I didn't—"

"Don't tell me you didn't," he hissed. "How else would he show up here? How would he know how to find me?" Henry looked up. The man still stood there awkwardly, looking in the opposite direction as if to give Henry a moment of privacy to process his presence.

"I don't know," Eliza said. "But I didn't call him. You have to believe me, Henry. I would never do that to you."

He felt her hand on his arm, but he shrugged it off. He was too far gone to be receptive to what little comfort she could offer.

"Henry, please . . . talk to me."

Henry shook his head. "There's nothing to talk about." He left her standing alone and walked back down the stairs.

William Harrison cleared his throat. "I guess I should have called first." His voice was gruff, weathered, with a faint twinge of a Southern accent.

"I'm sorry for your trouble," Henry said curtly. "But you shouldn't have called. You shouldn't have called, and you shouldn't have come."

Henry turned away and hurried around the corner of the building. He wasn't sure where he was headed, but when he reached the parking lot and saw his car, he knew he wanted to get farther away than just his own apartment. He pulled out his keys, and without so much as a glance back at the administration building, he climbed into his car and drove away from the father he hadn't seen or spoken to in twenty-five years.

Instead of driving toward Rose Creek, Henry went deep into the mountains, crossing into Nantahala National Forest. For nearly thirty minutes, he wove around the curvy mountain roads, trying to shake the image of William Harrison out of his mind. But it was no use.

He imagined Eliza on the porch, still speaking with him in her kind and generous way. The thought pulsed through him like fire, angering him to the point that he barely slowed enough to make it safely around an approaching curve.

At the next pull-off, an overlook that provided an expansive view of the mountains and the tiny dot of Rose Creek nestled neatly into the valley, he stopped the car and climbed out. It was cooler here because he'd risen several hundred feet in elevation.

He strode to the rock wall that rimmed the small parking area and sat down, looking out into the vast expanse of the mountains. They were so blue in the fading light of early evening, he almost couldn't tell where mountains stopped and sky started. The beauty of it all calmed him little by little until finally he was able to rationally consider why he was so angry in the first place.

For a moment, he wondered if perhaps Harrison had made contact with someone in his family, discovering his whereabouts from them. But he quickly dismissed the idea as impossible. No one in his family would have given out Henry's personal information without asking him how he felt about the matter.

Eliza's involvement, on the other hand, made perfect sense. Rockbridge was a small dot on a large map. It would never occur to anyone to look for it, and it was nearly impossible to stumble upon it by chance. She had insisted she wasn't involved, that she would never do that to him, but what other explanation was there?

If it was Eliza, she had crossed a line—gone far too deep into his personal life—and for what? Did she expect him to embrace the man like he was the long-lost father he'd always hoped to have? Henry wasn't like her.

It wasn't easy for him to handle his emotions even with people he'd known and lived with his entire life. To throw him in the ring with this man—the man who had signed away his right to be a father—and expect him to know what to say? It wasn't fair. It was cruel, even, for Eliza to do such a thing when she knew full well how strongly Henry felt about not having any involvement. He'd made himself perfectly clear.

Why hadn't she listened?

For the first time in weeks, his bitter anger still seething just under the surface, Henry finally felt justified in having pushed Eliza away.

Chapter 16

ELIZA STOOD JUST INSIDE THE door of the admin building and watched William Harrison; he'd been sitting on one of the porch's split-log benches since Henry had driven away forty-five minutes earlier. He was likely waiting, hoping Henry might return once he calmed down, but Eliza was afraid he was setting himself up for disappointment. Henry wouldn't come back until he was sure William Harrison was gone.

The man scratched his chin and glanced at his watch for the second time since Eliza had started watching him. She was trying to stay away—to keep as much distance as possible so Henry wouldn't accuse her of meddling, but William Harrison looked so sad it felt wrong to ignore him any longer.

Putting on a brave face, she pushed open the door and walked to where Henry's father still sat.

"Do you mind if I sit with you?"

"I don't mind." He shifted over to make room for her on the bench.

"My name is Eliza. I'm a friend of Henry's."

"I'm William Harrison, but I guess you already know that." He extended his hand. "People just call me Bill."

"Are you waiting for him to come back?"

"I don't know. I just came all this way. I guess I'm hoping if he calms down a little, maybe he'll want to see me."

"I'm sure it was quite a shock to see you standing there."

"I didn't expect him to recognize me. I saw his picture on the website, so I knew it was him, but I didn't think he'd know me. I thought I might have the opportunity to introduce myself, sort of explain who I am."

"You might have underestimated the family resemblance," Eliza said. "It's pretty amazing."

Bill kept his eyes down. "He looks exactly like I thought he would, like I always pictured him."

"He's a good man, Bill. One of the best I know." There was so much more Eliza wanted to say. She wanted to tell Bill about AJ, about Henry's teaching and writing. She wanted to tell him about Henry's goodness and compassion for people, for his steadying presence. But she couldn't do it; it wasn't her information to share.

"How did you know who I was?" Bill asked. "When you saw me, it seemed like you knew me."

Eliza almost felt ashamed to tell him how she knew. That was foolish though. He knew just as well as she did that he'd spent time in prison. What good did it do to pretend otherwise? "I saw your picture on the Department of Corrections website. Henry has seen it too. That might explain how he recognized you so quickly."

"So he *was* looking for me," Bill said.

Eliza shook her head. This wasn't a situation that sugarcoating would benefit. "No, Bill," she said gently. "Henry told me he had been adopted as a young child and that his only memory of you was when he came to visit you in prison. It was only curiosity that led him to look, but I don't believe he had any intention of seeking you out."

"I see." He leaned back against the wall of the building and shook his head. "Thing is, someone called. I answered the phone, but there wasn't anyone there. The caller ID said this place." He motioned to the building behind him. He sat up straight and looked at Eliza, a sudden fire in his eyes. "You know, I think about him all the time. I've always wondered if he would ever want to know me. I guess I hoped when I saw a number and a place I didn't recognize that maybe it would have something to do with him. I went down to the library, had 'em look up the name of the school on the Internet, and there he was." His voice trailed off as he slumped back into the wall once more. "I'm sorry. I didn't mean to say so much."

It must have been Henry who called, Eliza reasoned—called and then hung up. It surprised her to think he would do such a thing, but she hadn't made the call, and there was no one else who would have known to do so.

Bill glanced at his watch one last time. "Well, I guess I've waited long enough. I hope I didn't cause any trouble between you and Henry."

"I'm sure it will be all right," she assured him, though she was hardly convinced herself. "Are you sure you don't want to stay a little longer?"

Bill just shook his head. "It's mighty nice of you to suggest it, but if Henry has any of my blood in him, a couple hours isn't going to make a difference. I told myself I'd give him an hour, and then I'd head on down the road."

"But you came all this way. It seems such a shame to not even have a real conversation with him."

"'You shouldn't have called, and you shouldn't have come'? I believe that's about as real as it gets," Bill said. "It was nice to meet you, Eliza."

Eliza walked with him down the stairs and across the lawn to the visitor parking lot. Bill shook her hand one more time, said good-bye, and climbed into an old model truck that sputtered to life when he cranked the ignition. He revved the engine and slowly pulled onto the main road. Eliza watched him until his truck disappeared behind a curve. She shook her head sadly. How could it be right for things to end this way?

She couldn't erase Henry's past. She couldn't undo the feelings of hurt and anger that hung between Henry and Bill, but that didn't mean it seemed fair that after driving all this way, Bill would leave again with nothing more than a harsh couple of sentences thrown in his direction.

Even worse than the disappointment she felt over Henry's disastrous family reunion was the knowledge that he thought her responsible. How could he even think her capable of such willful deceit?

Tears fell freely now that Bill was gone, and Eliza felt close to crumbling. She hurried to her apartment then, not wanting to cause a scene any bigger than what had already transpired.

Henry would have to listen. He would have to let her explain. He simply hadn't made the connection between his own phone call and his father's arrival at Rockbridge. Eliza admitted she was pretty impressed with Bill's sleuthing skills. Henry would understand when she explained what had *really* happened. He would realize this wasn't her fault.

Except, maybe it *was* her fault. She was the one who had looked for Henry's father online in the first place. She was the one who had told Henry about the tattoo, who had suggested that maybe he ought to pursue a relationship with the man. She was the one who had meddled, who had projected her own happy ending with her mom into Henry's life, even though, clearly, it wasn't the ending he desired.

Guilt washed over Eliza, joining the anger and hurt already coursing through her. Inside her apartment, she went into the bathroom and splashed several handfuls of cold water onto her face. She washed off what little makeup was left and dried her face with a towel.

She had to get a hold of herself. She glanced at her watch and realized she and Flip were supposed to meet in just a matter of minutes to leave for

Rose Creek. He was meeting with the missionaries for the first time and had asked her to come along.

Wearily, she reapplied her makeup, taking extra care to cover the dark circles and splotchy red now surrounding her eyes. It would take all her energy not to think about Henry while they were gone. She could only hope that when she returned to Rockbridge, Henry would be home and willing to hear her out.

* * *

Fifteen minutes later, Eliza met Flip in the parking lot in front of the staff apartments. She glanced over at the empty spot where Henry usually parked.

Where are you, Henry?

"You all right, Eliza?" Flip asked.

She forced a smile. "I'm fine."

"I heard there was a bit of an uproar after staff meeting," Flip said casually. "Someone showed up to see Henry? Am I right in assuming it wasn't someone Henry wanted to see? Natalie said she saw him peel out of here like he was running from a tornado."

Eliza kept her eyes down, not wanting to reveal the depth of her feelings regarding the matter. "I don't want to talk about Henry's personal life, Flip. Are you ready to go?"

"Fair enough," Flip said. "I'm ready when you are."

They drove down the mountain in relative silence. At Andrew and Kate's insistence, they were meeting with the missionaries at the Porterfields' old farmhouse. Eliza had hesitated only because Kate's baby was due to arrive any day. She hadn't wanted to put more stress on the couple as they prepared for the birth, but Kate had assured her the distraction would be welcome.

Eliza knew she needed to do something to lighten the mood before they arrived at the Porterfields'. Flip had nothing to do with the drama she and Henry had experienced earlier; she ought to be able to put it from her mind for his sake. His meeting with the missionaries was a big deal, and she needed to be present, not just physically but mentally and emotionally as well. She took a deep breath and willed her focus onto Flip. "Are you nervous?"

Flip smiled. "Who, me? I don't know. You said the missionaries were pretty harmless. I expect I'll come out all right."

"I hope so," Eliza said. "It's just up here on the left." She pointed to the long gravel drive up ahead. "You'll like the Porterfields too. They're a great couple. Kate just joined the Church a few years ago, after she met Andrew."

"Was Andrew already a Mormon, then? I wonder if he had anything to do with her conversion." Flip gave Eliza a knowing look.

"You should ask her," Eliza said pointedly. "I'm sure it's not the first time she's heard it. I don't think her family was too happy about her baptism. She's probably had to defend her choice many times before."

Flip stopped the car and turned off the engine. "She doesn't have to defend anything to me. I'm sure she made the decision for the right reasons. I'm just saying, I expect the boyfriend didn't make it any harder."

Eliza rolled her eyes. She believed Flip when he said he'd never be so foolish as to join the Church just for her. But it was definitely implied that Flip thought his joining the Church would reignite the possibility of the two of them taking their friendship to a more serious level. Two weeks ago, Eliza might have considered it. But now? She forced the thought of Henry out of her head. If she let Henry in now, the rest of her evening was done for.

"Let's go inside," she said to Flip. "That's the missionaries' car. They're already waiting for us."

* * *

The missionaries did a wonderful job in their meeting with Flip. Flip's questions were thoughtful and revealed quite an extensive knowledge of world religious history and, much to his credit, an open willingness to consider the reality and truthfulness of the message the missionaries shared. Eliza scolded herself for doubting his intentions. It had been shallow of her to assume she was at the center of his decision.

As the discussion continued, Eliza went to the kitchen to find the Porterfields. Kate and Andrew had welcomed Eliza and Flip at the door and had invited them into the living room, but after that, they had made themselves scarce. Eliza was surprised. She thought the two of them would have wanted to join them, so when she heard noises in the kitchen, she thought she'd check to make sure everything was all right. She didn't want to overstay their welcome.

When she rounded the corner into the kitchen, she found Kate standing tensely at the counter, her hands gripping the edge of the worn tile countertop. Andrew sat at the table with his wristwatch lying flat on the place mat in front of him.

"Here we go," Kate said. She leaned forward and took slow, deep breaths, her eyes closed and her face tense. Eliza stood transfixed as she watched the couple. Andrew looked at his watch, then picked it up and moved to his wife's side.

"Four minutes apart." Andrew placed his hand gently on his wife's back. "Eliza," he said, acknowledging her presence in the kitchen doorway, "I think it might be time to wrap things up with the missionaries. Kate and I should probably head over to the hospital." Andrew's words were calm, but there was a nervous tremor in his voice that made Eliza want to smile.

"Oh, don't make them go, Andrew," Kate said, having breathed her way through another contraction. "Let them finish. They can just lock the door on their way out." She turned to Eliza. "I'm so sorry we didn't join you tonight. I wasn't feeling well all afternoon, but I really didn't think it was labor. Guess the baby fooled me, huh?"

Eliza laughed. "Don't apologize. I thought you were ridiculous for wanting us to come over tonight in the first place! Don't worry about us. You should go."

Eliza watched as the couple looked at each other, anxious smiles of anticipation on their faces. This was their first baby, and the excitement in the air was palpable. She followed them out of the kitchen and into the hall, where Andrew had already placed their bags, packed and ready for the hospital.

"Andrew," Kate said. "Can you go tell the elders we're leaving? You should say good-bye."

"Kate, I'm sure they're fine. We're having a baby. We can just leave—"

"Eliza's going to walk me to the car. Just say good-bye. I don't want to be rude."

Andrew gave his wife an exasperated look. "Fine, but you go straight to the car."

"Here," Eliza said, reaching for their bags. "I'll take these and make sure she gets there."

"'Go straight to the car'? Does he think I was planning a detour through the garden? You'd think it was him going into labor."

Eliza laughed. "I'm guessing you aren't the first wife to make that observation."

The women walked into the cool night air, pausing on the steps for Kate to breathe through another contraction before making it the rest of the way to the Porterfields' car.

"Distract me, Eliza," Kate said. "Tell me about your sister. Have you heard from her yet?"

Eliza had confided in Kate after Gina's disappearance, but there was no news to share. Gina still hadn't been in touch with anyone. "I wish I had something to tell you. I still haven't heard from her."

Kate's eyes were sympathetic. "Ugghh—I'm sorry, Eliza. I wish she'd just call you. Will you tell me when you hear from her?"

Eliza agreed to, amazed that her friend, as preoccupied as she was, had two spare thoughts for her missing sister.

"Talk to me about something else," Kate said. "What about you and Flip?"

Eliza shrugged her shoulders. "I don't know. We had dinner together once, but I was pretty clear I wasn't interested in dating someone who didn't share my faith."

Kate looked skeptical. "Is that why he's here?"

"I don't think so," Eliza said. "I told him he would be an idiot to consider something this serious if it wasn't for the right reasons. I *think* his interest is sincere. He's read a good bit of the Book of Mormon, and his questions are pretty detailed. But . . . I don't know. I'm not sure it even matters, really. I mean, he's a good guy. I like him, but I don't think we could have a relationship. I could have, at one point, but now . . ." Eliza trailed off.

Kate raised her eyebrows in question. "What changed? Is there someone else who's piqued your interest?"

Eliza looked up and met Kate's gaze. "No . . . I mean, yes . . . I don't know. I don't think it's going to work out."

Kate smiled. "Eliza, I see the way Henry looks at you. Knowing Henry, he might not realize he likes you, but trust me, he likes you."

Andrew came up behind the women, a look of shock and disdain on his face. "What are we doing?" he asked. "We're having a baby! Why are we still standing around talking?"

Kate laughed. "See? I just told Eliza you're acting like it's you having the . . . *ohhhhh!*" She leaned against the car.

"In the car," Andrew ordered. Kate held up a finger, breathing through the end of her contraction.

"Okay," she finally said. "Let's go." She smiled at Eliza, then willingly took Andrew's hand as he helped her into the passenger seat.

"Good luck!" Eliza called. "Send me a text when baby comes."

Flip and the elders had left the house with Andrew and now stood at the bottom of the porch steps having what Eliza quickly realized was a rather charged discussion on whether skiing was better in Colorado or Utah.

Elder Barker, a Utah native and avid skier, was giving it his best shot, but Flip argued pretty strongly for the virtues of Breckenridge as the best place to ski. They looked to Eliza and the other missionary, Elder Gerratt, to cast deciding votes.

A Southern California native, Elder Gerratt had little to offer. "You want to talk surfing, I'll weigh in with an opinion, but the ski slopes are all you." He slapped his companion good-naturedly on the back.

"Eliza?" Flip asked. "Care to weigh in?"

Eliza shook her head. "I've never been farther west than Kansas. You two are going to have to duke this one out on your own. Some other time though," she added. "I'm exhausted and need Flip to drive me home."

And . . . I need to find Henry.

"Thanks for coming with me," Flip said as they drove back to Rockbridge. "It was nice to have you there."

"I wish you could have gotten to know the Porterfields a little better," Eliza said. "They're wonderful."

"A bit busy tonight though, aren't they? That was exciting."

"Yeah." Eliza could tell Flip was trying to keep the conversation going, but her heart wasn't in it. She was consumed with worry for Henry— worry that he wouldn't listen when she tried to explain, worry that her snooping had completely undone their friendship.

* * *

Eliza slipped inside her apartment only long enough to drop her purse on the couch and wait for Flip to make it inside his own apartment. She had every intention of going to see Henry. It was just past nine thirty, and Eliza hardly cared what others thought, but she didn't feel like explaining to Flip why she was going to see Henry so late.

Moments later, she stood outside Henry's door and knocked softly. There weren't any lights on inside. Surely he hadn't gone to sleep already. She knocked again. After a few moments of waiting, she was about to turn away when the sound of shuffling inside kept her standing there just a bit longer. Henry opened the door and turned on the porch light. He looked at her, his face passive through the rickety screen door that graced every housing unit on campus.

"Hi," Eliza said. When he didn't respond, her words rushed out fast and steady until she'd said all she had come to say. "Henry, I didn't call him. I didn't contact him in any way. I would never do that to you. I would never go behind your back or involve myself in your personal affairs so obtrusively. Please believe me. Save the one search that I told you about, I never looked him up again. It was his caller ID," she continued. "He saw the school's name on his caller ID and looked it up on the Internet. When he saw you listed as a teacher on the school's website, he hoped you had been trying to get a hold of him. I don't know who called him, but I promise you, it wasn't me." She looked at Henry expectantly, not knowing what he might say but hoping, nonetheless, that he would say *something*.

"I called him." His voice rose with a quiet intensity as he spoke. "I called him because I was still living under the delusion that maybe I should try to be more like you." He stifled an angry laugh. "Well, live and learn, I guess. And that's exactly what I did today. I learned that your way of living is reckless and stupid and only leads to people getting hurt. You can't open doors just to see what's behind them or talk to people because you think they *might* be nice. You can't get in the car and drive five hours to pick up a drunk without the slightest clue as to what you're going to do with her when you get there."

"Now you're just being mean," Eliza said softly. She bit her bottom lip, hoping the pain might stop the tears she felt building beneath her eyes. She shook her head. "I'm sorry if I've caused you any pain, Henry. It was never my intention."

She turned and hurried down the porch steps. Before she reached her own apartment, she heard Henry's door click closed. When she looked back, she saw the light on his porch go dark.

Chapter 17

FOR HENRY, THE REST OF the week seemed interminable. When the weekend finally arrived, he was anxious to get away from Rockbridge and clear his head. Saturday afternoon, he took AJ hiking. They had a good time, but it didn't provide the head clearing Henry sought. Every time he looked at AJ, all he could see were those eyes—William Harrison's eyes looking out from his son's face.

It made him colder, more distant than he wanted to be, certainly more than AJ needed him to be. This only heightened his frustration. He'd had a breakthrough with Daniel by taking a risk and reaching out to him in a more personal way. And yet he felt incapable of making that same connection with his own son. He hoped church would prove a distraction, but, then, church was more complicated because he'd have to work on avoiding Eliza. He'd managed at Rockbridge pretty well, but the branch building was small. It would be hard not to pass her in the hallway at least once or twice.

On Sunday morning, Henry drove slowly down the mountain into Rose Creek. Heavy sheets of rain were falling from an iron-gray sky, forcing Henry to drop his speed to half the normal limit. The rain was making his trip near treacherous.

After rounding a sharp curve, Henry slammed on his breaks and swerved in order to avoid hitting a navy-blue SUV parked on the side of the road. It was obvious the driver had pulled over as far as possible—flush up against a steep bank that rose into a thick forest of trees—but the car still butted heavily into the road. With such poor visibility, it was sure to get hit. As Henry passed the car, he thought it looked familiar. A small decal in the back window confirmed his suspicion. The car belonged to Eliza.

Henry felt a knot of dread growing in his stomach. Where was Eliza, and why would she leave her car in such a dangerous location? He picked up his cell phone and confirmed what he already knew. He was still a few miles away from the nearest cell signal. If he didn't have cell reception, she didn't either.

If she'd run out of gas or had car trouble—the most likely scenarios—she wouldn't have been able to call for help. Henry shook his head. If he knew anything about Eliza at all, he knew she wasn't the kind of person who would simply sit still and wait for someone to find her. She would have left her car and tried to walk for help. But in this weather? The rain was heavy enough that Henry couldn't see more than ten or twenty yards in front of his car. The only thing easier than hitting Eliza's car by accident would be hitting *her*.

Please, God, just help me find her.

Henry pulled around the SUV and slowly crept forward, glancing off to either side of the road as frequently as he could safely manage in search of Eliza. A half mile later, he breathed out a sigh of relief as he saw her walking on the side of the road. He pulled up beside her and rolled down his window.

"Eliza, what happened?" He motioned for her to get in the car. "Come around and get in." He had to yell for her to hear him over the rain, but she must have heard or at least understood how ridiculous it would be for her to keep standing in the rain. She crossed in front of Henry's car and climbed into the passenger seat.

"Oh, I'm so wet, Henry! Your car will be ruined."

"Don't worry about the car. What happened?" he asked again. "Here, put this on." He reached into the backseat and picked up his suit coat. "You'll freeze just sitting there like that."

"No, Henry, not your nice suit coat. I'll be fine."

"I insist," Henry said. "Please, take it." She begrudgingly took his coat and wrapped it around her shoulders.

"Thank you." She sniffed and wiped her face with her hands. She was soaked head to toe. "I ran out of gas. Did you see my car? With no cell reception, I figured I had little choice but to try to walk into town. You never see anyone on these roads this early on a Sunday. I figured I'd wait all day if I just sat still. But then the rain started, and I'm wearing heels and—" She stopped and looked at Henry. "I'm so glad you stopped."

"Of course," Henry said.

"I feel so foolish. I knew it was going to be close, but I really thought I had enough gas to make it into town."

"It happens to the best of us," Henry assured her. He drove in silence for a few minutes, allowing the tension of their last conversation to creep into the car.

The fact that Eliza hadn't been the one to contact William Harrison directly did little to alter Henry's feelings. In his anger, he'd been foolish to look past the simplicity of caller ID and a little bit of online research—a very logical way for William Harrison to have discovered his whereabouts. But it was still Eliza's fault. The entire situation never would have come about had she not felt the need to stick her nose into his personal business.

Of course he wouldn't leave her stranded in the rain on the side of the road—stopping to help was the decent thing to do—but that didn't mean he had to go out of his way to be her friend. She'd shaken up his life quite enough. Henry slowed the car and turned into the driveway of Allison's childhood home.

"Are we not going to a gas station?" Eliza asked. "I thought you'd want to be rid of me before you picked up AJ."

"You're not going to a gas station," Henry said. "You can't go to church as soaked as you are. I thought you could stay here, dry off, and warm up, and I'll go take care of your car. I'll take AJ's grandfather along; he can drive it back to the house for you."

"Why does it seem like every time I need to be rescued, you're the one who shows up?"

"It's nothing. It's what anyone would do."

"It is not what anyone would do. You've been so kind to me. With all you did to help Gina, and now you're helping again this morning. I . . ." She thought a moment, then said, "I really am sorry for what happened, Henry. I'm so sorry that my actions have caused you pain in any way."

It wasn't something Henry wanted to talk about again. He'd replayed the moments of that afternoon over and over in his mind, and no matter how hard he tried, he couldn't remove Eliza from the middle of his frustration. He realized she hadn't meant to hurt him, but an apology couldn't change what had happened.

"Let's get you inside. I'm sure Allison has something you can borrow while your clothes dry."

They got out of the car and hurried up the concrete walkway and onto the porch.

"I hate that you're going to miss church as well," Eliza said as they waited for someone to answer the door. "You should at least be able to make it in time for Sunday School."

Henry glanced at his watch and only nodded.

Allison answered the door. Henry had to give her credit. If she felt surprise over finding him standing on the porch with a dripping wet redhead, she did a fine job of concealing it.

Henry hurried to explain, and Allison was gracious, inviting Eliza in and readily agreeing to Henry's plan.

When he and Jim left to get gas for Eliza's car, he had no doubt she would be well cared for. He expected that Lila, true to her grandmotherly nature, was already doting on Eliza, fixing her something warm to drink, making sure she was happy and comfortable.

There was an element of awkwardness to the idea of Eliza spending time with his ex-wife and ex-mother-in-law, but with her soaking wet and cold, it seemed the most reasonable option. Once her car was gassed up and ready to go, she could be on her way, and Henry could spend the rest of the day with AJ, as planned.

He still didn't know what he would do with the boy once church was over. The rain made their Sunday afternoons together difficult. He didn't mind just staying at Jim and Lila's house and visiting with him there, but it was easier for AJ to get distracted when he was home. When Henry had tried it in the past, he'd often found himself visiting with Jim and Lila while AJ had played video games or read in his room.

Fortunately, Allison at least made herself scarce whenever Henry had plans to hang around. Their relationship was civil, friendly even, but it had only just begun to not be a painful experience for Henry to be around her.

By the time he and Jim made it to a gas station and back to Eliza's car, the rain had stopped. Henry stood, his hands shoved deep into his pockets, as Jim slowly poured gas into the SUV's tank.

"She seems like a nice girl," Jim said.

Henry looked up. "Who, Eliza?"

"No, the other redhead you brought to the house this morning. Do you like her?"

Henry took the empty gas can from Jim. "No. I mean, I don't know. I'm sorry, Jim. This just feels like a weird question for me to be getting from you."

Henry watched as Jim turned and looked him right in the eye. "Son, I'm goin' to tell you something man to man, all right? I expect Allison will tell you herself before too long, but I don't want you to be blindsided." He shifted his weight and ran his fingers through his sparse gray hair. "Robert and Allison are getting married. He just asked her last night, and she said yes."

Henry's head started to spin. *Married? So soon?* It was painful to think that Allison was moving on to the point of marrying someone else when his wounds still felt so raw, but even worse were the implications of what her marriage would mean for AJ.

AJ living in another house.

AJ having another family.

AJ having another dad.

It was too much for him to process. For the second time in not even a week, Henry felt the need to turn his back on his life and flee. This time though, he couldn't run away. AJ was back at the house, waiting for him. He had to be a father, had to face the reality of his situation and fight for a better relationship with his son.

But how?

Chapter 18

ELIZA HEARD THE HUM OF Henry's sedan as it pulled into the driveway, followed by the throatier roar of her own SUV. She glanced out AJ's bedroom window and saw Henry and AJ's grandfather, Jim, making their way into the house.

"Look," AJ said, pulling her attention back to his collection of Legos. "This is the other one I wanted to show you. It has retractable wings, and if you pull on this lever right here, the wings will move up and down like it's really flying."

Eliza smiled. She was grateful for the attention and care she'd received from Lila, even the kindness Allison had offered, but it was all she could do to suppress a massive sigh of relief when AJ had asked her if she wanted to see his Lego collection. She had noticed the direction the conversation was heading with the two women and could tell she was mere moments away from a gentle yet pointed "define the relationship" kind of question regarding her friendship with Henry.

It wasn't that she was afraid of telling people she and Henry were just friends. They *were* just friends. But she was terrible at hiding her emotions. Her fear was that anyone who asked would be able to tell she wished they were *more* than friends. *But that will never happen now*, she thought sadly to herself.

"It's really amazing that you've built all of these. Does your dad like Legos too?"

AJ hesitated. "I don't know. We don't really talk about it."

"Why not?"

AJ turned his back and started fiddling with the wings of his ship. "He's busy, I think. I don't know if he really wants to be my dad anymore."

Eliza closed her eyes and placed her hand over her heart as if to stop the swift swell of pain she felt as she replayed AJ's words in her mind. Surely he didn't think that was how Henry felt.

"AJ, why would you ever think that? Your dad is my friend, and I know how much he cares about you. I'm pretty sure being your dad is his most favorite thing."

"I guess so," AJ said. "But now I'm going to live with Robert all the time, and he'll be my new dad. Why would *my* dad let that happen?"

So that was it. Eliza pulled out the chair to AJ's desk and sat down so she could look him right in the eyes. "AJ." She touched him gently on the shoulder. "Look at me." He slowly turned. "It's good that your mom and Robert have each other because Robert is just one more person who can love you and take care of you. But he won't ever replace your dad. Your dad would never, in a million, trillion years, give you up."

AJ stared at his hands, still gripping his Legos tightly. "Did he tell you that?" He looked up, his eyes hopeful.

Eliza nodded her head yes. "He sure did."

"Do you think he would like to see my ship?"

"Of course!" Eliza said. "In fact, I think he just got back. Why don't you go try to find him?" She watched as AJ darted out his bedroom door in search of his father. As she stood and pushed the desk chair back in place, she couldn't decide if her heart hurt more for AJ or more for Henry. As she left the room, a hand reached out and gripped her forearm.

She looked up. "Henry! You startled . . ." Her words trailed off when she saw his face. His eyes were red, his cheeks damp with tears. Clearly, he'd been standing outside AJ's door just long enough to overhear their conversation. In that moment, she knew her heart was definitely hurting more for Henry.

"I . . . uh . . ." he said gruffly. He shook his head and looked down, then raised his eyes back up to meet Eliza's. "Thank you."

Before she could respond, he turned and walked down the hallway, most certainly in search of his son.

* * *

Over the next couple of weeks, Eliza hardly saw Henry at all. Everyone at Rockbridge was busy. Though school remained in session year round, there was always a rush of new students in line with the traditional school calendar. Late August was generally the school's busiest time.

As Eliza got to know her new students and tailored her counseling sessions to meet their needs, she found herself wondering if she would ever get to have a real conversation with Henry at all. They exchanged pleasantries, talked about students when it was necessary, but their interactions were never personal. Henry was keeping his distance, avoiding the cafeteria and other common areas of Rockbridge. Even at staff meeting, he was in and out so fast there wasn't time to even attempt a conversation.

Eliza realized he had to be avoiding her on purpose. She had hoped, after the moment she'd shared with AJ, that Henry might be willing to let her back in, but he was apparently staunch in his determination to keep her out of his life as much as possible.

If she tried, she could work herself up, feeding the burn of Henry's words the last time they'd spoken until it flamed into anger. She could convince herself she was fine, better off even, *without* him in her life. But her resolve never lasted. All too frequently, her mind would drift. She'd find herself thinking about the sound of Henry's laugh or the way his face changed when he smiled. She wondered how things were going with Daniel and if Henry had managed to spend any more time with AJ.

Eliza was not the kind of girl to lose herself pining away for a man who clearly wasn't interested in a relationship with her. But with Henry, everything felt different. How long would it take to convince her heart it needed to move on?

She needed to focus on something else, even *someone* else.

"Eliza—just the woman I wanted to see."

Eliza turned and saw Flip walking purposefully in her direction. She was sitting on the side porch of the admin building, supposedly reviewing her notes from that week's counseling sessions and enjoying the cooling temperatures of the approaching evening. She smiled, wondering if the answer to her dilemma was right there in front of her. Flip had been on excursion the past ten days. The group must have just returned.

"I'd give you a welcome-back hug, but I'm guessing you stink."

Flip stopped right in front of her. "I don't know." He raised his arms dramatically to take a whiff under his armpits. "It's not that bad. Wait . . . yes, sorry. It is that bad."

"Go shower, Flip! What's so important it couldn't wait for a bath?"

"I suppose it could have waited. But you can't blame me for wanting to see you, now can you?"

"Of course not," Eliza said. "I love having friends who smell. What woman isn't charmed by the enticing aromatic blend of body odor, smoke, and dirt?"

Flip sat beside her on the bench of the picnic table. "I always knew you were my kind of girl." He nudged her gently with his elbow.

Eliza blushed. She'd been working hard to keep things with Flip on a strictly friend basis. He'd had several more meetings with the missionaries, even attended church with her once. But she still didn't want to complicate things with romance.

Of course, considering her feelings for Henry, it was also important to Eliza that she not lead Flip on. Now she wondered if it wasn't better to push her hesitations aside. Flip *did* seem serious about the Church. And he was clearly far more interested in her than Henry had ever been.

"So what's up?" she asked.

"Well, I was hoping I could catch a ride to church with you tomorrow. And then after, I carved a wee something for the Porterfields' new babe. I thought we might take it over and drop it off." He handed Eliza a small wooden teddy bear, about six inches tall. The detail was exquisite, the wood smooth and polished in Eliza's hand.

"Flip, you made this? It's beautiful!"

"Oh, it's nothing. It just helps pass the time when you're sitting around a campfire."

"Kate and Andrew will love it. It was nice of you to think of them."

"So, what do you say? Are we on for Sunday?"

"I think that sounds perfect. I've got something for the baby too, so that works out well. Once we're in town tomorrow, I'll send Kate a text to make sure we can stop by."

"It's a date." Flip looked at Eliza, a conspiratorial twinkle in his eye.

"It's not a date," she said, rolling her eyes. "It's church."

"Yes, yes, I know. It's only church." He was still smiling. "I'll see you in the morning." He stood and headed toward the staff apartments.

"You better shower before then," Eliza shouted after him. "You can't ride with me if you still stink!"

Flip raised his hand in acknowledgment without turning around.

Eliza sighed.

She *did* like Flip. He was thoughtful, kind, funny. She always had fun when they were together. What was holding her back? Her mind drifted to the moment in her aunt's kitchen when she'd kissed Henry.

Yeah. That's enough to hold me back.

Chapter 19

HENRY STOOD AT THE END of the hallway and watched as Eliza and Flip entered the Relief Society room for Sunday School. He'd spoken with the missionaries earlier that morning, and they had confirmed that Flip was talking seriously about picking a baptism date. Henry had to work to hide his surprise.

If Flip was sincerely interested in the gospel, that was great. If not? Henry had seen it too many times. Conversion for the wrong reason only resulted in failed expectations and disappointment.

He couldn't help but think of Allison. He'd been so sure she wasn't joining the Church just for him. But in retrospect, he wondered if that wasn't precisely what she had done. Maybe not just for him but because it was what everyone had expected her to do. It seemed a natural next step in their courtship. Only without the roots of her own testimony to hold on to, when things got tough and she let go of him, she let go of her faith as well. Henry wouldn't wish the same experience on anyone—especially Eliza.

Just before priesthood, Henry walked to where Flip was sitting a few pews ahead of him and sat down.

Flip looked up. "Hello, Henry," he said. "How are you?"

"I don't want to see Eliza get hurt."

Flip seemed taken aback. "I can't imagine anyone wanting Eliza to get hurt. What's your point?"

Henry leaned forward, resting his elbows on his knees. "I guess what I'm trying to say is I think it's great that you're here, that you're thinking about being baptized, but I've experienced firsthand how it can end when baptism doesn't happen for the right reasons. This is too big of a decision for you to be doing it for anyone other than yourself."

"You Mormons sure aren't very encouraging," Flip said.

"Please don't misunderstand my meaning, Flip. I really think it's wonderful that you're learning and that you want to be baptized. I guess I just want to make sure you understand. This is a big deal. You can't do this for Eliza. It will never work in the end."

"Henry, my friend, would you believe you're not the first person to have this conversation with me? Even Eliza herself has threatened to stop speaking to me altogether if I even hint that I'm doing this for anyone other than myself. I understand. Trust me."

Henry could see the sincerity in Flip's eyes. "In that case," he said, extending his hand, "welcome to the branch. Really, Flip. It's a good thing you're doing."

"Now, that's more like it." A broad smile stretched across Flip's face. He took Henry's hand and gave him a friendly clap on the back. "I will be honest with you though . . . if you don't mind."

"Of course not."

"I'd be lying if I didn't tell you I'd like for things to work out for Eliza and me. I'm certainly not doing this for her, but if she happened to be a part of a package deal, I wouldn't be disappointed."

Henry took a deep breath and leaned back in his chair. "I'm not sure I understand why you're telling me this."

"Out of respect, of course. I'm pretty sure Eliza's felt something for you. If there's been anything between you in the past, I thought I better let you know where I stand."

Henry was silent for a moment. He thought about the kiss he'd shared with Eliza and the strength of the emotion he'd felt when he'd heard her talking with AJ about Allison's impending marriage.

But then he thought of the expression on her face as she'd stood on the other side of his screen door listening to his tirade about how awful a person she was, how terrible he found her approach on life. He'd hurt her. He knew that and regretted it deeply.

Henry had never spoken such hateful words. It was completely out of character, and he'd spent hours reflecting on where he'd found the venom he'd thrown at her that night. It had been a rough day, yes, and he felt justified in the anger he'd experienced, but he'd had no right to be so unkind. He knew he needed to tell her that. He just didn't know how.

Still, an apology wouldn't change how different they were. No matter the intensity of Henry's feelings, he would be lying to himself if he didn't acknowledge that Eliza would be better off with Flip. Flip could make Eliza happy *without* asking her to compromise. Henry shook his head. "There's nothing between Eliza and me. There never has been."

"Really?" Flip's voice was infused with doubt. "Well, I guess that's even better."

* * *

A week later, Henry listened as Dr. Adler closed their staff meeting.

"Eliza, Henry, could the two of you stay for a few extra minutes? We need to discuss something that concerns you both."

Henry looked at Dr. Adler and nodded, then glanced at Eliza, his eyebrows raised in question.

She shrugged. Apparently she didn't know what this pertained to either. After the rest of the staff had cleared the room, Dr. Adler motioned for the two of them to join her at the head of the large conference table.

"Ordinarily," she began, "this is not something I would specifically ask of any of my staff members. But the truth is, this matter concerns a student who is the granddaughter of an old friend of mine. The granddaughter, Amber, is having a difficult time right now and could benefit from a stay at Rockbridge. I offered as much, encouraged her, even, to consider bringing her to visit the school. Her only hesitation has to do with Amber's faith. When I told her we had nondenominational services here on campus that Amber could easily attend, she told me that wasn't quite what she had in mind. My friend and her granddaughter are Mormon.

"Now, again, I realize this is quite an unusual request, and I do understand if either one of you is uncomfortable with what I'm asking. But as I'm sure you're both aware, being Mormon is much more than just a definition of where you attend church on Sunday. My friend believes that Amber's faith should be a large part of her therapy, which is where the two of you would come in. Eliza, you would obviously be responsible for Amber's counseling. I'll make sure she's yours, both for individual counseling and all group sessions she attends. Henry, your role would be more of secondary support. My friend mentioned something about priesthood blessings. I'm a little out of my depth here, but is that something you could provide should the need arise?"

Henry nodded. "Of course. That wouldn't be a problem."

Dr. Adler breathed a sigh of relief. "That's good. In addition, and this is probably the largest sacrifice I'm asking you to make because it requires you to bring work into your personal life, I'd like it if you could facilitate Amber's attendance at your church every Sunday." She leaned back in her chair. "What do you think?"

Henry looked at Eliza and waited for her to respond. She had to agree to far more than he did, though he didn't doubt she would be willing. It wasn't in Eliza's nature to turn down something like this simply because of a little inconvenience.

"I'd be happy to help in any way I can," Eliza said. "In fact, it will be a wonderful privilege to incorporate my faith into my therapy. When does Amber arrive?"

Dr. Adler smiled. "I knew I could count on you both. You know, my friend was surprised to hear that way out here in Western North Carolina I had even one Mormon staff member who would be willing to help. To have the two of you is nothing short of a miracle. Amber will be here at the end of this week, so hopefully we'll all be prepared by then." She stood. "There's just one more thing," she said as she stepped toward the door. "This situation will require a bit of discretion. After all, Amber will have the privilege of leaving campus immediately rather than having to earn it like her peers. We must be clear from the start that these outings are for church meetings—Sundays only at first. Once she's proved she can behave, we can include other church-sponsored activities, youth-group meetings, and things of that nature. Under no circumstances is it to appear that Amber receives any special treatment from either of you. I realize that will be difficult given the requests I've made, but I feel confident you'll both find a way to be solicitous of her unique needs without being unfair to the other students." She started to leave, then turned back to face them. "Are we good?"

Henry and Eliza nodded. "We're great," Eliza said. When Dr. Adler was gone, she turned to Henry. "Wow. This must be some friend of Dr. Adler's. I'm surprised she's going to such lengths to accommodate her."

"It seems like you'll be the one going to such lengths," Henry said. "Faith-based therapy hardly seems like too much to ask, and her tagging along to church on Sunday isn't a big deal, but I don't know, Eliza. The youth have a lot of activities. Once she's able to attend them all, that's a lot of trips into Rose Creek. Since it wouldn't exactly be appropriate for me to shuttle her back and forth alone, it'll be you doing most of the driving."

Eliza's face fell. "I hadn't necessarily thought of that," she said. "But that's no matter. This is an incredible opportunity. Do you know how frequently I feel a desire to incorporate my faith into the conversations I have with these kids? I mean, I do to some extent, as much as a general nondenominational acknowledgment of God's existence allows, but to really, truly talk about repentance and forgiveness and the plan of salvation . . . This is the kind of therapy I would really love to do."

"Well, then, I'm glad you'll have the opportunity. I'll help you any way I can."

Eliza looked at him just long enough to make him uncomfortable. He'd been doing a pretty good job of avoiding her and had created a measure of distance he imagined made it easier on them both. With all the time she'd been spending with Flip, and now with his knowledge of Flip's intentions, surely it was better for their friendship to fizzle into something more like acquaintances. Associates, perhaps? But she wasn't looking at him like an associate.

"I've missed hanging out with you, Henry."

Of course she would say something like that.

"I've been meaning to ask you about Daniel. How are things going with him?"

Henry smiled out of relief to be discussing something work related and also because speaking of Daniel made him genuinely happy. "Things with Daniel are great, actually. He's been writing some of the most incredible things. We're talking—even about things that don't have anything to do with English. I never expected it to go as well as it has. How's Flip?" He shifted the conversation back into Eliza's court. Talking about other men would keep them from getting too personal. "Has he decided on a date for his baptism?"

"The second Sunday in October," she said. "His father will be visiting that week, so he thought it would nice to wait and have the baptism while he's here."

"That's really great," Henry said. And he meant it. It was wonderful the way Eliza had been so willing to share her faith and how receptive Flip had been in response.

"Yeah, it is great. At first I wasn't so sure about Flip, but now? He's surprised me in more ways than one."

Henry wondered if that was a loaded statement. But then, it wasn't his place to wonder.

He stood.

"Well, it's been nice catching up. Just let me know if I can do anything to help with Amber. I'll talk to the branch presidency to let them know they can expect her arrival. I can let the Young Women presidency know as well, if that would help."

"That would be great. But, Henry, wait . . . Before you go . . ."

He hesitated but finally turned to face her.

"I just wanted to say I'm sorry about Allison. I'm sure it isn't easy, and I just want you to know I'm here for you if you need someone to talk to."

Henry had done about all the talking regarding Allison's marriage that he could stand. After AJ's conversation with Eliza, he'd confronted Allison about what he'd heard. Surely she hadn't given AJ the impression that Robert was going to be his new dad—except, she pretty much had.

"It's not that I told him Robert would be replacing you," Allison had said. "I just said Robert would be his dad now too and he would be living with us full-time."

"I'm sure his seven-year-old mind easily understood that," Henry shot back. "He sure seemed comfortable with the idea when he was telling Eliza he didn't think I wanted to be his dad anymore."

"Fine. I should have been more definitive. But let's be real. He only sees you a couple of times a week. He'll benefit from having someone around *every day*. Robert really cares about AJ; he's going to be a great stepdad."

The words stung Henry to the very core. "I didn't sign up to live away from AJ," he said, anger seething under the surface. "I didn't want us to be apart, didn't want us to live like this. You did, Allison. You split us up. You decided to put us through this hell."

"Right. Because a marriage falling apart is always completely one-sided."

The conversation had gotten worse from there. It had been the same argument they'd had multiple times, and it never accomplished anything.

In the weeks since, every time Henry was with AJ, he felt almost paralyzed with fear. He wanted to reach out to him, reassure him over and over again that he wasn't going anywhere, that he loved him and would always be his dad, but the right words never came. AJ seemed to be pulling away, so much so that Henry wondered if he wasn't *excited* about having Robert as a dad.

Henry looked at Eliza. It had been so easy for her to offer AJ reassurance and to promise that Henry loved him and would always be there. But, then, that was what Eliza did. For her, loving was easy.

"Eliza," he finally said with a heavy sigh. "About what you said to AJ, about Allison's marriage . . ." His words were slow and deliberate.

"I just want you to know I appreciate what you said. Sometimes I don't feel like there are many people in my corner. It was nice feeling like you understood."

"It was nothing."

"I also need to apologize. I've been meaning to for quite some time, and I just haven't found the right moment. I shouldn't have said what I did that night, after my . . . after William Harrison showed up. I realize you weren't involved and you didn't deserve my wrath. I'm sorry if I hurt your feelings."

"Henry, it's already forgotten."

He'd known she wouldn't be angry. She'd handled far worse things in life and managed not to hold a grudge; it wasn't surprising that forgiving him for his poor judgment and angry comments wouldn't even give Eliza pause. But he was still glad to hear her say it. It was important to him, regardless of their status as friends or acquaintances or *anything*, that she not think poorly of him. It frustrated him to realize that all the distance he'd created between them did little to dampen the importance she claimed in his life. It wasn't supposed to be that way. She wasn't supposed to *matter* so much.

"Right, well, thanks for that, I guess. I appreciate your willingness to understand." Henry picked up his bag and slung it over his shoulder.

Escape. He definitely needed to escape.

"I should go," he said. "I'm sure I'll see you around." He turned and hurried from the room without glancing back.

Chapter 20

ELIZA WATCHED FROM HER OFFICE window as Amber climbed the main porch steps of the admin building. She dragged a large black suitcase, stopping on each step to heft it up beside her. She was several inches shorter than Dr. Adler, who climbed the stairs beside her, and had a narrow, petite frame that reminded Eliza of her old roommate, Lexie.

Eliza had always felt like the Jolly Green Giant when she'd stood next to Lexie. Even though they'd worn similar sizes and had frequently shared clothes, Eliza had much broader shoulders and stood several inches taller than Lexie, who just barely made it past five feet.

It's no wonder she can't get her suitcase up the stairs, Eliza mused. *It probably weighs more than she does.*

When they stopped at the top of the stairs, Amber turned, allowing Eliza to see her face. She had long blonde hair that hung straight down her back and pleasant, pretty features. Eliza was surprised to note that for the most part, she looked rather normal. For a brief moment, the girl even smiled.

It wasn't a hard and fast rule, but first days on campus weren't generally the best days for many students. The first day was overwhelming, often filled with tears and words of anger and criticism as parents left and kids realized their reality was very different from what it was the day before.

In contrast, Amber looked nothing but completely complacent. Her curiosity officially piqued, Eliza turned and left her office to meet Dr. Adler and Amber as they came through the front door.

"Ah," she heard Dr. Adler say. "Here comes Eliza. She will be your counselor here at Rockbridge. You'll be meeting with her in an hour or so, after you've had the chance to unpack and settle in."

Eliza smiled expectantly at Amber but received only a brief nod in return.

"Eliza, can you walk Amber over to the girls' dormitory? Rachel is expecting her." Dr. Adler turned to Amber. "I'm so glad you're here at Rockbridge. Things will be hard for the first couple of weeks. There are a lot of rules and expectations, but we're very clear about what they are. The harder you work to remember them, the easier things will become. Just remember, every single person here is on your team. We are all fighting *for* you, not against you."

Dr. Adler said good-bye and left Amber in Eliza's care.

"Can I help you carry anything?"

"I got it," Amber said.

"Okay; just follow me." Eliza headed out the back door of the admin building and started across the brick footpath that led to the girls' dorm. Amber followed closely behind.

"Who's Rachel?"

"She's the girls' dorm manager," Eliza said. "When you're not with a counselor or in class, she's the one in charge. And you'll like her. She's really fun. I've even heard girls say with Rachel around, every night feels like one big slumber party."

"Sounds thrilling."

"That's the boys' dorm just over there," Eliza said, ignoring Amber's sarcasm. "And the girls' dorm is the building just past that. When we get there, Rachel will help you unpack. It isn't an option to do it without her."

"Why? So she can see all my stuff? Are you afraid I'm trying to smuggle in razor blades and pain pills?"

"Yes," Eliza said. "We are."

For a moment, Amber seemed taken aback by Eliza's honesty, but it didn't last. "Whatever," she finally said, rolling her eyes. "I don't care who searches my stuff. I didn't bring anything."

Rachel opened the dormitory door just as they approached the porch steps. Eliza turned Amber over to Rachel and returned to her office. She had an hour before Amber would be back for their first session—time Eliza wanted to use to gather her thoughts. She wasn't nervous, but surely Dr. Adler would be paying extra close attention to her progress with Amber. Eliza wanted to do her best.

* * *

"So how's the new girl?" Natalie sat on the long split-log bench next to Eliza, nudging her when she asked the question. It was a typical Friday

night at Rockbridge, and Flip had built a campfire in the fire pit behind
the staff apartments, where people gathered to talk, eat, and decompress
from the strains of the week's work.

"She's good," Eliza said. "Our session went pretty well today. She's in
better shape than most when they arrive."

"She didn't punch me when I took away her iPod," Rachel said as
she sat down on the other side of Eliza. "For that, she's already one of my
favorites."

"Look at you," Natalie said to Rachel. "You've been let out of your
cage!"

As one of the dorm managers, Rachel had the least amount of freedom
in the evenings. When the students were in their rooms, so was she. She
laughed at Natalie's comment. "Would you believe Dr. Adler herself came
over and offered to give me a break for a while? I love that she still enjoys
spending time with the girls, especially when there are marshmallows to
roast."

"You get extra time with this one, though, don't you?" Natalie asked,
turning the conversation back to Eliza. "She's really going to go to church
with you every Sunday?"

"It was a condition of her grandmother's," Eliza said. "And really,
I don't mind. Trouble is, *she* seems to mind. She wasn't exactly thrilled
when I told her church attendance wasn't an option."

"She'll be all right," Flip said from across the fire, "once she realizes
how fun it is to hang out with you all the time."

Natalie leaned over to Eliza, speaking low enough that only she
could hear. "So, yeah—how's that 'friends only' thing going with Flip?"

"We *are* just friends."

"Says you," Natalie said. "But for him? It's a done deal. He's totally in
love with you. The end."

"He is not," Eliza said. "It's not like that at all."

Rachel leaned over to join the conversation. "It's all right, Eliza. She's
only ribbing you because she wishes Flip would look at *her* that way
instead of you."

"Seriously? You have a thing for Flip?" Eliza looked at Natalie and
tried to read her expression.

"No," she said quickly. "I mean, I did, at one point, when he first
started working here, but it never really . . . I guess it just sort of fizzled out
over time."

"Did you ever tell him?"

"Of course she didn't tell him," Rachel said. "That would require her to actually *talk* to him. I'm pretty sure that's never happened."

"Oh, come on. That's not true. I talk to Flip all the time. About work or . . . work." They all laughed. "I've just never been very good at talking to guys. Casual conversation is hard enough. You want me to tell a guy I have feelings for him? Yeah, that's not going to happen."

Eliza could relate to that. She would rather die a slow and painful death than tell Henry how serious her feelings were. But that was only because she was certain he didn't feel the same way.

"You should tell him," she said to Natalie. "Ask him out; tell him you'd like to go see a movie."

"No," Natalie said. "I'm pretty sure that ship has sailed. Besides, he really does have feelings for *you*. It's written all over his face every time he looks at you. I'm not getting into the middle of that."

Eliza looked up and caught Flip's gaze across the fire. He *was* looking at her with a kind of intensity that made her want to look away. The same old question coursed through her mind. Could she develop feelings for Flip? Could their friendship turn into something more?

As if to answer her question, Henry appeared from around the corner of the apartment building and headed toward the campfire.

Natalie noticed him as well. "Well, miracles never cease. It's Henry coming to join the party."

It was true. In all the Friday-night campfires Eliza had enjoyed since her arrival at Rockbridge three months before, Henry had never been there.

"Now all we need is for ole' Gerald to show up and stand everything on its end," Flip said.

Everyone laughed. Gerald never did anything but grumble about the Friday-night fires. His apartment, at the end of the building, was closest to their gathering space. It wasn't a Friday night if Gerald didn't open his window at least three times to complain about them all making too much noise.

Eliza was pleased when Henry stopped in front of the empty bench next to Eliza.

"Do you mind if I join you?" he asked.

"Please do," Eliza said. "How are you?"

"I'm good. I met Amber this afternoon."

After Amber's counseling session, Eliza had walked Amber over to the conference rooms, where she would meet her teachers.

"How did it go?"

"She was very polite. I was completely surprised when I looked over her transcripts. Her grades were decent before she moved to Georgia, but once she started school there, she completely tanked. She didn't have a single passing grade for an entire semester."

Eliza nodded. "Her parents went through a difficult divorce, and she ended up moving to Georgia to live with her grandmother. That was a year ago, and she's been struggling pretty much since then. I believe her grades were probably one of the largest reasons her grandmother decided to send her here. I actually think she's a good kid—just angry and hurt and lost. It's like she's decided the world is a really ugly place, you know? She doesn't want to see the good. I'm going to change that though," Eliza said. "Or I guess I'm going to try, at least."

Henry smiled and shook his head. "I don't doubt it. If anybody can, it's you."

He spoke the words lightly, like he was simply making conversation, but given their recent conflict, Eliza was pleased to hear him speak highly of her in any regard.

"Hey, Eliza!"

Eliza looked up. Jeff was hurrying across the parking lot in her direction. "You got a call. Somebody named Gina? She says it's urgent."

Eliza stood. Gina was on the phone? It was the first anyone had heard from her since she'd disappeared in Knoxville. She hadn't contacted anyone, not her mom, not Barbara. Eliza stood frozen in place while her mind raced through the possibilities.

Her first thought was that Gina was either stranded or in need of money. Of course, she hoped it was something more, but if the past was any indication of the present, Eliza shouldn't expect much from the phone call. A warm touch on her arm brought her back to reality.

It was Henry, leaning close, a concerned look on his face. "Are you all right? Do you want me to come with you?"

His sincerity nearly melted her out of her shoes. Of course she wanted him to come with her. She wanted him to go *everywhere* with her. But that wasn't anything he wanted to hear. She shook her head. "Thanks, but I'll be okay."

She hurried over to Jeff. "Can I take it in my apartment?"

"She's on the main line, but if you run, I'll kick it over to your place. It'll only ring four times before going to your voice mail, so you better hurry."

Eliza's phone was ringing when she made it to the foot of her porch steps. She took them two at a time and made it inside just before the fourth ring.

"Hello? Gina?" She was out of breath, both from her race back to her apartment and the adrenaline pounding its way through her veins.

"Hey," Gina said.

Eliza paused. Jeff had said the call was urgent, but nothing about Gina's casual, lackadaisical greeting seemed urgent at all.

"Hey," Eliza said, her nervous energy suddenly deflated.

"So, I'm back at Mom's."

Eliza hooked the leg of the bar stool at the edge of the counter with her foot, pulling it closer so she could sit down. "That's good." She was hesitant, still unsure what to make of the phone call.

"She thought I should call you," Gina said.

"I'm glad you did. I've been worried about you."

"Yeah, about that . . . I'm sorry I bailed. That wasn't cool."

Eliza breathed out a frustrated sigh. They were the same apologies, Gina's halfhearted attempts to keep her family on her good side. She'd say whatever she had to say to keep her safety net in place.

"You stole from Henry."

"I'll pay him back."

"What, that's it? You'll pay him back? He's my friend, and he went to a lot of trouble to try to help you."

"What do you want me to do, pay him interest?" Her voice was raised, her tone sharp.

Eliza sighed again. "Let's not do this, Gina. You didn't call so we could fight. I'm glad you're home safe."

Gina didn't respond, allowing the silence between them to grow for several more seconds.

"I've been sober for ten days," she finally said.

Eliza sat up straight, her weariness immediately replaced with a faint sense of hope. "Gina, that's really great." She tried to soften her tone.

"That's sort of the reason I called. Mom seemed to think : . . Well, she made it sound like maybe you might still be able to help."

"Help . . . how?"

"If I want to go to rehab," Gina said. "Is it too late for me to go to that place in Raleigh?"

Eliza couldn't believe what she was hearing. At first she hesitated to believe her sister. She expected the sullen, sarcastic Gina from the first five minutes of their conversation. But this was different. Was it possible her sister was actually reaching out for help?

When Eliza didn't respond right away, Gina kept talking. "Look, I realize I was terrible to you, and you don't have to help me, but I just . . . I think I'm ready now." She suddenly sounded small, her voice more childlike than Eliza had ever heard it. "I don't want to do this anymore, Eliza. I'm just so tired."

Eliza wanted to believe her sister was completely sincere. But there was only so much she could do. "Gina, I can't leave work again," she said. "I can call, I think, or have Henry call, but I can't take you to Raleigh."

"No, you don't have to take me. Mom said she would drive me over."

Eliza was happy to hear that her mother was willing to be involved. If Gina's rehabilitation was going to stick, she would need their mother's support. Eliza's hope was growing stronger. Maybe this time it would actually work out.

"I can't make any promises, but I'll see what I can do, okay? Listen though, if you can't get into Hazelwood, you can go somewhere else. You know that, right? There's help out there."

"I know," Gina said. "I'm not going to give up this time. I promise."

Chapter 21

"HEY, HENRY, YOU GOT A free hand?" Henry turned and saw Andrew Porterfield standing in the doorway of the branch president's office. He had a briefcase in one hand, a diaper bag slung over his shoulder, and an infant car seat on the floor at his feet.

Henry smiled. "Of course," he said. "I remember those days."

Andrew still wore the goofy grin of a new dad experiencing the bliss of being in love with his daughter. He picked up the carrier and extended it to Henry.

"Would you mind walking the baby down to Kate? She's in the Relief Society room, I think. I've just got to finish up this interview before the baptism starts."

Henry took the baby and lifted the carrier high enough that he could see the tiny face of the sleeping newborn. He watched as she grunted and yawned, her eyelids fluttering open for a brief second, then closing again.

Henry laughed. "It's a rough life you've got there, little one." He looked back at Andrew. "You want me to take the diaper bag too?"

"Oh yeah, here," Andrew said. "Hey, are you staying for the baptism?" He took a step closer to Henry, glancing cautiously in both directions. Somehow, Henry suspected there was more to Andrew's question than simple curiosity.

Henry raised his eyebrows. "I was planning on it."

Andrew only nodded. "So it seems like Flip and Eliza are pretty good friends."

Ah, Henry thought. *So that's where he's heading.*

"They are good friends," Henry said. "Though I believe Flip has hopes for something more."

"And you're good with that?" Andrew stood with his hands on his hips, a look of mild incredulity on his face.

"I'm not sure it's actually any of my business." Henry tried to avoid eye contact, but Andrew was unrelenting.

"Really? It's not your business at all?"

Henry sighed, resigned to the fate he'd given himself. "No."

"Well, I'm sorry to hear that. I thought the two of you seemed like a great fit." Andrew stepped into his office, then turned back once more. "Let me just tell you this. I know you've got a complicated past, Henry, but just because the past is complicated, it doesn't mean your future has to be. Some things are worth fighting for."

Henry shook his head as he walked down the hallway, the baby carrier swinging gently as he walked. What did Andrew know about whether or not he and Eliza were right for each other? And how could his past not affect his future? To him, everything seemed so completely intertwined, so completely . . . complicated.

After delivering the sleeping newborn to Kate, Henry went to find a seat at the back of the chapel. Flip's baptism would start in just a few minutes. The chapel was filling nicely; many members had chosen to stay after the regular block to support Flip and welcome him into the branch.

Henry watched as Eliza sat down, Amber close by her side. As he watched them, an uncomfortable feeling swelled up in his gut. They were leaning their heads together, whispering and smiling, talking animatedly about something that was obviously very interesting to them both. They were interacting as if they were friends. He supposed there wasn't anything wrong with the two of them being friendly, but if the lines between them started to blur, he worried things might become more difficult for Eliza.

But Eliza was a good counselor. Henry felt confident she had things under control. Perhaps he ought to consider it a good sign that Amber was smiling *and* attending a church function at the same time. Maybe Eliza really was changing Amber's opinion about things.

When the prelude music stopped, Henry motioned to AJ, who had been sitting with his friend Jeremiah's family, and asked him to come back and join him. AJ obliged but didn't try to hide his disappointment that he didn't get to sit with his friend. Henry knew it was perfectly natural for a seven-year-old kid to want to sit with his buddy, but every time AJ wanted to choose someone else over him, he couldn't help but feel a little sting.

Flip's baptism was much like every other baptism Henry had ever attended. The missionaries who had been responsible for teaching him spoke and performed the baptism, and Eliza shared her testimony. There was a special musical number a group of Primary children sang, and Andrew spoke for a few minutes to officially welcome Flip into the branch.

Much to Henry's surprise, the most compelling moment of the service was when Flip stood and spoke about the process of his conversion. He talked about reading the Book of Mormon while out on excursion and trying to find the courage to pray about it. It was clear his words were heartfelt and sincere. Henry felt remorse for having ever doubted him.

As Flip continued to speak with the slight Irish lilt in his voice and his genial, self-deprecating humor, it took only a few minutes for him to completely charm the entire room. It was a side of Flip Henry had never really appreciated and one he had to admit he could easily see making Eliza happy. Above everything else, Henry couldn't help but notice that Flip seemed utterly and completely *un*complicated.

When the branch gathered in the cultural hall for refreshments, Henry took AJ's hand and went in search of Flip to offer him his congratulations. In the hallway, he passed a group of young women, one of whom was Amber.

"Are you kidding?" he heard Amber say. "Of course I'll be there. I've got her eating out of my hand."

Amber's words stopped Henry in his tracks. Righteous indignation filled him as he thought of anyone trying to take advantage of Eliza's kindness. He tried to tell himself Amber could have been talking about anything—about *anyone*. But instinctively he knew it wasn't just anyone. He would have to talk to Eliza about it later.

Flip was in the cultural hall when Henry found him finishing a conversation with a small flock of overly enthusiastic Relief Society sisters.

"I think they like you, Flip," Henry said with a grin. "It was a nice baptism," he continued, his voice sincere. "Congratulations."

"Thanks, Henry. I'm glad you were here." Flip glanced down at AJ, standing slightly behind Henry. "I don't believe we've had the pleasure of meeting," he said. "I'm Flip."

"Is that your real name?" AJ asked.

"It's not," Flip said. "My real name is Frederick Finnegan Marshall, but since that's such a mouthful, I've been Flip since I was about your age."

"Why does your voice sound different?"

"AJ, don't be rude," Henry said gently.

"I'm not being rude; I'm just asking. His voice sounds different."

Flip only laughed. "It does sound a bit different. AJ, do you know where Ireland is?"

AJ nodded. "It's next to Britain across the English Channel from France."

Now it was Henry's turn to laugh. He could tell it wasn't the answer Flip was expecting. Before the divorce, AJ had a globe in his bedroom that he and Henry would look at together every evening before bed. Henry would spin it around until AJ would stick out his finger and yell stop, then they'd talk about whatever place his finger had landed on.

Their geography lessons had been mostly rudimentary, but they had named countries and bodies of water enough that many of them had stuck.

It was a painful realization—a guilt-inducing stab just behind Henry's ribs that blasted through the haze of his own suffering and etched out a new picture of his son with such crystal clarity Henry nearly gasped. He hadn't thought about those moments with AJ or attempted to re-create them, even in the smallest part, one single time since the divorce. As he watched his son in animated conversation with Flip, he wondered how he had managed to venture so far off course. How had he let the sting of Allison's betrayal keep him from recognizing the pain of the one person who didn't deserve to hurt at all?

* * *

The following afternoon, Dr. Adler met Henry in the doorway of his classroom just after he'd finished for the afternoon. "Henry, do you have a quick minute?"

"Sure," he said. She pulled his classroom door closed behind her.

"I'm going to be perfectly frank," she said. "Eliza has suggested that Amber be approved for our final wilderness excursion of the season. They leave at the end of this month, and I'll be honest, I'm not sure Amber will be ready in time. Ordinarily, it takes students quite a bit longer to be ready for excursion. Eliza feels there are reasons to fast-track Amber through the program, and while her reasons seem valid, there's something I can't quite put my finger on, some doubt that's hovering off to the side that I can't make sense of. I'm wondering if you can provide some insight."

"I don't really feel qualified to make a judgment of that sort," Henry said. "Amber is doing well in class, working very hard . . ."

"Of course, of course," Dr. Adler said. "It's not a judgment on Amber I'm asking you to make. What I'm afraid of is that in asking Eliza to take Amber to and from church every week and in giving them so many opportunities to spend time together, I've crafted a situation where Eliza has formed a bit of an attachment to the girl. I worry, perhaps, that her judgment is a bit clouded, muddled by her own feelings and desires for Amber's success."

Henry shook his head. He immediately remembered the remarks he'd overheard in the hallway at church the day before and the casual way he'd seen Eliza and Amber interact. But he couldn't be certain that all he had observed was completely accurate. Having not had the opportunity to discuss it with Eliza, it didn't seem right to share his concerns with Dr. Adler.

He chose his words carefully. "Eliza is a good counselor. Even with the unusual circumstances of their relationship, I haven't seen anything that would make me think to question her judgment. I feel certain she has Amber's best interests in mind."

It wasn't necessarily a lie. He *did* think Eliza had Amber's best interests in mind. He would feel better revealing the rest of his concerns directly to Eliza.

Dr. Adler smiled. "Well, perhaps you're right," she said. "Thank you, Henry. It makes me feel a bit better to hear you say so. Will you tell me, though, if you see anything that might indicate otherwise?"

"Of course," he said.

She moved to the door. "Oh, and, Henry," she said, glancing back, her hand resting on the knob. "I've heard wonderful things about the progress you've made with Daniel. I know you've had your doubts about how you fit here at Rockbridge, but I hope you are feeling better about things. I know I am."

Funny, Henry *had* been feeling better about things. He didn't love the turmoil surrounding William Harrison's appearance at the foot of Rockbridge's front steps, and his relationship with AJ still felt fragile, but work-wise, it had been a good summer. He'd found his footing with a few more students and was feeling a more natural rhythm to his teaching. He reasoned he'd only needed a little more time to adjust and settle in, but in the back of his mind, he knew his progress stemmed from something more.

That something more was Eliza. He'd had the insight to pray about Daniel because of Eliza. He'd had the courage to get personal, to take risks because of Eliza. Her influence was the biggest reason he'd been able to accomplish so much. Of course, that was far more than he could ever explain to Dr. Adler. He settled instead on simple acknowledgment.

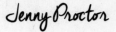

"Thank you. I'm feeling much better about things and have no intention of giving up."

"Well, that's good," Dr. Adler said. "Rockbridge wouldn't be the same without you."

Chapter 22

THE WEEK AFTER FLIP'S BAPTISM went by in a blur. Eliza was busier than she had ever been at Rockbridge. Her counseling load was maxed out—in fact, all of Rockbridge was maxed out. There wasn't room for a single new student, which left everyone feeling like they couldn't let their guard down even for a second.

In addition to work, Eliza was driving Amber into Rose Creek for weekly youth activities. It had taken only a couple of weeks before Eliza felt like Amber deserved the added opportunity to leave campus. After a few sessions, Amber had morphed into the most compliant, good-natured student Eliza counseled.

So many students were in such a difficult place when they came to Rockbridge. Amber was like a breath of fresh mountain air in comparison. And Eliza wasn't the only one who thought so. Everyone enjoyed being around her. She'd grown close to several of the other girls and was quickly building friendships with the youth from church.

It was only when Eliza tried to get Amber to talk about her family that things got ugly. Today they sat together outside, enjoying their counseling session in the sunshine of the October afternoon. At least, *Eliza* was enjoying their session.

Amber was sullen, her eyes dark, her arms folded tightly across her chest. They were discussing her parents' divorce, something that had clearly shaken her world in a way that had left her feeling bruised and battered from within.

"Tell me why you're angry," Eliza said gently. When Amber didn't answer right away, Eliza let the silence pool between them. She'd learned that sometimes it took the hardest answers a long time to make it to the surface.

"I'm angry because I feel like it was all a lie," Amber said.

"What was a lie? Their relationship?"

"Well, that, but everything they ever told me about love—eternal marriage, the temple, looking for my eternal companion." Her words were laced with sarcasm. "Why teach me all of that if none of it matters anyway? What's eternal about our family now?"

"But it doesn't always end that way," Eliza said. "Sometimes it does, yes. But we live in an imperfect world, Amber. We're all doing the best we can, and when we don't measure up, the Savior is there to make up the difference. When we fail, even when marriages fail, the Atonement covers it all."

"My parents weren't doing the best they could," Amber said. "If they were, they would still be together."

Amber's words might very well have been true. But that didn't change how important it was for her to find forgiveness for her parents.

"Can we talk about something else now?" Amber flopped back onto the grass behind her and stretched her arms over her head.

"Like what?"

"Like Dawson," Amber said, her voice a little dreamy.

"Dawson Peterson? From church?"

"He's amazing, isn't he? I think he's in love with me, and I know he wants me to be at the stake dance on Halloween. What do you think? Is there any chance I'd be able to go?"

"Amber, it's not likely. Stake dances are all the way in Asheville, which is a long way from Rockbridge. You are already afforded so much more leeway when it comes to leaving campus. A dance is pushing the rules a little too far. Aside from that, you'll likely be on excursion at the end of the month."

"You're not really going to send me into the woods, are you?"

Eliza smiled. "Trust me. It's a good thing. You'll be surprised how much you'll learn about yourself out there."

"I suppose you always know what's best." Amber's voice was light enough that Eliza couldn't tell if she was being sarcastic or not. "You know, I think maybe you're right about my parents," Amber continued. "Maybe they really do deserve to be forgiven."

Eliza raised an eyebrow. There was something unsettling about Amber's tone. She'd switched so rapidly from sullen to cheerfully compliant that Eliza couldn't help but doubt her sincerity. It suddenly felt like she was watching a play—and Amber was the lead actress.

* * *

Later that evening, Eliza heard a quiet knock on the screen door of her apartment. She looked up from the progress reports spread out on the coffee table in front of her and smiled when she saw Henry standing on her porch.

"Hi," he said. "You busy?"

Eliza shook her head. "Not at all. Come on in."

He opened the squeaky screen door and let it swing shut behind him.

"How are you?" He sat on the couch beside her.

"I'm swamped. It's all I can do to keep up with all this paperwork. What about you? Have you adjusted to a heavier load?"

"I think so," Henry said. "It *is* a lot of paperwork though. That was hard to get used to when I started teaching here."

"What was your job like before you came to Rockbridge? You taught high school, didn't you?"

Henry nodded. "Classic American literature—eleventh grade English."

"Did you love it?"

"You know, it's funny," he said. "I remember thinking it was so hard to teach high school, to deal with the kids and handle all the drama. In retrospect, what I dealt with then was nothing like what I've faced here at Rockbridge."

"I'm sure," Eliza said. "Things seem like they're going better for you though, aren't they? I mean, Daniel is doing better, and I'm hearing good things about your classes from other students."

"I hope so." He hesitated. "I do feel better about things—at work, anyway."

Eliza longed to ask him what he meant. Instead, she bit her lip and let the moment pass.

"I got a call from my uncle." Henry seemed happy to change the subject. "He said the funding worked out for Gina—three months free of charge."

Eliza smiled. "I meant to tell you! I've just been so busy. It's so wonderful though, isn't it? My mom drove her over last week. She said it was a beautiful place, Henry. I hope you realize how grateful we are to you for your help."

Henry only nodded.

"So listen," he said. "I ran into Dr. Adler the other day, and she asked what I thought about Amber's progress."

"In your class? Her grades have been good, haven't they? She just showed me the paper she wrote about *The Scarlet Letter*. She was really proud of the A you gave her."

"She deserved an A. It was a good paper. But Dr. Adler didn't want to talk about Amber's grades."

"Then what did she want to talk about?"

Henry sighed. "She wanted to know if I'd ever seen the two of you behave in such a way that would indicate you consider Amber more of a friend than your patient."

Eliza shook her head. She hated the word *patient*. It made her think of sick people in hospital beds. The kids she worked with every day didn't belong in hospital beds. They needed love and support and help, but they weren't patients.

"What did you tell her?"

"I told her I had tremendous confidence in your ability as a counselor and that I thought if you trusted Amber, then Amber must deserve to be trusted."

Eliza was gearing herself up for a rebuttal, but after hearing Henry's comment, all she could manage was a simple, "Oh. Well, thank you."

Henry wasn't finished though. She could tell by how intensely he was still staring at her.

"That's what I told Dr. Adler, Eliza, but I have to admit you *do* spend a lot of time with Amber, taking her to and from church. When I see you together, it seems like you *are* friends. And also, I overheard Amber say something in the hallway after Flip's baptism. Now, I realize I wasn't a part of the conversation, but if she was discussing you, and I think she was, then I have reason to believe she's taking advantage of you. At least, she's trying."

"What did you hear her say?"

"She said she had you eating out of her hand."

Eliza leaned back into the sofa cushions and folded her arms across her chest. She remembered the observations she'd made of Amber earlier that afternoon. Was it possible Amber was treating this like one giant game? Saying and doing the right thing in order to get what she wanted?

"Just because she's trying to take advantage doesn't mean she's succeeding, Henry. I promise. I do like her, and I do enjoy her company, but I haven't lost control of the situation."

"Just be careful," Henry said. "Dr. Adler wonders if she's asking too much of you."

"No," Eliza said. "I don't think so. Though I do have to remind myself to be objective. I appreciate her concern and yours too, but I think I'm okay."

"And you think she's ready for excursion?"

Eliza considered the question. "I think she has to be. I don't know what else will humble her."

The shrill ring of the telephone hanging on the wall in the kitchen punctuated Eliza's words. Her heart jumped. The ring indicated an irregular phone call. It was short and sharp and repeated in fast intervals.

"It's an emergency call," Eliza said. She stood and hurried to the phone.

"Yes?" she answered as she picked up the receiver.

"Eliza, get to the girls' dorm. There's been an overdose, I think. I don't know what's happened. The paramedics are on their way." Rachel's voice was hurried and frantic.

"Rachel, who is it? Is she still breathing?"

"It's Rebecca. She's breathing, but I can't get her to wake up. She's completely limp. Get Natalie too, will you? The girls are all scared."

"We'll be right there," she said.

She turned to Henry. "I'm going to the girls' dorm. Can you go get Natalie? Tell her to come right away?" She pulled on her tennis shoes and raced out the door of her apartment, not even waiting for Henry to respond.

Rachel met her at the door of the dormitory. "She's in here," she said, leading Eliza down the hall and into one of the girls' shared bedrooms. Rebecca lay on her bed, her head tilted back, her arms thrown out to either side. She was obviously drugged, but as Rachel had indicated, her breathing was still steady and regular.

Eliza's mind raced. No one was allowed access to medication of any sort without approval and supervision. What had the girl taken, and how had she found it? She started looking around the room. The desk to the right of Rebecca's bed was neat and tidy, with nothing noticeably out of place, and the trash can beside it was empty.

Eliza went to the closet and opened the doors. She pushed the clothes aside and moved the shoes, looking for anything out of the ordinary.

There it was.

Eliza pulled the empty pill bottle from the inside of one of Rebecca's tennis shoes. When she turned the bottle over, her heart nearly stopped. She recognized the bottle. It was a generic brand of ibuprofen, a significant fact because it was a store brand sold at grocery stores in Tennessee. Eliza carried a bottle just like it in her purse . . . or she had carried *this* bottle in her purse.

Moments later, the EMTs arrived. Eliza gave them the bottle of ibuprofen, explaining where she had found it. As they worked to secure Rebecca for transport, Eliza found Rachel. "Natalie will stay here in case anyone needs to talk," she said. "I'll ride to the hospital with Rebecca."

"Is she going to be all right?"

"An ibuprofen overdose won't kill her," Eliza said. "I know that much. The paramedics said her vitals were stable, so I think she's going to be fine. Have you talked to the Adlers?"

"They aren't home, and I can't get either cell phone. I've left messages with them both."

"We're ready to go," one of the paramedics said.

"I'm coming with you," Eliza said. She turned to Rachel. "I'll keep you posted."

As she left the room and followed the paramedics down the hall, she heard a voice calling her name from behind. "Eliza, wait!"

She turned. Amber stood there, her eyes rimmed with red and filled with tears. Her obvious distress confirmed Eliza's suspicions. There was only one student who would have had the opportunity to take something from Eliza's purse. That one student was Amber.

"I didn't think . . . I just . . . I'm so sorry, Eliza. Rebecca told me she gets headaches all the time but that no one here ever lets her take anything. I was just trying to help. I didn't think she'd take them all at once, I swear. If I thought that, I never would have taken them from your purse." The words tumbled out, tears streaming freely down Amber's face.

"Rebecca is going to be fine," Eliza said coolly. "But you stole from me, Amber. You stole from me and put someone's life at risk. We'll talk about this later. Until then, you are on suspension from all activities. Do you understand?"

Amber only nodded. Eliza turned and hurried outside, where the paramedics had just loaded Rebecca into the ambulance. The paramedic in the back offered Eliza a hand, helping her into the truck, then pulled the door closed.

Oh, Amber, Eliza thought to herself. *What have you done?*

Chapter 23

HENRY STOOD IN THE PARKING lot of Rockbridge, his hands thrust deeply into his pockets as he watched the ambulance pull away. He turned and saw Jeff walking across the now-quiet lot to join him.

"Do you know what happened?" Henry asked.

"No details," Jeff responded. "Only that it was Rebecca and it was some sort of overdose. Eliza's gone to the hospital with her."

"Overdose? What did she take?"

"Eliza found an empty bottle of ibuprofen in her closet. We can't be sure until they get her to the hospital, but I think it's safe to say that's what it was. The question is, where did she get it?"

Henry knew how closely the students were monitored. It would be extremely difficult for any student to get their hands on any sort of medication unless a staff member let their guard down, creating just the right window of opportunity.

An uneasy feeling swelled in the pit of Henry's stomach. "I'm going to drive down to the hospital." Henry spoke more to himself than to Jeff, who still stood beside him.

"What, right now?" Jeff asked.

"Eliza left in the ambulance without even putting her jacket on. Besides, she'll need a ride back to campus. The ambulance doesn't exactly make round trips."

"True," Jeff said. "But I doubt she'll be coming home tonight. She'll stay with Rebecca."

"Probably," Henry said. "But once the Adlers get there, they may want to send her back. I'll go just in case."

When Henry arrived at the hospital forty-five minutes later, he found Eliza slumped in a corner chair in the waiting room, biting her fingernails with savage fury, her eyes staring emptily at the blank wall across from her. When she saw him approach, her face instantly brightened.

"Henry, what are you doing here?"

"I thought you might need your jacket and your purse. And here"—he handed her a water bottle and a pack of peanut butter M&M's—"fortifications in case it's a long night."

"Thank you. That's really kind of you."

"How's Rebecca doing?" Henry sat down in the chair beside her.

Eliza sighed. "She's going to be fine. They were able to wake her up, which is a good thing, though she's terribly groggy and disoriented. Now that she's awake, she's likely to experience some pretty severe gastrointestinal pain, and they need to monitor her pretty closely to make sure her liver and kidneys don't shut down, but for now, she looks okay."

"Jeff said it was ibuprofen?"

"Oh, right," Eliza said. "I didn't tell you that part, did I? I found the empty bottle in her closet. Doctors confirmed that's what's in her system."

"Eliza, where did she get it?"

For a moment, she wouldn't raise her eyes to meet his. When she did, it wasn't hard to recognize what she was feeling. "It was mine." She was dejected, more than Henry had ever seen her before. Considering the journey they'd taken together to retrieve an alcoholic sister and cajole her into rehab, that was really saying something.

"Amber took it from my purse while we were at church last Sunday and gave the bottle to Rebecca."

"Are you sure?"

"I'm sure," Eliza said. "Amber told me herself before I left for the hospital. She said Rebecca was always complaining of getting headaches . . . that she was just trying to help."

Henry was relieved. Stealing wasn't a good thing, but when he considered the alternative—one that involved Eliza's giving Amber or Rebecca the drugs herself—he was actually glad it *had* been thievery. "Do you believe her?"

Eliza looked surprised by his question. "Who, Amber? Of course I believe her. Why would she lie about something like this? She came to me and confessed. If she wanted to lie, why seek me out and tell me what happened?"

"Eliza, I don't mean to cast shadows on her character, but you have to think about this objectively. If Amber knew you found the bottle in

Rebecca's room and realized you could have recognized it as your own, is it possible she lied to paint the prettiest picture possible on top of a much uglier truth?"

"But why else would she have taken it? Her story makes sense."

"Have you ever heard Rebecca complain about headaches?"

Eliza crossed her arms defensively across her chest. "No, but . . ." She closed her eyes and rubbed her hand across her forehead. "Maybe I'm not being objective. But why would she lie?"

"Does she want to go on excursion? Maybe she was trying to get into trouble, hoping she'd be kept back."

"She doesn't want to go," Eliza agreed. "That's something to consider. But where does Rebecca come in? I can believe Amber's lying, but I can't imagine her wanting Rebecca hurt."

"Fair point," Henry said. "Maybe she *was* just trying to be a good friend to Rebecca. But whether her actions were well intentioned or not, Amber's not afraid to bend the rules because she's counting on your being lenient. She completely violated the relationship she has with you and took advantage of your kindness."

"You're probably right," Eliza said. "Maybe I have been too trusting, too lenient. But when you're attending church with someone, you don't spend a whole lot of time thinking about how you better not leave your purse in the chapel while you run to the bathroom."

Henry could tell she was weary.

"I understand what you're saying," she continued. "I get it, all right? From now on, I'll be more careful." Grabbing her purse and jacket that Henry had left beside her chair, she stood and stalked off down the hall.

There was an edge to her voice that Henry had never heard before, and he wondered if he'd made a mistake in coming. Come to think of it, why *had* he come? He couldn't put it into words—that tangible feeling that drew him to Eliza and made him feel as if it were his responsibility to make sure she was all right.

He couldn't name it, but he also couldn't ignore it.

* * *

An hour later, the Adlers arrived at the hospital. Eliza was with Rebecca when they arrived, so Henry walked them down to Rebecca's room. He motioned for Eliza to join them in the hallway, then stood back while she gave the Adlers a rundown of everything that had happened.

When Eliza explained how Rebecca had come to have the medication in the first place, Dr. Adler did little to hide her frustration. Henry felt guilty for his scolding Eliza. He should have known she'd get it from her superiors. He was just the English teacher. What did he know? When the Adlers entered the room to see Rebecca, Henry looked at Eliza. "You okay?"

She shrugged. "It wasn't as bad as I expected, nothing I didn't deserve."

"I'm still sorry you had to go through it," Henry said. "I shouldn't have said anything earlier. It wasn't my place to be critical."

"No, no, you were right. I shouldn't have been so defensive. Let's just call it even, okay?"

"Eliza?" Dr. Adler called from inside the room.

"Don't go yet," Eliza whispered to Henry before she ducked back into the hospital room. She reemerged a few minutes later, her jacket and purse in hand.

"Dr. Adler is going to stay here tonight." She slipped on her jacket. "Frank offered to take me home, but I told him you were still here. Do you mind if I catch a ride with you?"

"Not at all," Henry said. "That's a large part of why I came, since I was pretty sure the ambulance wasn't likely to bring you home."

"Yeah, they don't really make round trips, do they?" Eliza said with a smile.

"That's exactly what I said."

Once they were settled in the car and driving back up to Rockbridge, Henry asked, "So what happens to Amber now?"

"I'll have to discuss everything with Dr. Adler tomorrow, just to make sure she agrees, but I've already told Amber she's suspended from all activities. She'll lose all her free time and have extra chore rotations. She'll have to work hard to earn back my trust."

"Will she still go on excursion?"

"I don't know. At this point, I think I should defer the decision to Dr. Adler. Obviously, there could be trust issues. But with all the extra opportunities church has given her, I'm just not sure she's been shaken up enough, you know? I still think excursion might be the only thing that can get through to her."

It was late, nearly midnight, when Henry pulled his car into the parking lot at Rockbridge, and it felt much like the night he and Eliza had returned from Tennessee.

"So when will you hear from Gina? Is she allowed to communicate with you during her therapy?" he asked as they climbed out of the car.

"Not at first," Eliza said. "Eventually, as she progresses, she'll be able to e-mail and then call. It still seems surreal to me to think about her being there, you know? I've wanted this to happen for so long; I can't believe it actually is. I just hope three months is long enough."

"You don't think it will be?"

"I don't know." Eliza let out a long sigh. "I want it to be. I guess I just think about her going back home with Mom after the three months is over. How will she not fall back into old patterns and old habits? If she's around her old friends, won't they try and lure her back into her old ways?"

Henry leaned on the hood of his car. "I suppose. But isn't that the risk everyone takes when they leave rehab? You have to start living a normal life sometime. And that's what they will teach her at Hazelwood—how to live her life normally, how to say no to her old ways."

"You're right. I know you're right. If we were talking about someone else, I would be offering the same encouragement. I just know Gina's track record. That, and she's my sister. How do I not worry?"

"You do worry," Henry said. "It's what we do when we love someone. I don't think there's a way to turn it off."

For a moment, Henry remembered the feelings he'd had at the hospital, his unnamed need to be there for Eliza, to make sure she was cared for. His own thoughts echoed back in his head. *It's what we do when we love someone.*

Love.

Love?

It took him a moment to realize Eliza was speaking again.

"I'm going to see my mom in a couple of weeks," Eliza was saying. "My old roommate is getting married, so I have to go back to Tennessee to do the bridesmaid thing. We're planning a phone call that weekend. Maybe it will make me feel better to hear Gina's voice and let her tell me how much better she's doing."

Eliza stood in the dim glow of the street lamp that lit the small employee parking lot. Her arms were wrapped around her waist, her hands tucked inside her jacket.

"You're cold," Henry said. "I should let you get inside."

"I love the cold," she responded. "Cold means fall is officially here. I've never seen anything more beautiful than these mountains when the leaves are changing color."

For a moment, they stood in silence. Though he tried to prevent it, Henry couldn't stop his mind from thinking of her, a wave of impulsive fire darting across the kitchen and touching her lips to his. As he looked at her, her skin glowing in the lamplight, he had to resist the impulse to pull her to him and kiss her again, this time because *he* wanted it. His stomach nearly dropped when he looked in her eyes and realized that was precisely what she wanted him to do.

"I'm gonna go," he said hoarsely. "I, uh . . . Good night." He took a step backward and started to turn.

"Henry, wait." Eliza lunged forward and caught his hand. "I don't understand why you're running away. What are you so afraid of?"

Henry kept his face turned away, but he left his hand in hers.

"Henry, I want this. I want *you*."

He pulled his hand away, feeling more conflicted than ever. "Eliza, I don't know what to say. I just . . . I'm sorry."

He turned and walked to his apartment, wondering if he'd done the right thing. Every time he was with Eliza, it was becoming increasingly difficult to ignore his feelings. He'd used logic and reason to determine their future. They could never be anything more than friends.

But his heart wasn't catching up.

Not when she looked at him like she just had, when her touch alone was enough to take his breath away.

Chapter 24

ON FRIDAY AFTERNOON, AFTER HER counseling sessions, Eliza found herself on the back deck of the admin building, drawn by the warm sun and the hope of some peace and quiet. It was late in the afternoon, and though the sun was settling toward evening, there was just enough light left to bathe the last row of picnic tables in a pleasing glow.

On a whim, instead of just sitting at a picnic table, Eliza dropped her work bag, kicked off her shoes, and climbed on top, stretching out with her head resting on her bag, her legs crossed comfortably with one foot kicking in the air. She placed her arm across her eyes to shield them from the sun and, all at once, felt perfectly relaxed. Several minutes passed.

"It's a bit brazen, don't you think, lying on a table right outside the director's window? What kind of example are you setting for the students?"

Eliza turned her head and saw Flip standing there, a quirky grin on his face.

"The director could hardly argue with how magnificent it feels to lie in the sun at the end of a long day. As for the students, there are plenty of other tables if anyone would like to join me."

Flip laughed. "Well, enjoy it while it lasts. I can stand here and see the shade creeping up on you. Another ten minutes and the sun will be behind the trees, and your pretty perch might start to feel a bit chilly."

"Then please do be quiet for my last ten minutes of warm toes."

"How 'bout this?" Flip said. "I ask you to go out with me, you say yes, then I let you get back to your sunshine."

Eliza pushed up on her elbows. "On a date?"

"Yes, a date, and I'll not let you call it anything different this time either. Are you off tomorrow? Let's take a picnic up onto the parkway. The trees are still blazing with color. We could hike, eat . . . It could be fun."

Eliza would be lying if she said she hadn't expected this moment to come. Flip had convinced Eliza he hadn't joined the Church for her, and she believed him. But he'd never been shy about his intentions. Now that faith was no longer a reason for her to say no, it was only natural for him to ask.

She tried to be objective. Here he was, an active, bona fide, and official Mormon, funny, charming, with bonus points for being handsome, and he was asking her out on a date.

Could she say yes?

Her mind flashed back to the look on Henry's face two nights before when she'd told him it was him she wanted. It still stung to think of him pulling his hand away and turning his back.

It had been a long time since Eliza had shed any tears over a man. But that night, she'd called Lexie—it had taken three tries to wake her up—and indulged in an exhausting cry that had left her feeling empty and alone. She had to get over her feelings for Henry.

"I'm not working Saturday," she finally said. "I'd love to go out with you."

"Splendid," Flip said. "I'll come by for you at eleven. Hey, how's Rebecca? Is she back from the hospital yet?"

Eliza glanced at her watch. "Actually, she should be getting back any minute now. I should probably head over to the dorms to meet her and Dr. Adler."

"So she's all right, then?"

"Physically, she's fine. It's a pretty big step back in her therapy though. I'm still trying to figure out how I'm going to tackle it all."

"Hey, Liza," Natalie said from the back door of the admin building. "Dr. Adler just pulled up. I figured you'd want to talk to Rebecca first, yeah?"

"Yeah, I'm coming," Eliza said. She climbed off the table and stepped back into her shoes.

"So I guess I'll see you Saturday," Flip said with a grin.

"And probably ten times before then," Eliza said, "seeing how we live and work at the same place."

"Yes, but Saturday is a date, which makes it far more important. I'm already counting down the hours."

Eliza smiled and willed herself to feel a similar sense of excitement. There wasn't a single good reason why she couldn't go on a date with Flip and have a nice time.

Not one single reason at all.

* * *

After an extensive counseling session with Rebecca, Eliza went to check on Amber. She was handling her probation with what Eliza considered to be far more grace than was typical. Still, Eliza wondered if she actually felt the weight of what she'd done wrong. She was apologetic, of course, but every time they talked about it, Eliza thought she almost seemed dismissive, like there was hardly a reason to keep mentioning it at all.

When Eliza arrived at Amber's dorm room, she found the door open. Amber was alone in her room, sitting cross-legged on the bed, a book in her lap.

"Hi." Eliza leaned on the doorframe. "Where's your roommate?"

"Cleaning the bathroom, I think," Amber said. "It didn't pass inspection the first time, so Rachel is making her do it again."

"Do you mind if I come in?"

Amber sighed and placed the book on the bed beside her. "Nope."

"How are you feeling?"

"Bored." It was an obvious reference to her lack of activity over the past couple of days. She was able to attend class, go to her counseling sessions, and eat, but nothing else. "Oh, I meant to ask you," Amber said, suddenly perking up. "I'm supposed to take marshmallows to the mutual activity next Wednesday night. Can you take me by the store on our way to the church?"

"I'm sorry, Amber," Eliza said, "but your probation includes your Wednesday night Church activities. You'll still attend with me on Sundays, but that's it."

"That's not fair." Her voice was still calm, but it wasn't hard to pick out the angry undertones pulsing through her. "I thought Church activity was supposed to be a part of my therapy."

The last word, *therapy*, was said with obvious distaste and sarcasm. It validated Eliza's earlier observations about Amber's experience at Rockbridge. Simply put, her life was too normal. Attending church every Sunday, meeting with friends on Wednesday nights, spending time with Eliza—so far, Rockbridge had required little sacrifice on Amber's part.

She was doing better than she did at home only because Rockbridge provided so much structure that she had little choice but to follow the rules. But rehabilitation wasn't just about following rules. It was about changing perspectives and helping teenagers see themselves in a different way, a more productive way.

Amber's self-view wasn't changing at all.

She wasn't answering the hard questions. She wasn't changing *herself.*

As her counselor, Eliza was the one to blame for that.

Church was important. Amber needed the fellowship and the opportunities for spiritual growth that Mutual provided, but she seemed to treat it as nothing more than an event on her social calendar. It was time to shift Amber away from those things she recognized as "special treatment." A weekly trip into Rose Creek to hang out with other teenagers was *definitely* special treatment.

"I thought my grandmother insisted I attend church on Sundays and Wednesdays."

"I called your grandmother first thing this morning. She knows what happened, and she supports my decision. Until you can earn back my trust, you will leave campus only on Sunday mornings. Understood?"

Amber slumped onto her pillow and folded her arms tightly across her chest. "Fine," she said coolly. "You know they'll miss me though, right? The leaders, my friends—what about their trust? Won't I be letting them down?"

"I can speak with your youth leaders and make sure they understand."

Amber breathed out a frustrated sigh. "So what about excursion? You're not still sending me into the woods, are you?"

Eliza considered the question. She and Dr. Adler had been discussing it at great length over the past two days. They recognized the risks but had ultimately decided the experience would benefit Amber a great deal. "You're still going on excursion. You'll leave next Thursday."

* * *

At 7:32 that evening, the phone in Eliza's kitchen started to ring. Eliza had missed dinner in the cafeteria that night because of an extended meeting with Dr. Adler, so she'd gone home to fix herself an omelet; otherwise, she might have missed the call. But she never could have prepared herself for the voice she heard on the other end.

"Is this Eliza?" a gruff male voice asked.

"Yes, it is."

"Eliza, this is Bill Harrison. Do you remember me? I'm Henry's . . . I used to be Henry's father."

Chapter 25

"I DON'T UNDERSTAND," HENRY SAID. He shifted his laptop off his knees, placing it on the couch cushion beside him. "Why on earth would he call *you*?"

Eliza sat perched on the edge of the armchair diagonal from Henry, her hands fidgeting nervously in her lap. It was the first time they'd spoken since she'd told him how she felt. He couldn't be certain, but it seemed like she was trying very hard *not* to make eye contact.

"I think he was afraid you wouldn't speak to him, wouldn't listen if he tried to leave you any messages."

"And I guess you talked to him that day, didn't you? Told him your name—that's probably all he needed to find your number."

"He waited for an hour or so to see if you'd come back. He just looked so sad; I felt like I needed to check on him. We only spoke for a few minutes, and he was very kind, apologetic that he might have caused any trouble. He left not long after that."

"Did he"—Henry swallowed hard—"Did he say anything about me?"

"When he called?"

"No. That day, after I left. Did he say anything about me then?"

"He said you look exactly like he'd always pictured you."

Henry took off his glasses and rubbed his eyes. The room around him felt small and warmer than normal. He stood up, agitated, and went into the kitchen. He poured himself a glass of water and gulped it down, then tried to take several slow, deliberate breaths.

"Henry, I didn't tell him anything about you," Eliza said. "I told him you were a good man, but I didn't tell him anything personal."

"You didn't mention AJ?"

"Of course not. That's not my information to share."

Then why did he call?

Henry couldn't imagine any reason why he would want or need to know what William Harrison had told Eliza. He didn't know the man and had no desire to get to know him. What could he have possibly said that would change Henry's mind about that? He looked at Eliza, still sitting awkwardly in the living room, and sighed. "What did he tell you?"

"He's sick," Eliza said.

"Sick? What kind of sick?"

"He didn't give me any specifics, just that he wasn't doing well." She took a breath. "Henry, I think he's dying. He didn't say as much, but the way his voice sounded, it . . . it was like he was trying to clear the air, you know? Like he needed to make some final statement. In the end, he never did say anything. I asked if he wanted me to tell you he called, but he said no. He said it had been a mistake, that you would never want to see him."

"Did he want to come back here? To Rockbridge?"

Eliza shook her head. "He's sick—too sick to travel. I think he wanted to ask you to come to him."

Henry let out a frustrated laugh. "Well, that's not likely to happen."

"Why not?" Though Eliza's voice was small and quiet, the weight of her words settled on Henry like concrete miles thick.

Why not?

Why not?

Why not?

"He's not my father, Eliza. We've had this conversation before. Why would I go see him? What would I even say if I did? 'Gee, thanks, Dad. So happy you had such an easy time giving me away'?"

"Who told you it was easy for him? How do you know that's how he felt? Maybe there's a different story here that you don't know. Maybe that's why he wants you to come see him. Maybe he wants to tell you how he really feels."

"Maybe so." Henry collapsed back onto the couch. "Or maybe he's not really sick at all and he's manipulating the both of us."

"To what end?" Eliza said, the pitch of her voice edging upward. "What would be the purpose of that?"

"I have no idea what the purpose would be, but I know this man spent most of his adult life in prison. I can't trust him just because you thought he seemed kind."

"That's true," Eliza said. "You shouldn't have to trust him." The weight of the words she *wasn't* saying hung heavy between them.

"But you still think I should go see him."

Eliza shrugged. "If it were me, I'd want the closure of knowing what he had to say."

Closure? Henry *had* closure. He was perfectly fine living his life without a single thought for William Harrison. The matter was and always had been closed. It seemed like going to see him would bring the opposite of closure. It would open old wounds and galvanize the hurt Henry had experienced as a child all over again.

Eliza moved from the chair and sat down next to Henry on the couch. "Do your parents have any idea that Bill has contacted you?"

"Bill? He goes by Bill?" Henry asked, momentarily distracted. Eliza nodded. Henry shook his head. "I thought about telling them, but I don't want to upset my mom, you know? This guy is very much a part of her past too—a past I'm pretty sure she's put behind her. I could never expose her to anything that might bring her pain."

"That says a lot about the kind of man you are," Eliza said. "But even though I've never met your mom, I'd venture a guess she'd do anything to keep *you* from feeling pain too. She's the one person who might be able to add a bit of clarity about this man and what his intentions might be."

"I don't know if I can do it." Henry was sure his mom would talk to him. She'd tried in the past, and it was always Henry who had stopped her.

What Henry feared more than anything was that starting down this road would inevitably land him square in the middle of William Harrison's living room, having a conversation he never thought he would need or want to have.

Except, maybe it was a conversation he *did* need to have. That was the most terrifying thought of all.

"Thanks for telling me," Henry said, looking over at Eliza. Reflexively, he reached for her hand. Her skin was warm to his touch, and she looked up, surprise in her eyes. He felt his heart skip. Just as quickly as he had reached for her hand, he dropped it. How many times would he make the same mistake? She wasn't his to touch. She would *never* be his.

He stood. "I, uh, I should . . . I've got some stuff . . . some writing I was meaning to do. You —" He turned and looked at her. "You should probably go."

Eliza kept her eyes down as she walked to the door. With her hand on the knob, she turned and finally looked at him once more. "You can't just keep running away, Henry." And then she was gone.

Somehow, he knew she was talking about more than just William Harrison.

Chapter 26

ELIZA WAS FIDGETY AS SHE and Flip drove up to the parkway on Saturday morning. If she wasn't retying her tennis shoes, she was tugging at the drawstrings of her hoodie or fiddling with her hair. It was stupid, really. If she could just relax, she was sure she would have a good time. She wondered, though, if she even *wanted* to have a good time.

"Are you all right?" Flip glanced over at her.

She forced a smile. "I'm good. Where are we hiking?"

"I thought we'd go to Graveyard Fields. Have you ever been there?"

Eliza shook her head. "That's where you picked those blueberries earlier in the summer, isn't it?"

"Yeah, the blueberries are great in the summertime. There's a nice hike down to this amazing waterfall too, with big boulders everywhere. I figured we'd hike down and eat lunch at the base of the falls."

"Sounds perfect." And it did sound perfect. It shouldn't be hard for her to enjoy herself.

Relax, Eliza. Just try and relax.

"I heard Amber's going on excursion," Flip said. "You think she can handle it?"

"No," Eliza said. "And that's exactly why I think she needs to go. I've been too easy on her, I think. So far, Rockbridge hasn't required enough of a sacrifice. If she could just get away from it all—away from her comfort zone, her friends, away from this boy Dawson . . ."

"Who's Dawson?"

"The Peterson kid at church—tall, with the curly hair."

"Oh, right. I did see them talking last Sunday."

"And that's just it. Rockbridge has such strict rules about things like that, but with her leaving campus every week, I feel like she's treating this more like summer camp, albeit a really strict summer camp, but still. I hope excursion gives her the wake-up call she needs."

Once they started hiking, Eliza nearly forgot she was on an actual date with Flip and fell naturally into the old patterns of their friendship. They laughed and talked and enjoyed the crisp autumn air and sunshine. After lunch, Eliza sighed and leaned back on the smooth surface of the large rock where they spread their picnic.

"How could anyone ever want to live anywhere but here?"

"Every place has its charms," Flip said. "But I agree. I've traveled to a lot of places, but these mountains are the most—" He stopped as if to find the right word.

"Glorious," Eliza said, finishing his sentence for him. "Simply glorious."

"You know, I used to wonder why they called them the Blue Ridge Mountains," he said. "You only have to drive the parkway once on a clear day to figure it out."

Eliza agreed. "I noticed when we were driving up that even with the fall colors looking so bright, the distant mountains, the ones touching the horizon, still look blue."

When Flip didn't say anything in response, Eliza began to grow uneasy.

Flip was only quiet when he was preparing to say something important enough that it wouldn't just roll off his tongue. Her heart quickened. She knew they couldn't keep pretending like they *weren't* on a date. He surely intended to do something, say something that would take things a bit further. As the silence stretched between them, Eliza felt with growing certainty that *this* was the moment. This was the moment she had to decide if she really wanted to be on a date with Flip in the first place. She'd been giving it her very best effort, but if she was honest with herself, she knew her heart wasn't in it. She liked Flip too much to push him away completely but respected him too much to pretend she didn't have reservations about getting more serious.

So where did that leave things?

"So," Flip began. "How long have you been in love with Henry?"

Eliza sat up quickly, her eyes wide with surprise. "I don't . . . Why would . . . ? How did you even . . . ?" She couldn't find the words to form a coherent sentence. Her cheeks burned with embarrassment as she struggled to respond. Flip moved beside her and put his arm reassuringly around her shoulders.

Eliza took a deep breath. "How did you know?"

"I only had my suspicions," Flip said, "but you certainly just confirmed them with that reaction."

"Am I that obvious?"

Flip laughed. "Eliza, you've been avoiding me for weeks, save today. You're trying mighty hard not to look me in the eye, which means you're hoping things don't get too personal. And furthermore, every time I see you and Henry together, you can't stop staring at him. I held on to a glimmer of hope when you agreed to go out with me today, but I'm not a fool. I can tell your heart is somewhere else."

"I don't stare," Eliza said. "I . . . Do I stare?"

Flip laughed again. "I'm sure I only notice because I'm busy staring at you."

Eliza's heart sank. "Flip, I'm so sorry. I haven't meant to hurt you. I just . . . With Henry, it just sort of happened. I didn't try to fall in love with him."

"Oh, don't worry about me," Flip said. "I saw it coming. It's not like I didn't have time to get used to the idea."

"Thank you for understanding. It means a lot."

"Does Henry know?"

Eliza was quiet for a moment. "He knows," she finally said. "I mean, I'm not sure he knows how serious my feelings are, but I pretty much told him that I felt . . . something. He just keeps running away though. I don't know what else to do but assume he doesn't feel the same way."

"This is Henry we're talking about. Perhaps he's running because he *does* feel the same way. I like the man, even more now that we've been going to church together, but his life's not exactly a sunny-day picnic. You, with your red hair and confident smile, you've probably got the man scared out of his wits."

"So now I'm scary? I don't want him to be afraid of me."

"He's not afraid of you," Flip said. "He's afraid of *loving* you."

"He told you as much, huh?" Eliza gave Flip a gentle nudge with her elbow.

"Sure," Flip said. "We had a cozy chat over the fire pit last weekend . . ."

"You did no such thing," Eliza said, her tone light and playful. "Henry would never say anything like that to you."

"True. But that doesn't mean I'm not right." He stood and started gathering the remains of their picnic. "You should talk to him again. Tell him to man up."

Eliza looked at the smooth surface of the rock between her feet. "Maybe," she said. But she knew she never would. The pain she had suffered when he'd rejected her the first time was still fresh in her mind. She wouldn't ever sign up for that again.

Chapter 27

FOR NEARLY A WEEK, HENRY mulled over Eliza's suggestion. His initial reaction was to keep his mother out of it. But she was the only person who could give him any insight into what William Harrison—Bill, as Eliza had called him—was really like.

Henry also wanted to talk to his dad. All this thinking about his biological father left him feeling a little deprived, a little disconnected from his adoptive father, and he found himself feeling an intense desire to reconnect—to make sure the ties that bound the two men were still strongly secured.

Friday afternoon, a week after Eliza told him of Bill's call, he was in the car on his way to Winston-Salem just thirty minutes after his last afternoon class was finished. The momentum of his decision to go carried him all the way to his parents' driveway, where he now sat wondering if he should have called ahead to let his parents know he was on his way.

He could see they were home. His father's truck was parked off to the side of the house, and his mother's sedan sat in the open garage.

Still, he didn't go inside. There was a certain inevitability of going in that kept him glued to his seat, his hands resting on the steering wheel. He sat there staring straight ahead until a loud thump on the driver's side door made him jump. He turned to see the shaggy blonde face of his parents' golden retriever staring at him through the window of his car.

Now he had to go inside. If the dog had found him out, it wouldn't be long before his parents discovered him as well.

"Hello?" Henry called as he opened the front door. "Mom?"

His mother, Julie, appeared in the hallway, a dishcloth in her hands. "Henry! What are you doing here?" She hurried to him, reaching her arms up and around his neck. "What a wonderful surprise!"

"Hi, Mom," Henry said. "It's good to see you."

"Where's AJ?" she asked, finally releasing him from her embrace.

"He's with Allison," Henry said. "I thought I'd come alone this trip."

Henry tried to drive AJ to Winston-Salem two or three times a year to see his grandparents. It wasn't frequent enough, he knew, but it was difficult to get away from Rockbridge, and lately it seemed that more and more of AJ's weekends were filling up with Robert-related activities.

"Is everything all right?"

"Things are fine. Am I really only allowed to come see you if I bring your grandson?"

"Of course not," she said, smiling. "We just like it better when you do."

"Where's Dad?"

"He's out back trying to fix the lawn mower. Go say hello and tell him to come inside. I'm just about to get dinner out of the oven. Did you eat? There's enough here we can share."

She turned to go into the kitchen, then paused and looked back at Henry. "You know, it's funny," she said. "I haven't cooked a pot roast in months. What on earth made me buy one at the store this morning? 'A pot roast,' I said to myself. 'Who cooks a pot roast on a boring old Friday night?' I bought it anyway though, and now here you are to enjoy it with us. Suddenly, a pot roast seems perfectly appropriate."

"Thanks, Mom," Henry said. "Pot roast sounds wonderful."

After dinner, Henry did the dishes. He was slow and deliberate, knowing that as long as the dishes weren't done, he didn't have a reason to join his parents in the den, where he knew they'd want to know what had brought him all the way home.

He'd dodged their questions pretty deftly at dinner, but it wasn't a charade he wanted to keep up. As he dried his mother's heavy roasting pot and returned it to its home next to the stove, he let out a weary sigh. It was time. He walked into the den and turned the large leather chair in the corner so it faced his mother, who was sitting on the couch reading a book.

Julie must have noticed the seriousness of Henry's actions. "Hey, Tom?" she called, closing her book. "Why don't you come into the den? I think Henry needs to talk to us."

When his father finally joined them, Henry took a deep breath and sat down. "Two months ago, Bill Harrison showed up at Rockbridge." He watched his parents stiffen.

"I don't understand," his mom said. "He just showed up? How did he even know that's where you work?"

"My picture is on the website." He kept his eyes down, afraid that if he looked his parents in the eye, they might see he wasn't telling them the entire truth. "A simple Google search probably told him in a matter of minutes where I was working and how exactly to get there."

"Did you speak with him?" Tom asked.

Henry took a deep breath and looked into his hands sitting open on his lap. "Only for a moment," he said. "I was so surprised to see him, so taken aback, I told him I had no desire to see him, and then I fled."

"Oh, Henry," Julie said. "I'm so sorry."

Henry gave his head a slight shake. "You know, I pretended for so long that he didn't exist. I have a father." He looked up at his dad. "I felt no need to make room in my life for this man I don't even really remember. But then I saw him standing there, and I . . . I can't decide if what I felt was just anger or confusion or, I don't know, fear, maybe? But that just makes me mad to think about because I don't want to feel *anything*. This man didn't want me. Why does he deserve even a sliver of consideration from me?"

"Henry, is that what you think? That he just didn't want you?" Julie looked at him, her eyes wet with tears. "It's time for you to let me tell you about Bill Harrison."

Chapter 28

It felt like the perfect time for Eliza to be going out of town. The last excursion group had left the day before, which meant things at Rockbridge felt relatively quiet.

"Who's getting married, again?" Natalie asked. She was standing in the parking lot beside Eliza's car.

"It's my old roommate, Lexie." Eliza loaded the last of her bags into the back of her SUV. "We lived together for a couple of years when I was in Nashville."

"And you'll be back when?"

"I'll leave Tennessee on Tuesday, just after lunch. I should be home by five or six."

"Don't hurry. We'll be fine until you get back."

"Thanks, Nat. And you have my cell number, right? You'll call me if anything happens?"

"Nothing is going to happen. But yes. I'll call you."

Two hours later, Eliza was out of North Carolina and driving across the eastern portion of Tennessee. She was excited to see Lexie and was looking forward to spending Monday and Tuesday with her mom.

Eliza had received an e-mail from Gina earlier in the week. She would call on Sunday afternoon when Eliza and Beverly were together. Eliza was excited to talk with her, to hear her voice. The updates she'd been getting from Gina's therapy team were encouraging; she was making wonderful progress, had even started painting again. Eliza hoped it wasn't too good to be true.

Lexie was waiting in the lobby of the hotel when Eliza arrived.

"What are you doing here?" Eliza gave her friend a hug. "Aren't you busy?"

"Are you kidding?" Lexie said. "My mother isn't letting me lift a finger. She and the wedding planner have handled everything. I practically begged to come meet you just so I could feel useful."

"And you're okay with that? With your mom running the show?"

"Better her than me," Lexie said. "Wedding stress gives me hives."

Eliza laughed. A bride willing to surrender her wedding plans to her mother? Lexie might be the first in history.

Lexie picked up one of Eliza's bags and slung it over her shoulder. "Come on," she said. "Your room is just down the hall from mine."

Eliza had hesitated when Lexie had told her the entire bridal party was staying at the hotel in downtown Nashville, where the reception would be held. Her mom lived just a few minutes outside the city. Why spend money on a hotel room she didn't really need? But Lexie—or Lexie's mom, Eliza now realized—was persistent. Everything would be easier if everyone was staying together, and Eliza wasn't expected to pay for her room. When Eliza saw the posh suite she'd be enjoying for the weekend, she was glad she'd finally caved and agreed to the plan.

"It's nice, huh?" Lexie motioned to the room around her. "I've got to admit Mom really knows how to do this kind of stuff right."

Eliza kicked off her shoes and climbed onto the bed. "Yeah, I could get used to this."

"Of course, everything must feel luxurious after coming from the great outdoors."

"I don't work in the great outdoors," Eliza said. "I work in a perfectly comfortable air-conditioned office."

"That just happens to *be* in the middle of nowhere, *in* the great outdoors."

Eliza laughed. "I really love it. It's everything I thought it would be and more."

"You sound like you belong on a travel brochure."

"I mean it though," Eliza said. "I really do love it. I love my work. Being with these teenagers. It's the most challenging, rewarding thing I've ever done."

"Your work completely inspires me," Lexie said. "You know I mean that. Now spill the real goods. I need an update on the English teacher."

Eliza sighed. "Who, Henry? He's good, I guess."

"How are the two of you? Just friends?"

"Yeah," Eliza said softly. "Just friends."

"Well, all the better," Lexie said. "Jason has seven thousand old mission companions coming to the wedding. I'm sure a few still have to be single."

"Jason's mission companions are probably all four, maybe even five years younger than me. He's only been home, what, eight, nine months?"

"A little longer than that," Lexie said. "But still. Age hardly matters anymore. You're going to look fabulous in your bridesmaid dress. You'll turn heads everywhere you go."

"I don't know about that," Eliza said.

"Trust me," Lexie said. "You'll be amazing."

"Isn't that the kind of thing I'm supposed to say to *you*?"

"Maybe, but your heart is broken, and I'm worried about you. I just want you to have a good time this weekend."

"Lexie, you're too good to me—too good in general. I'll be fine this weekend, and *you* are going to be amazing."

Lexie's mother had wedding festivities scheduled back to back for the entire weekend. Through it all, Lexie was gracious and kind, making an extra effort to ensure Eliza was having a good time. Eliza appreciated her friend's efforts, particularly through a weekend that was supposed to be all about Lexie. But Eliza was also happy to leave the busyness of the wedding behind. When she pulled into her mother's driveway on Sunday evening, she was looking forward to a quiet couple of days with her mom.

She took her time pulling her suitcase out of the back of her SUV and walked slowly to the porch. The door was unlocked, so she let herself in. "Hello?" she called. "I'm here! Where are you?"

Her mother came blustering around the corner, wearing a painting smock and holding paint brushes in both hands.

"Eliza, I'm so glad you're here! Come on. Gina just called. I've got the phone on speaker."

"Mom, wait. How is she?" Eliza asked.

Her mother turned around and smiled. "Eliza, she's wonderful. I feel like I'm getting to know her for the first time. She sounds so . . . so alive."

Eliza hugged her mom, ignoring the fact that she was likely getting paint all over her clothes. "I'm so glad, Mom."

The call with Gina was strained at first. Eliza tried to be supportive, asking Gina questions about how she was faring. What was she doing to stay busy? Was she attending group therapy? Was she allowed to leave Hazelwood's campus? After ten minutes of rather uncomfortable conversation, Beverly asked Gina to hold on and pulled Eliza into the kitchen.

"You have got to stop this," her mother said.

"Stop what?" Eliza wrinkled her eyebrows at her mom, her arms crossing her chest.

"Stop treating your sister like she's your patient. What's with all the questions? She's doing great. I told you that. Why don't you try and talk to her like a sister? Like someone who isn't a mental-health professional doing a follow-up interview?"

Eliza sighed, forcing the tension out of her shoulders. "You're right, Mom. I'm sorry."

"Don't apologize to me. Just go back in there and *be* her sister."

It was a novel idea. And yet Eliza wasn't sure how. She'd never really *been* Gina's sister, save their earliest years of childhood. It seemed odd to try to start now.

"Eliza, she wants so much to have your approval. I know you're only asking questions because you care; just take it easy on her. Maybe ask her something not rehab related? There are times to be tough and times to be nice. You were tough when the situation required it, but now? She just needs nice."

"How do I ask her something not related to rehab? She's *in* rehab. What else does she know?"

"But your questions sound so clinical. Ask her about her friends, the view from her window—anything!"

When they went back into the other room, Eliza asked Gina to tell her about the friends she'd made. The longer they talked, the easier it became. After a small pause in the conversation, Gina said, "I'm supposed to tell you how much I appreciate what you did. I mean, I'm supposed to tell you as a part of my therapy, but I also want to tell you because I really mean it. Three months ago," she continued, "I was in a really dark place. I'm not sure I would have gotten out if you hadn't been willing to fight for me. So . . . thanks."

Eliza took a deep breath. "You're welcome."

"And also," Gina said, "I don't want you to feel like you have to look out for me anymore. I mean, I've got this. I'm not going back to where I was."

"I'm your sister, Gina," Eliza said. "How am I supposed to stop looking out for you?"

"Look out for me because we're sisters and that's what sisters do. But you don't have to worry anymore. Not like you did before."

It was incredible how different Gina sounded. She really *was* a different person. But to stop worrying? Eliza had been worrying for so long that it had become a defining part of who she was. Gina was a big part of why she'd gone into counseling in the first place, because she'd felt such a strong need to try to help people.

But maybe sometimes it was okay to let go. Maybe sometimes people had to make the hardest choices on their own.

* * *

The next morning, Eliza's cell phone rang just after 7:00 a.m. She was still sleeping—a perk of being away from Rockbridge—and the phone startled her awake.

"Hello?" she said groggily.

"Eliza, it's Natalie. Something's happened. I think you might need to come back."

Eliza sat up in bed, her pounding heart forcing her wide awake. "What happened? Is everyone all right?"

"I'm afraid not," Natalie said. "It's Amber. She's missing."

Chapter 29

HENRY LEANED BACK IN HIS chair and covered his face with his hands. "I don't know if I can," he said. "I don't know if I *want* you to tell me about Bill Harrison."

To listen to his mom would require a deconstruction of the wall Henry chose to live behind. It was safer to blame his biological father—safer to assume he was the one in the wrong, to believe he deserved to be despised. What if the things Henry had been telling himself his entire life weren't true?

"Of course you can," Julie said. "That's why you're here, isn't it?"

"I guess so," Henry said quietly.

Tom rose from the couch. "I'm going to give the two of you a little privacy." He leaned down and kissed his wife on the forehead.

"Dad, wait. You don't have to go."

His father shook his head. "It's fine. This is a story I know well enough to know it's easier for your mom to tell without me here." He walked past Henry, then turned back. "Henry, I want you to remember something. No matter what happens—whether you see Bill again or not—you are my son. I made a promise to God to love you as my own, and that's what I've done. This man? He doesn't change that, doesn't change the commitment I have to you. Do you understand?"

Henry stood and, in a rare display of affection, wrapped his arms around his father. "Thanks, Dad," he said.

He moved to the couch and sat beside his mom. She reached for his hand and held it gently between her own.

"Your father . . . your *biological* father," she amended, "wasn't a terrible person. He was misguided and confused and had terrible impulse control, but he wasn't an evil person, if that makes sense. We met when I was just seventeen and he was twenty-one. I was young and foolish, and he was . . . an adventure." She stifled a laugh. "It about killed your grandparents when I started spending so much time with him. They begged and pleaded for me to stop, but I was so foolish, Henry. I thought I was good enough and smart enough to be good, even if I chose to keep bad company. That's not to say Bill didn't try. He told me he would clean up his life for me, and for a while, just before you were born, he did. But I should have known it would never stick."

She hesitated for a moment as if trying to decide what to say next. "Henry, I was six months pregnant with you when Bill and I got married. When your grandfather found out about the pregnancy, he told Bill he had two choices. He could get his act together and marry me, or he could disappear for good."

"So he married you," Henry said. "He married you because of me."

She nodded her head. "I think he knew it was the right thing to do. But it was no good. He tried, but he simply couldn't shake off his old life. I look back now and try to figure out what he was so afraid of, why he was so restless all the time." She shrugged her shoulders. "It's no matter now. We limped along through life for a couple of years until just before your second birthday. That's when things went from bad to worse. Bill started drinking, started staying out later at night, started spending all of his free time with his friends."

"Mom, wait," Henry said. He wasn't sure he wanted to hear the rest of the story—not until one thing was perfectly clear. "Before you go on, please just answer one question. Did he . . . Did he ever hit you?"

"Not once." She answered without pause. "He wasn't a violent man. He was foolish and impulsive and stupid, but he never would have hurt me or you. That kind of malice just wasn't in him."

Henry took a deep breath. It was the thing he had feared more than anything. If this man had done anything to hurt his mom, it might be more than he could forgive.

"One night," his mom continued, "Bill was at a bar with his friends. He was drunk—drunk enough that when his friends dared him to steal a car from the parking lot, he did just that. Just a mile from the bar, he turned into a residential neighborhood. From what the police told me, he lost control of the car and careened over the sidewalk and into a yard where a woman was standing with her dog. The dog was killed instantly and the woman nearly so. She survived but was paralyzed from the waist down as a result of the accident."

"And that's what landed him in prison," Henry said.

His mother nodded. "The first time, anyway. A year or so after that, we divorced, and three months later, I met Tom."

Henry sat quietly trying to process his mother's confession. It wasn't as dreadful as he had imagined. True, Bill Harrison had made some stupid, careless decisions, but he wasn't a monster.

"Henry, Bill didn't give you up because he didn't want to be your father. He gave you up because he knew he couldn't be. I'd met someone else, was moving on with my life, and I think he wanted you to be able to move on with me. He knew it was the best thing for you—that Tom would be a much better father than he could ever be. We decided when he signed the papers and relinquished his rights as your father that it would be better for everyone involved if it was a clean break, if he didn't see you at all. I guess looking back I realize breaks like that are never really clean after all."

"I look just like him," Henry said quietly.

His mother smiled. "You do. You're a little taller, but there is a very strong resemblance, to be sure."

"Is it . . . hard for you to look at me? I mean, to see me without thinking of him?"

"It's never hard to look at you. I certainly have regrets about some of the decisions I made in the past, and not all of my memories regarding Bill are happy, but I still wouldn't change anything. Those years gave me you. How could I want to change a single thing about that?"

Henry felt a peace settle over him that was unlike anything he had ever experienced. All his life he had been living with a cloud of darkness in the corner of his heart. It wasn't big enough to fill him—to keep him from experiencing joy and happiness in other parts of his life—but it was always there, always lurking in the corner, threatening to overshadow the light. Henry didn't realize how oppressive that cloud had been until it was gone. He took a deep breath and reached over to hug his mom.

"I'm sorry I didn't let you tell me all of this sooner."

"You had to be ready," Julie said. "I knew you'd let me know when it was time."

"So, Bill called the school again last week," Henry said.

"Did you speak to him?"

Henry shook his head. "He called my friend Eliza. He didn't think I would want to speak with him. He's sick, Mom. Eliza thinks he might be dying."

"Does he want to see you?" she asked.

"He stopped short of saying as much, but Eliza said that's what it sounded like to her."

"Are you going to go?"

He looked at his mom and shook his head with a sigh. "I don't know. I have to think about AJ too. This guy's been in and out of prison his entire life. I don't know anything about him, if I can trust him. What do you think I should do?"

"It's a decision only you can make, Henry. Just ask yourself what you think you might regret the most. It's certainly possible you'll regret it if you go and it isn't what you expect. But it's also possible you'll regret not going even more."

* * *

Later that night, Henry joined his father on the back deck. They sat in companionable silence for several minutes.

"Did Mom tell you Bill's sick?" Henry finally asked.

"Hmm," his father murmured. "Have you decided what to do?"

"Not yet." After a few more minutes of silence, he asked, "Dad? What would you do?"

His father kept his eyes on the yard and scratched his chin, looking thoughtful. "Well, I don't know what else Bill has been up to the past thirty years, but if he's been in and out of prison like you said, it's probably safe to bet it isn't much. I expect you're probably the best thing that man ever did. If he is dying, it might not be such a bad thing for him to lay eyes on you one more time before he goes."

"I'm having a hard time convincing myself that he deserves even that much," Henry said. "I mean, for so long, he's been the bad guy; he's been the man I've blamed for not wanting me, for not caring about me. How do I rewrite twenty-five years of feeling that way in one afternoon?"

"Forgiveness is a choice, son. You have to carry around the burden of blame only as long as it takes you to give it over to the Lord. Go see the man. The best thing you can give him on his way out of this world is your forgiveness."

Chapter 30

ELIZA PULLED INTO THE PARKING lot at Rockbridge but was unable to make it to her usual spot. The sheriff's department had a staging area set up on the west side of the lot, where search teams were being coordinated and deployed. Eliza found a spot off to the side and got out of the car. Her movements were slow and deliberate, her only defense against the panic rising in her throat, threatening to overtake her altogether.

As she walked over to the staging area, Eliza watched what looked to be the first wave of search teams arriving back, exhausted and disheartened by their lack of progress.

Excursion sites were remote. They were accessible only by foot and were generally ten to twelve miles into the forest, away from Rockbridge. It meant that anyone who was searching was walking quite some distance to do so.

Eliza heard a helicopter flying overhead and looked up. Of course. They would be searching for her by air as well. A wave of nausea overcame her, nearly sending her to her knees. Amber was out there somewhere, alone in a sea of mountains and valleys that continued for miles and miles. She could easily wander for days without finding another soul. Eliza took slow, deep breaths and willed the uneasiness to pass. They simply had to find her. Eliza couldn't bear to imagine what it would mean if they didn't.

"Eliza!"

Eliza turned to see Dr. Adler, who was striding purposefully across the parking lot.

"I'm sorry you had to cut your trip short," she said.

"No, no, it doesn't matter. Is there anything new that I should know?"

During the drive, Eliza had spoken with Natalie and learned the basics of what was known about Amber's disappearance. She'd gone to bed with everyone else but had disappeared from camp sometime in the middle of the night.

"We don't know anything more," Dr. Adler said. "They haven't found any clues indicating which direction she might have gone, so we're pretty much searching blind. I want you to think about the things Amber has told you. Is there somewhere she's trying to go? Is there something she's trying to tell us? If we can understand her motive, it might help us find her sooner. Can you think of anything significant?"

Eliza tried to think. "I . . . I don't know. She was never excited about excursion. She was worried about the food, about having to walk so far. I don't know why she would have left on her own."

"What about her friends from church? Is this something she could have arranged with them?"

Eliza shook her head. "That doesn't make sense. She hasn't seen or spoken with them since Rebecca's overdose. And before that, she didn't know she was going on excursion. But wait . . . at the church . . . there is a dance this weekend. It's been planned for so long that I know she knew about it. She even told me she wanted to go. Maybe she's trying to get to Rose Creek?"

"Rose Creek is a long walk from where she was camped," Dr. Adler said. "Of course, she's obviously not using the best judgment or she wouldn't have left camp in the first place. Maybe she thinks if she can get to the parkway, or to a forest service road, someone will stop and pick her up."

"Dr. Adler, we have to find her. What if we don't find her?" Eliza felt the panic creeping into her voice.

"Stop," Dr. Adler said. "We cannot afford to fall apart. I've notified Amber's family about what's happened. Her grandmother should be here in the next hour, and her parents are arriving sometime tomorrow. When they arrive, I want you to stay with them, make sure they are comfortable and cared for and have everything they need."

Eliza nodded her head. "I understand."

"In the meantime, start making phone calls. Call her friends from church. Do any of them know anything? Be sure to tell them that if they hear a single word from her, they are to call you immediately."

"Of course," Eliza said. It made sense, what Dr. Adler was asking her to do. But the thought of sitting idly by at Rockbridge when she could be out searching the woods made Eliza want to scream.

Dr. Adler must have sensed her discomfort. "Eliza, the people searching know what they're doing. Frank and Flip are both out there. They *know* these woods. If anyone can find her, they will."

Eliza nodded and used the back of her hand to wipe away the tears spilling onto her cheeks. She wanted to believe Dr. Adler, but it wasn't hard to see the doubt that clouded the older woman's eyes.

"Did she take anything with her? Any food? Water? Does she even have a coat?"

"She took a day pack with her," Dr. Adler said. "A couple of water bottles and a handful of granola bars were missing, but that's it."

Eliza shook her head. How was one teenage girl with a few meager supplies and some extra water bottles going to survive on her own?

Eliza couldn't help but feel guilty. Clearly, she'd made a massive error in judgment in sending Amber on excursion. Why would Amber ever risk venturing into the woods on her own? For a dance? For a boy?

Eliza suddenly felt desperate to be alone. She hurried to her apartment and shut the door firmly behind her. In her living room, she dropped to her knees beside her couch and, through her tears, offered a pleading prayer to her Father in Heaven. "Just let them find her," she prayed. "Please keep her safe until they do."

* * *

Forty-eight hours later, there was still no sign of Amber. Eliza had called everyone she could possibly think of that might have had information, but no one knew anything at all.

Even Dawson had sounded innocent enough. He insisted they hadn't made any official plans, and he never would have supported or encouraged her running away from Rockbridge. Amber's grandmother and parents were now on campus, watching the activities of the search with fear and trepidation. When dusk fell on the second day and the search parties had started to trickle back in, Eliza's heart sank lower than it ever had before. When Flip emerged from the woods, weary and worn, it was more than Eliza could bear.

She reminded herself that Dr. Adler had been in favor of Amber's excursion trip, had supported Eliza's suggestion from the start. But Eliza couldn't shake the feeling that if she had handled Amber's counseling better, they would never have wound up in such difficult circumstances.

Eliza should have been more in tune. She should have understood what Amber really needed. The guilt Eliza felt was eclipsed only by the thought of Amber being out there somewhere, cold, hungry, and completely ill-equipped to take care of herself.

And it's my fault, Eliza thought to herself. *Amber could be* dead, *and it's all my fault.*

* * *

Eliza wasn't sure if he would want to hear from her. But through the turmoil of the past forty-eight hours, she'd longed for Henry's steadying presence. She needed him to look in her eyes and tell her everything was going to be okay. Somehow, it felt like if he said it, she'd have to believe it was true.

Wherever he was, Henry wasn't answering his phone. It took three tries for Eliza to find the courage to leave him a voice mail. "Henry? It's Eliza. I know you're out of town, but I wish you were here. There's something going on. Amber has run away, and I just . . . I don't know. I think my head works better when you're around. I miss you, Henry. I hope you're coming home soon. Please . . . come home."

Chapter 31

HENRY PULLED HIS CAR INTO a gas station just three miles away from Bill Harrison's home. It was an unusually warm afternoon for the fall, warmer than the mountains, especially, and Henry found himself uncomfortably hot.

He was annoyed when he realized the catch on the gas pump that held the nozzle trigger in place was missing, leaving him with no option but to stand in the heat, feeling the sweat bead up on the bridge of his nose.

Wiping the wetness away with his free hand, he stood and stared at his reflection in the window of his car. He tried to conjure up the aged face of his biological father—remember the details etched in his memory from their brief encounter at Rockbridge earlier in the summer. If he tilted his head just right and wrinkled his forehead, he could see him in his own face in the window.

The gas pump clicked, and Henry sighed. There was nothing to hold him back now. He was out of excuses, out of reasons to stay away from Bill Harrison. But that didn't make it any easier to get back in his car and drive the short distance left between them.

By the time he pulled down the gravel drive, with the GPS on his phone confirming he had arrived at his destination, his heart was beating so quickly he had to take several slow, deep breaths before even feeling comfortable enough to get out of the car. He said a quick, silent prayer, then sat for a moment staring at the small house in front of him.

The house was green stucco with a terra-cotta tile roof and cement-slab front porch. Landscaping was almost nonexistent. The lawn was mostly dirt. A few straggling patches of grass clung to life here and there, and a row of meager shrubs hugged the exterior wall of the house.

The only spot of brilliance in the otherwise drab surroundings was a vibrant oak tree, its leaves flaming red, standing in the far corner of the yard. The sun shone brightly on the tree, creating the impression that it was light itself, glowing with its own source of brilliance and warmth.

Henry closed his eyes. The beauty of the tree felt like a gift from God—a reminder that someone far greater than Henry was in control. With renewed vigor and a calm heart, Henry got out of his car and walked to the front door of the little house. Before he lost his nerve, he raised his fist and knocked three times, sharp and quick. Immediately, his heart started racing again. He was surprised when it wasn't Bill Harrison who opened the door but an elderly woman instead.

"Hello?"

Henry cleared his throat. "Hi, I, um, was looking for William Harrison— uh, I mean, Bill. Is he home?"

The woman was quiet for a moment, her gaze resting purposefully on Henry's face. "Henry?" she said softly.

"Yes, ma'am. I'm Henry Jacobson."

He offered his hand, and she took it, limply, then turned and glanced over her shoulder. "You better come inside."

Henry followed her into the living room, sparsely furnished but clean and well kept.

"I'm Bill's sister, Stella. Can I offer you something to drink? Tea? Water?"

"No, I'm fine," Henry said. "Thank you."

"Are you sure? Maybe just a glass of water?"

Henry sensed a growing feeling of unease in the woman. She stood in front of the couch, looking almost longingly at the kitchen. It felt as if she were looking for a way to escape.

"I'm really fine," Henry said again. "Is everything all right?"

The woman sighed and sat down directly across from the couch, where she motioned for Henry to sit.

"There's quite a resemblance," she said. "You've got the look of him, that's for sure."

Henry nodded. "I realized as much when he came to Rockbridge— that's the school where I work—a few months back. I'm afraid I wasn't in a state of mind to speak to him properly then."

The woman's face was passive, her eyes cast down. "He told me," she said. "He didn't blame you though. Said he never should have surprised you like that."

"I was surprised," Henry said. "But I shouldn't have been rude."

Stella leaned back in her chair and grasped her hands in her lap. Henry could tell she was preparing to speak and wondered if her words would bring clarity or perhaps more confusion to the oddity their interaction was turning out to be.

"I always told Bill he shoulda looked you up sooner," she said. "But he'd have nothing of it. He said it was your life and you deserved to be happy without having him meddle in your affairs. I told him he was your daddy, had every right to call you up and ask you how the day was, but he wouldn't hear it. Then one day, somebody called the house—" She paused and raised her eyebrows in question. "It was you, wasn't it?"

Henry only nodded.

"Well, that phone call got him all worked up, said he knew in his gut it was you trying to call. So he went down to the library and had the woman at the research desk look up that school of yours, the name he'd seen on the caller ID. Sure enough, there you were." She shifted in her seat and, with her lips pursed, looked at Henry pointedly. "If I could be so bold," she said, "why did you call if you didn't have anything but rudeness for him in your heart? He only came to see you because he believed you had tried to call."

"I was scared," Henry said simply. "I called because I was curious, but then I got scared." Somehow, it felt easier being honest with a stranger.

His answer seemed to satisfy her enough that she continued with her story. "Well, after he came home," she said, "things just went from bad to worse."

Henry's unease heightened. "I'm not sure I understand."

Stella's lips tightened into a thin line across her face. "Bill knew he was sick, see? But it was like he suddenly stopped caring, stopped fighting after he went to see you."

"I still don't understand," Henry said. "Did Bill . . . Is he . . . ?"

"You came too late. Bill died last Thursday."

The words settled over Henry like bits of broken glass. He certainly hadn't been looking forward to a reunion with his biological father, but he never would have chosen for it to end this way. This was awful—like severing a limb and, instead of stitching up the wound, leaving it open, gaping, a mess of raw flesh and blood.

"Was . . . ?" Henry's voice cracked, and he cleared his throat, starting again. "Was there a service?"

"Just a small one down at the funeral home," Stella said. "He wouldn't have wanted much fanfare."

"I wish you had called me about the service," Henry said, his voice now more controlled. "I would have liked to attend."

"Well, I guess you missed your chance, son." Stella didn't try to hide the contempt in her voice. It was clear she held Henry responsible for her brother's untimely demise.

"All my life," Henry said, speaking more to the floor than to the woman who sat across the room. "All my life I believed he didn't want me. I remember the look on his face when he signed those papers, when he . . . I just . . ." He didn't know how to finish. How could he express in words what he didn't understand? He felt angry and disappointed, confused and overwhelmed, but mostly he just felt sorry—sorry that he'd missed speaking to his father, sorry that it was his own anger that had kept him from doing so.

"I'm sorry I was late," he said. "I'm so sorry I didn't get the chance to speak with him." Henry felt a catch at the back of his throat—a sob he had no desire to release in the presence of . . . his aunt? She certainly wasn't treating him as someone she regarded as family. He cleared his throat and stood.

"I guess I should get going," he said. "It was kind of you to let me in. And I am sorry, truly sorry that you've lost your brother."

He didn't wait for her to get up. He hurried across the room and pulled the door open. He suddenly felt desperate to escape, to be far away from the wretched living room, from the contemptible woman who blamed him for the death of a man he didn't even know, from the hot, boiling anger raging inside him. Once inside his car, the last shred of Henry's reserve crumbled away, and for the first time in more years than he could account for, he allowed himself to cry for the man he had never known as his father.

Several minutes later, he sat with his hands resting on the steering wheel, his head leaning forward on his hands. The sun was heavy, hanging low in the sky, and was no longer visible from where Henry sat. As a result, the house and yard were cast in dreary shadow. Crying had felt rather cathartic, and Henry found himself in a sort of peaceful stupor. He was startled when he heard a soft tap on the driver's side window. He looked up and saw Stella standing beside the car, a small box in her hands. He sniffed and wiped his eyes with the back of his hand, then rolled down the window.

"Sorry," Henry said. "You probably thought I'd left."

"It's not that he didn't want you," Stella said. Her voice was still distant, but it no longer had the edge that had dominated their previous conversation. "He just wanted what was best for you. He wanted you to have a life he knew he couldn't give you."

Henry nodded. "I understand that now."

"Here." Stella handed him the box she was holding in her hand. "It isn't much, just whatever made it into the newspaper. Even when he was locked up, he had me keep an eye on the papers in case you ever showed up."

Henry opened the box and found a handful of newspaper clippings—a picture of his state championship Little League team, his graduation picture announcing him as a Morehead scholar finalist, his wedding announcement with Allison.

"I just thought you might like to have them," Stella said.

"Thank you." Henry placed the clippings back in the box. "I appreciate your giving them to me."

Without another word, Stella turned and headed back toward the house. But then she hesitated and walked back to Henry's window.

"Are you all right?" she asked.

Henry nodded. "I think I'm going to be just fine." Only this time, he actually believed it.

* * *

Back at his parents' home, Henry was grateful that his mother and father were out for the evening. He was still trying to make sense of his afternoon and wanted, even needed to be alone for a while. He sat on the back porch swing, his feet propped on the small wicker table in front of him, and stared into the darkness of his parents' backyard.

Across the lawn, a family was having a party, the privacy fence between the yards not enough to keep the happy noises from drifting over to where Henry sat. The bursts of laughter and upbeat music somehow brought Henry comfort, as if to remind him that happiness was always within reach.

The funny thing was that Henry knew what Stella had told him was true. His adoption really had been the very best thing that could have happened. Why, then, had he allowed himself to carry his anger through life like a millstone hung about his neck?

A moment of clarity buzzed through him like a jolt of electricity. Anger was easier. He was angry because if it wasn't his father's fault for leaving him, then it was his. And that was what he'd been afraid of all his life—that he wasn't good enough, that the people who got close to him would all decide he wasn't worth sticking around for.

It was what his father had decided. It was what Allison had decided. And if he let Eliza get too close, it was what she would eventually decide too.

And yet the contents of the little box tossed on the seat beside him indicated otherwise. He flipped through the newspaper articles one more time. Henry would never have the opportunity to know Bill Harrison. But it wasn't too late for him to forgive and move past the bitterness that had always accompanied the man's name.

In the peaceful dark of his parents' porch, Henry slipped quietly off the swing and lowered himself to his knees. With the neighbors partying cheerfully in the background, Henry offered a prayer of marked sincerity.

Into Jesus's waiting arms, he turned over the anger and crippling fear he'd been hiding behind for so many years. He turned over the animosity he felt toward Allison. He pleaded with the Lord to help him bridge the distance keeping him from AJ. And then he thought of Eliza. He smiled inwardly as he realized how desperately he'd been trying to run from her, to keep her out of his heart.

But Eliza was a force of nature. There *was* no stopping her.

Henry opened his eyes. "I'm in love with Eliza," he said out loud. He threw his head back and laughed. Standing up, he ran into the yard and just short of the fence that kept him from the party guests on the other side, he cupped his hands around his mouth and yelled, "Hey! I'm in love with Eliza!"

The noise of the party was too loud for anyone to have noticed, but Henry didn't care. He felt himself a new man. He was lighter, happier than he had been in years. Realizing he'd never concluded his prayer, he looked heavenward. As he gazed at the stars, he talked to his Father in Heaven once more. *Help me be worthy of her*, he prayed. *And if you could manage it, perhaps you could help her love me too.*

* * *

The next morning, after an early breakfast with his parents, Henry left for Rockbridge. He missed AJ and wanted to see him. And, of course, he wanted to find Eliza. Or did he? In the brightness of morning light, it seemed a little more difficult for him to so readily admit his feelings. What if she didn't feel the same way? What if he'd waited too long and she'd fallen in love with Flip? The questions kept swirling as he pulled onto the interstate that would take him back into the mountains.

Remembering that his cell phone had died the night before, he pulled it out of his pocket and plugged it into the car charger. He hoped there weren't any messages from Rockbridge. His fellow faculty had been gracious when it had come to filling in for him in spite of his hasty departure. He hoped they hadn't had any trouble in his absence. To his relief, there were no messages from anyone, except Eliza. He listened to her message once, and then again and again.

He couldn't close the distance between them fast enough.

Chapter 32

FLIP STOOD ON THE CREST of the ridge, his arms folded resolutely across his chest.

"Flip, there's no way she would have headed down that ravine," Frank Adler said. After two days of searching, both men were beginning to feel a little tense. Flip knew that time was running out. Amber would have had a small amount of food with her, and water was easy enough to find in the forest, but what little she'd taken wouldn't have lasted her this long.

As they looked down the steeply declining slope of the mountain, Flip was having a hard time convincing Frank it was the way they should go to continue their search.

"She would have looked for the easier way," Frank continued.

"I'm not so sure," Flip said. "I've just got a feeling, Frank. I think I have to ask you to trust me on this one."

Frank was quiet for a moment. He ran his fingers through his graying hair and stared at Flip, his eyebrows raised. "Okay," he finally said. "Lead the way, then."

Together, they descended the ravine one treacherous step at a time. When they reached the bottom, they moved a short distance apart and started walking through the dense undergrowth of the forest. Like this, rather than walking side by side, they had a better shot of catching any clues that would lead them to Amber's whereabouts.

An hour later, Flip was beginning to question his intuition. The terrain was awful—thick and tangled and steep. If it was difficult walking for the two of them, it seemed near impossible for someone with Amber's inexperience to have made it through. Flip cast his eyes upward. "God, help me," he said softly. "Help me find her."

"Flip, I think we need to change our direction," Frank called. "This is getting too rough."

Flip stopped and looked over at Frank. He didn't want to admit he might have led them astray, but Frank was likely right. He waited while Frank made his way over to where he stood.

Stay on course.

Flip heard the voice as clearly as he'd heard Frank call out to him just moments before. Though he'd never experienced a prompting of the Spirit with such crystal clarity, he didn't doubt this one for even a moment. The peace and assurance that washed over him was confirmation enough. God knew where Amber was, and Flip was close. He knew they had to be close.

"No."

"No, what?" Frank asked.

"Forgive my being bold, but we can't change course. She's close by. I know she is."

"You can't know that."

"No, but God can, and He's the one I'm listening to."

Ten minutes later, they found her. She was curled into a ball, leaning against the base of a tree, and appeared to be asleep. She was dirty and a little pale but otherwise looked to be unharmed. Flip knelt beside her.

"Amber? Amber, can you hear me?"

Her eyes fluttered open, and she tried to push herself up to a sitting position.

"She needs water," Frank said. He passed a canteen over Flip's shoulder. He took it and held it to Amber's lips.

"Here, drink this," he said.

Amber took the water and drank. She still hadn't spoken and had a dazed, frightened look about her.

"Amber, look at me," Flip said. "We've found you. We're going to get you out of here. Do you understand?"

Amber looked into his eyes for several seconds before nodding her head and bursting into tears. A few yards behind Flip, Frank was on the radio, communicating their location to the sheriff's department. After a moment, Amber reached for Flip's arm.

"My ankle." Her voice was cracked and quiet, almost a whisper. She pulled at the leg of her pants, sliding it up above the top of her hiking boot. The boot was still on her foot, but the laces were loose enough it was easy for Flip to see the mottled blue-and-green bruises extending up her leg.

"When did this happen?" Flip asked gently.

"I don't know," Amber said. "Yesterday, I think."

"Did you walk on it at all?"

"I tried, but I couldn't . . ."

"Frank," Flip said, "I think her ankle is broken."

Frank nodded in acknowledgment. A moment later, he walked back to where Flip still knelt beside Amber.

"Two miles north, there's a clearing large enough for them to land a helicopter. If we can get there, they'll be able to get us out."

"All of us?" Flip asked.

"They said there would be room. We'll fly straight to the hospital in Rose Creek. Amber needs a doctor."

"Let's move out, then," Flip said.

* * *

Henry moved through the chairs in the hospital waiting room to where Flip sat in the corner. Flip looked exhausted—his legs were stretched in front of him, and his head was leaned against the wall. His eyes were closed, but Henry couldn't imagine he was actually asleep in such an uncomfortable position.

"Hey, Flip."

Flip opened his eyes and sat up. "Hello, Henry. You've missed all the excitement."

"I just got back in town. They said you found her?"

"Who's they?" Flip asked.

"I called the school. Is Amber all right?"

"She's got a broken ankle, and she's dehydrated, but other than that, she's doing fine."

Henry was glad to hear that Amber was faring so well. He'd worried about her and was relieved to know she'd been found safe and whole, but he'd also agonized over the anguish her disappearance must have caused Eliza. He hesitated to ask what he *really* wanted to know, but only for a moment. He'd wasted too much time letting fear dictate his decisions. "How's Eliza?"

"I don't rightly know," Flip said. "I came to the hospital in the helicopter and haven't seen her. My guess is she's on her way down the mountain right now. Have you not been up to Rockbridge at all, then?"

"I *just* got back," Henry said. "I came here first, thinking she . . ." He didn't finish his sentence, but it didn't seem to matter. A shadow of understanding passed across Flip's face. He knew exactly whom Henry had come to the hospital hoping to see.

"So, Henry," Flip said, "seeing as how I've been scouring the woods for three days and I'm tired, hungry, and desperate for a bath, what do you say you give me a lift back up to the school?"

In any other circumstance, Henry wouldn't have hesitated to say yes. Flip, more than anyone, deserved a ride home after all he'd done the past few days. But if Henry took Flip home, he'd likely miss Eliza. Still, it would give him the opportunity to talk with Flip privately, something he knew he needed to do *before* he told Eliza how he felt. Maybe it was better this way after all.

"Of course," Henry finally agreed. "I'd be glad to give you a ride."

When they arrived back at Rockbridge, Henry instinctively looked for Eliza's car, but he wasn't surprised when he didn't find it. There was no way she hadn't gone to the hospital. Once out of the car, Flip said good night and headed toward his apartment.

"Flip, wait," Henry called. "Can I talk to you for a minute?"

"We were in the same car for thirty minutes, man. We talked the whole time."

"I know," Henry said. "But . . . I need to talk to you about Eliza, about what I told you."

"What did you tell me?" Flip stood with his hands pushed deep into the pockets of his cargo pants, an expression of wry amusement on his face.

It confused Henry—it seemed like Flip was in on a joke that Henry still hadn't figured out.

"I told you there wasn't anything going on between us. And there wasn't then, not really, and well, there might not be *now*, but—" He ran agitated fingers through his hair. "It's just that Eliza isn't supposed to be with you." He filled his voice with every ounce of conviction he could muster. "She's supposed to be with me."

Flip smiled. Pulling his hands out of his pockets, he took a step toward Henry and put a hand on his shoulder. "Henry, it's about time you figured it out."

"What's that supposed to mean?"

Flip turned toward his apartment once more and shook his head. "Talk to Eliza," he called over his shoulder. "You should wait up for her. She'll want to talk to you tonight."

Chapter 33

ELIZA SAT IN A CHAIR at the foot of Amber's hospital bed and leaned back. It was the first time she had relaxed in three days. When Amber's family finally left to get something to eat, Eliza was left to keep watch. Now that she and Amber were alone, she wasn't sure she was ready for a conversation and hoped Amber would sleep a little longer.

The truth was that Eliza was still so angry she wasn't sure if she could speak with Amber properly—as a counselor—without losing her head. Running away had been a stupid, stupid thing to do. She could have died. Had Flip not found her, *she would have*. Eliza was angry with Amber, but she was also angry with herself for misjudging the situation.

"Hey."

Eliza looked up. Amber was awake.

Ready or not.

She stood and moved to her bedside. "Hey," she said. "You're awake. How are you feeling?"

"Like I need to pee," Amber said. "I think they've got me hydrated again." She pointed to the IV bag hanging from the pole next to her. "Think they'll take this thing out now?"

Eliza smiled. "I'm sure they will as soon as they know you're good to go."

After a nurse came and helped Amber to the bathroom, Eliza pulled her chair close so they were sitting just a few feet away from each other.

"Amber," Eliza began, "I owe you an apology."

Amber raised her eyebrows but didn't say anything.

"I never should have sent you on excursion. Had I been doing a better job as your counselor, I would have realized it wasn't the best thing for you. Instead, I put you at risk, and for that, I'm sorry."

Amber sniffed and closed her eyes, wiping away newly formed tears with the back of her hand. "No," she said. "It was me. I was just so mad that you sent me. I figured if I had to go, maybe I could turn it into my chance to get away. I just—" She shook her head. "It was the stupidest thing I've ever done in all my life. I'm so, so sorry."

"Where did you think you were going to get away to?"

"Rose Creek," Amber said. "I didn't want to stay gone forever, just for the weekend."

Eliza shook her head. Venturing into the mountains alone, with little food and no shelter, thinking she could walk all the way to Rose Creek? It was utter and complete idiocy—a lack of judgment that only a child could have. Eliza reminded herself that Amber *was* still a child. She hadn't thought about the harsh conditions of the mountainside. She hadn't thought anything through at all.

"You're lucky to be alive, Amber. Do you realize that?"

The girl looked at her hands. "Yes," she said, "but it wasn't luck."

"What do you mean?"

"After I hurt my ankle, I was out of food and water, and I couldn't walk anymore. I sat down. I even felt too numb to cry." She kept her eyes down, her fingers busy picking at the threads of the loose blanket draped across her lap. "But I wasn't too numb to pray," she said. "I prayed and prayed for I don't even know how long, and then suddenly, I knew I was going to be okay. I knew if I stayed where I was that Flip would find me. God told me he would find me."

Eliza reached forward and took Amber's hand in hers.

"I don't want to be stupid anymore," she said, the tears flowing freely. "I want to make good choices and be happy, and even though I really love you, I don't want to go back to Rockbridge. I want to be with my family. I don't want to be mad at them anymore."

"Oh, Amber," Eliza said gently. "I think your family would like very much to have you home."

Dr. Adler stuck her head around the door of Amber's hospital room. "Eliza? Can I speak with you for a moment?"

Eliza got up and joined her boss in the hallway.

"The doctors want to keep her overnight just to be sure she's all right, but then they'll discharge her in the morning."

Eliza nodded. "That sounds good. She told me she wants to go home with her family. She says she's tired of being mad at them and wants to work things out."

"Well, that's good, because her family has already made it perfectly clear that they want to take her home with them." There was a measure of disappointment in her voice.

"Dr. Adler, I'm so sorry about all of this. I feel directly responsible. I made a bad call, and I know that."

"Eliza, we all made bad calls," the director said. "I ignored rule after rule, trying to accommodate the desires of an old friend, allowing Amber far more liberty to leave campus than what I would typically allow. We both sent her on excursion. You only made decisions I gave you free rein to make."

Eliza breathed an inward sigh of relief. "I won't be so foolish again," she said. "I can assure you of that."

"No," she said. "Nor will I."

* * *

Eliza pulled into the parking lot at Rockbridge, weary to the very core. She was looking forward to a good night's rest, but that hardly mattered when she discovered Henry sitting on the front stoop of her apartment. She stopped in front of him.

"Henry, it's so cold out. What are you doing out here?"

"I didn't want to miss you," he said. "I just got back into town."

"Do you want to come inside?"

He nodded. "That would be good, that is, if you're not too tired. I know it's been a long three days."

"The longest of my life. But no, I'm not too tired. Please come in."

Eliza tried to read Henry's face for clues. What was he doing here? Why was he waiting for her? What was so important that it couldn't wait?

"I got your message," he said a little awkwardly. "I'm sorry I wasn't here sooner."

She unlocked her apartment, and the two of them went inside.

"No worries," she said. "I guess all's well that ends well, right?"

She could tell Henry was nervous. He took off his jacket but remained standing in the living room, looking quite sheepish.

"Here." She motioned for him to sit with her. "Come sit down."

"Thank you." He followed her to the couch. "Did you speak with Amber? How is she?"

Eliza managed a weak smile. "She's going to be fine. She's lucky."

"Flip told me how he found her. It's pretty amazing."

"I haven't talked to Flip," Eliza said. "What did he say?"

"Frank kept insisting they go a different way, but Flip said he felt a prompting that told him to stay on course, so he did. And then he found her."

Eliza smiled. "Amber tells a similar story."

For a moment, neither of them spoke. Something was going on. Eliza could tell there was something Henry wanted or needed to say.

"So what's going on with you?" she asked. "What took you out of town so suddenly?"

Henry took a deep breath. "I went to see Bill Harrison."

Eliza's eyes grew wide. "I can't believe you went! How did it go?"

"It was awful," Henry said. "He died six days before I got there. I met his sister, this puzzling woman who was mean and condescending and treated me as if I was the reason he had died."

"Oh. I'm so sorry. That can't be what you expected."

"It wasn't, but don't be sorry," Henry said. "I mean, be sorry he died. *I'm* sorry he died, but it was sort of amazing anyway. I've decided I don't have to be mad at him anymore. I don't have to run scared. He had his reasons for doing what he did. I always told myself that, but I actually *see* it now."

"That sounds pretty profound."

"It was. It is," Henry said. "There will always be things I regret, you know? I wish I could have apologized for the way I spoke to him that day. I wish I could tell him I understand the choices he made, and I hate that my own anger kept that from happening. But forgiving him was just as much about me. Carrying around all that bitterness—I don't want to do it anymore."

Henry ran his hands through his hair and leaned back against the couch cushions. "Things have to be different now. I realize I have to try harder with AJ. I have to fight for our relationship and let him see every single day how important he is to me. And then . . ." Something about the way he looked at Eliza made her feel as if the tone of the entire conversation was about to change. His eyes were bright and held an undercurrent of buzzing energy Eliza was certain she'd never seen in Henry before. "There's also something else I realized while I was away."

Eliza's heart started to pound.

Henry cleared his throat. "What I'm trying to say is . . . I mean, I know you said . . . and maybe you've changed your mind, but . . ." He shifted in his seat, so visibly uncomfortable Eliza almost wanted to laugh. "I just want you to know," he continued, "that is, if you *haven't* changed your mind—"

"Henry." Eliza reached for his hand, cutting off his words completely. "You could save yourself a lot of trouble if you would just kiss me."

It was all the invitation he needed. He closed the distance between them and, taking her face in his hands, kissed her fully and completely. When their lips parted, Henry remained close, his forehead leaning against hers. She reached up and wrapped her arms around his neck.

"I've been waiting for you to do that for a really long time," she said.

"I guess I've been a little obtuse."

Eliza shrugged and smiled. "Maybe a little."

"I'm in love with you, Eliza. I don't want to be scared anymore. I don't want to hide from anything. I just want . . . you. I want you to be with me. I want you to read my book," he said, laughing now. "I want you to know AJ, to be a part of his life. I—" He stopped. "I'm saying too much. Am I scaring you?"

"You're not scaring me." She shook her head.

He leaned in and kissed her again.

"Henry, I love you too," she said. "I've loved you for so long."

"I felt like there were mountains between us—these impassable barriers that were meant to keep us apart. We were too different. My life was too complicated. But I was wrong. All this time I've been so very wrong. I realize now there's not a mountain in this world I wouldn't climb to get to you."

Eliza placed her hand on Henry's cheek.

"Thank you for not giving up on me," he said softly.

Eliza smiled. "I never will."

Chapter 34

ALLISON AND ROBERT WERE MARRIED at Christmastime. They sent Henry and Eliza an invitation to the ceremony, but Henry didn't feel it necessary to go. He did, however, want to pick AJ up afterward. He had something for him—a surprise he was eager to share.

On the evening of Allison's reception, he stood anxiously by his car, waiting for Eliza to join him.

"I'm coming, I'm coming!" she called as she hurried down the steps of her apartment. "I got a late start."

"It's okay." Henry slipped a hand around her waist and pulled her to him, kissing her softly. "You look lovely."

"Thanks," Eliza said. "So what's the surprise? The suspense is killing me."

"You'll find out soon enough," Henry said. "Let's get going. I don't want AJ to have to wait too long."

Henry pulled into the circle drive of Rose Creek's country club and stopped outside the large double doors. The reception was happening just inside. It was here he was supposed to meet AJ.

"I'll just go in and see where he is," Henry said. "Actually, do you want to come in with me? If I have to crash my ex-wife's wedding reception, I should at least do it with a beautiful woman on my arm."

Eliza rolled her eyes. "You're not crashing anything. You could have gone to the wedding if you wanted. You *were* invited, after all."

"Yes, but does anyone really want their ex-spouse at their wedding?"

"I suppose not," Eliza said. "Well, let's go, then."

They got out of the car but didn't actually have to go inside. Lila met them at the door, holding on to AJ's hand as he danced to the music streaming out through the open doorway.

"Hi, Dad," AJ said. "Want to come dance?" He let go of his grand-mother's hand and started twisting—literally doing the twist. "Look what Mom taught me," he said with enough enthusiasm to make everyone laugh.

Henry crouched in front of his son. "That's really great, AJ, but we'll have to dance another time. Right now, I have a surprise for you."

"A surprise? What is it?"

"Well, if I told you, it wouldn't be a surprise, now would it? Go get in the car. We'll leave as soon as I say good-bye to your grandma."

AJ twisted his way to the backseat of Henry's car and buckled himself in. Henry turned his attention to Lila. "Thanks, Lila."

"Oh, you're welcome." She turned to Eliza. "It's nice to see you again, Eliza."

"Likewise."

Henry watched as Lila pulled Eliza into an embrace.

"You're taking good care of him, I hope," Lila said.

Eliza smiled. "Of course."

"Dad!" AJ called from the car. "I want my surprise!"

"All right," Henry said. "Let's get going."

* * *

Eliza wondered what Henry was up to. She could tell he was driving in circles, delaying their arrival at wherever it was they were headed. As they made the same right turn for the third time, AJ finally caught on.

"Dad," he said, "we've been here before. Are you driving in circles?"

Henry laughed. "Maybe."

AJ leaned back in his seat and let out a dramatized sigh. "Dad, come on!"

"Okay, okay, we're almost there."

They were in a part of Rose Creek Eliza had never seen before. It was a quaint neighborhood, modest homes with manicured yards and a friendly sidewalk lining the street. And then Eliza realized where they were going. Sure enough, Henry slowed the car and pulled into the driveway of a little white house with dark-blue shutters. The porch light was on, casting just enough light into the yard that Eliza could see a child-size soccer goal sitting in the grass.

"Whose house is this?" AJ asked.

"Why don't we go inside and see?" Henry said.

Eliza followed a few steps behind, allowing Henry the opportunity to enjoy the moment with AJ. Henry unlocked the door, ignoring the constant questions AJ was volleying his way. "Why do you have a key, Dad? Did someone give you a key to their house? Do I know who lives here?"

Once inside, Henry looked down at AJ. "Why don't you look around and see if you can figure out whose house this is?"

"Okay!" He dashed off down the hallway, looking for clues.

Eliza moved to Henry's side and slipped her hand into his. "This is really amazing," she said.

Henry smiled. "It's been so hard not to tell you. But I wanted it to be a surprise for you too."

Eliza looked at him. What was he trying to say?

"Dad! Dad!" AJ came running down the hallway at full speed. "There's a room back here, and it's *full* of Legos. They're everywhere! It's the coolest thing I've ever seen! Come see!" He turned and raced back down the hall.

Henry laughed. "After you," he said to Eliza.

She followed AJ down the hall and entered what could only be described as the most incredible Lego-themed bedroom she had ever seen. There were shelves full of Lego sets already built. There was a massive steamer trunk against the wall that was full of miscellaneous pieces. There was even a giant Lego head sitting on the dresser.

"Dad, look," AJ said, holding up the giant head. "You put all the random pieces in the Lego head and it sorts them for you. Isn't that cool?"

"It's very cool," Henry said.

"How did you do all of this?" Eliza whispered under her breath. "This is incredible."

"Dawson Peterson outgrew his Lego collection," Henry whispered back. "Most of this was his."

"I still don't think he's made the connection," Eliza said. "He doesn't realize this is all his."

"Hey, AJ," Henry said. "What's that say on the wall over there?" He pointed just above the bed. AJ turned. On the wall just above the head-board, in Lego-made letters, was AJ's name.

"It says *AJ*." He froze. He turned to his dad, eyes wide with excitement. "Is this my room? Dad! This is your house? This is so awesome!" Henry bent down just in time to catch his son, who was now throwing himself across the room and into his father's arms.

"Now you can come stay with me any time you want," Henry said. "You can come for the weekend or any other time. Would you like that?"

"Yes, yes, yes!" Without any prompting or any music, AJ jumped onto his new bed and started to dance the twist.

"I think you've made him a little happy," Eliza said.

Henry only smiled.

"You know," Eliza said, "seeing you like this, being all happy loving your son, it makes me really, really love you."

"Is that so?" Henry leaned down and whispered softly in her ear, "I have something for you too." With a glance over his shoulder to make sure AJ was happily occupied with his Legos, Henry took Eliza by the hand and led her back down the hallway and into the dining room. On the table, there was a single sheet of paper. Henry picked it up and handed it to Eliza.

"What is this?" She skimmed over the paper's contents.

"It's a job description," Henry said. "It's a job offer, really—the job Dr. Adler is willing to give you if you want it."

Eliza looked up, puzzled. "I don't understand. This sounds a lot like the job I already have."

"There is one small difference. See?" He pointed to the bottom of the page. "With this job, you don't have to live on campus."

"But that doesn't make any sense. Dr. Adler knows she needs counselors on site at all times. Why would she let me live somewhere else?"

"She says you're too good to lose. She's willing to hire another counselor to cover the residency and let you shift into a supervisory role, still counseling and working with your students but helping others with theirs too. It's a promotion, Eliza. It's a good thing."

"Of course, I see that. This second part—it lists the new responsibilities. I'm just trying to figure out how it will all work out. I mean—"

"Eliza, stop," Henry said gently. He pulled the paper from her hands and set it back on the dining room table. "You're kind of missing the point."

"What?"

"Why would I care so much about you living off campus unless I wanted you to live here with me?"

"Henry? Are you . . . ?"

"Proposing? Yes, I am." To Eliza's surprise, Henry darted into the dark kitchen, then returned with a large stack of paper in his hand. Around the paper, there was a single piece of twine tied in a knot. Tied to the twine was a beautiful diamond ring. Holding the stack of paper, Henry dropped to one knee.

"I thought I knew what love was. I thought I'd found the kind of love that would make me happy. And I guess in some ways I had. But there was so much I didn't know, so much I was afraid of knowing. Until I met you. You changed everything. You changed *me*. Will you marry me?"

Eliza smiled through her tears, nodding her head yes. "Of course; of course I will." Henry stood up and handed her the stack of paper. While she held it, he untied the ring.

"Is this your book?"

"It's *a* book," Henry said. "A new one. I finished it only last week. I've been writing . . . I feel like I haven't really slept in weeks, but I wanted to finish it. It's for you. This one I wrote for you."

"Thank you, Henry."

Henry grasped her hand and gently slid the ring onto her finger.

It was a perfect fit.

About the Author

JENNY PROCTOR WRITES FROM HER home in the mountains of Western North Carolina. She loves being a mom, loves being a writer, and loves being a Mormon in the South. Jenny is convinced that the four basic food groups should be fruit, bread, cheese, and chocolate and consumes plenty of each, quite often together. When she isn't writing, Jenny likes to run, swim, and bike (because it balances out the bread, cheese, and chocolate).

Mountains Between Us is a reflection of Jenny's love for the Blue Ridge Mountains. She believes the mountains have a way of filling people and making them happy and hopes to share a little of their majesty and spirit through her words.

Jenny's first book, *The House at Rose Creek*, was released in 2013. To learn more about Jenny, visit her website at www.jennyproctor.com.